LEADING THE WITNESS

What Reviewers Say About Carsen Taite's Work

Practice Makes Perfect

"This book has two fantastic leads, an attention-grabbing plot and that sizzling chemistry that great authors can make jump off the page. While all of Taite's books are fantastic, this one is on that next level. This is a damn good book and I cannot wait to see what is next in this series."—*The Romantic Reader*

Pursuit of Happiness

"I like Taite's style of writing. She is consistent in terms of quality and always writes strong female characters that are as intelligent as they are beautiful."—*Lesbian Reading Room*

Love's Verdict

"Carsen Taite excels at writing legal thrillers with lesbian main characters using her experience as a criminal defense attorney." —*Lez Review Books*

Outside the Law

"[A] fabulous closing to the Lone Star Law Series. ...Tanner and Sydney's journey back to each other is sweet, sexy and sure to keep you entertained."—*The Romantic Reader Blog*

A More Perfect Union

"[*A More Perfect Union*] is a fabulously written tightly woven political/military intrigue with a large helping of romance. I enjoyed every minute and was on the edge of my seat the whole time. This one is a great read! Carsen Taite never disappoints!"—*The Romantic Reader Blog*

"Readers looking for a mix of intrigue and romance set against a political backdrop will want to pick up Taite's latest novel."
—*Romantic Times Book Review*

Sidebar

"*Sidebar* is a sexy, fun, interesting book that's sure to delight, whether you're a longtime fan or this is your first time reading something by Carsen Taite. I definitely recommend it!"—*The Lesbian Review*

Letter of the Law

"Fiery clashes and lots of chemistry, you betcha!"—*The Romantic Reader Blog*

Without Justice

"Another pretty awesome lesbian mystery thriller by Carsen Taite."—Danielle Kimerer, Librarian, Nevins Memorial Library (MA)

"All in all a fantastic novel…Unequivocally 5 Stars…"—*Les Reveur*

Above the Law

"…readers who enjoyed the first installment will find this a worthy second act."—*Publishers Weekly*

"Ms Taite delivered and then some, all the while adding more questions, Tease!! I like the mystery and intrigue in this story. It has many 'sit on the edge of your seat' scenes of excitement and dread (like watch out kind of thing) and drama…well done indeed!"
—*Prism Book Alliance*

Reasonable Doubt

"Another Carsen Taite novel that kept me on the edge of my seat. …[A]n interesting plot with lots of mystery and a bit of thriller as well. The characters were great."—Danielle Kimerer, Librarian, Reading Public Library

"Sarah and Ellery are very likeable. Sarah's conflict between job and happiness is well portrayed. I felt so sorry for Ellery's total upheaval of her life. …I loved the chase to find the truth while they tried to keep their growing feelings for each other at bay. When they couldn't, the tale was even better."—*Prism Book Alliance*

Lay Down the Law

"Recognized for the pithy realism of her characters and settings drawn from a Texas legal milieu, Taite pays homage to the prime-time soap opera *Dallas* in pairing a cartel-busting U.S. attorney, Peyton Davis, with a charity-minded oil heiress, Lily Gantry." —*Publishers Weekly*

"Suspenseful, intriguingly tense, and with a great developing love story, this book is delightfully solid on all fronts."—*Rainbow Book Reviews*

Courtship

"Taite (*Switchblade*) keeps the stakes high as two beautiful and brilliant women fueled by professional ambitions face daunting emotional choices. …As backroom politics, secrets, betrayals, and threats race to be resolved without political damage to the president, the cat-and-mouse relationship game between Addison and Julia has the reader rooting for them. Taite prolongs the fever-pitch tension to the final pages. This pleasant read with intelligent heroines, snappy dialogue, and political suspense will satisfy Taite's devoted fans and new readers alike."—*Publishers Weekly*

"Carsen Taite throws the reader head on into the murky world of the political system where there are no rights or wrongs, just players attempting to broker the best deals regardless of who gets hurt in the process. The book is extremely well written and makes compelling reading. With twist and turns throughout, the reader doesn't know how the story will end."—*Lesbian Reading Room*

Switchblade

"Dallas's intrepid female bounty hunter, Luca Bennett, is back in another adventure. Fantastic! Between her many friends and lovers, her interesting family, her fly by the seat of her pants lifestyle, and a whole host of detractors there is rarely a dull moment."—*Rainbow Book Reviews*

Beyond Innocence

"Taite keeps you guessing with delicious delay until the very last minute…Taite's time in the courtroom lends *Beyond Innocence*, a terrific verisimilitude someone not in the profession couldn't impart. And damned if she doesn't make practicing law interesting."
—*Out in Print*

The Best Defense

"Real Life defense attorney Carsen Taite polishes her fifth work of lesbian fiction, *The Best Defense*, with the realism she daily encounters in the office and in the courts. And that polish is something that makes *The Best Defense* shine as an excellent read."—*Out & About Newspaper*

Nothing but the Truth

Author Taite is really a Dallas defense attorney herself, and it's obvious her viewpoint adds considerable realism to her story, making it especially riveting as a mystery. I give it four stars out of five."—Bob Lind, *Echo Magazine*

Do Not Disturb

"Taite's tale of sexual tension is entertaining in itself, but a number of secondary characters…add substantial color to romantic inevitability"—Richard Labonte, *Book Marks*

It Should be a Crime—Lammy Finalist

"Taite, a criminal defense attorney herself, has given her readers a behind the scenes look at what goes on during the days before a trial. Her descriptions of lawyer/client talks, investigations, police procedures, etc. are fascinating. Taite keeps the action moving, her characters clear, and never allows her story to get bogged down in paperwork. It Should Be a Crime has a fast-moving plot and some extraordinarily hot sex."—*Just About Write*

Visit us at www.boldstrokesbooks.com

By the Author

Truelesbianlove.com
It Should be a Crime
Do Not Disturb
Nothing but the Truth
The Best Defense
Beyond Innocence
Rush
Courtship
Reasonable Doubt
Without Justice
Sidebar
A More Perfect Union
Love's Verdict
Pursuit of Happiness
Leading the Witness

The Luca Bennett Mystery Series:
Slingshot
Battle Axe
Switchblade
Bow and Arrow (novella in Girls with Guns)

Lone Star Law Series:
Lay Down the Law
Above the Law
Letter of the Law
Outside the Law

Legal Affairs Romances:
Practice Makes Perfect

LEADING THE
WITNESS

by
Carsen Taite

2019

LEADING THE WITNESS
© 2019 By Carsen Taite. All Rights Reserved.

ISBN 13: 978-1-63555-512-7

This Trade Paperback Original Is Published By
Bold Strokes Books, Inc.
P.O. Box 249
Valley Falls, NY 12185

First Edition: October 2019

Credits
Editor: Cindy Cresap
Production Design: Susan Ramundo
Cover Design By Jeanine Henning

Acknowledgments

Thanks always to Rad and Sandy for making this publishing house a home. To my intrepid editor Cindy Cresap—thanks for all the work you do behind the scenes to make my work shine.

Georgia, thanks for our daily word count check-ins and for always offering an encouraging word when I'm struggling with the process.

Ruth and Paula, thanks for being my literary lawyer pals, always available to strategize. And, Paula, special thanks to you for reading drafts of this story right up until the moment I turned it in. You're a top-notch pal and I treasure our friendship.

Thanks to my wife, Lainey, for always believing in my dreams even when they involve sacrificing our time together. That you are always available to brainstorm book ideas and plot points is a total bonus. I couldn't do this without you and I wouldn't want to.

And to my loyal readership, thank you, thank you, thank you. Every time you purchase one of my stories, you give me the gift of allowing me to make a living doing what I love. Thanks for taking this journey with me.

Dedication

To Lainey. I'll follow where you lead.

CHAPTER ONE

The moment Detective Reese shifted in his seat, Catherine knew she'd won. The move was subtle, and she doubted the jury in their post-lunch haze even noticed it, but she saw it for what it was, and knew exactly how to expose his discomfort at having to lie to prove up the case against her client.

Catherine stood for effect but remained at the defense counsel table and made a show of picking up a heavy file and flipping through pages. "Please pick up the binder next to you," she instructed him, keeping her voice polite and even, "and turn to State's exhibit D7."

While he flipped the pages, she risked a quick glance at the prosecution table. Starr Rio, chief prosecutor for the felony courts in Travis County, was the lead attorney for the state. Her usual role was supervising the felony trial prosecutors under her command, but she had a habit of keeping the headline-grabbing cases. Rumor had it Starr was planning to announce a run for district attorney in the upcoming election, and every win she racked up between now and the start of her campaign was money in the bank. Money that Catherine intended to rob from her.

"I found it."

At the sound of the witness's voice, Starr looked up from her notepad and locked eyes with Catherine, who did her best to hide her own discomfort at the scrutiny. She took her time turning back to the witness, unwilling to let Starr see her unease. "Detective, please describe to the jury what you see in this photograph."

He narrowed his eyes, likely surprised at the open-ended question and assuming it was a trap. It was, but not the kind he could escape while he was seated in full view of the jury. She looked back down at the file in her hand while he fumbled to answer.

"This is a photo of the crime scene."

She waited, allowing her silence to push him to say more.

"It's the living room of Angela Knoll's house, taken from the entry to the kitchen." He held it up and pointed to the left of the photo. "You can see here," he pointed, "the coffee table is turned over and several items are scattered around the room which led us to believe there had been a physical altercation."

"Tell us what else you see, Detective. I'd like you to cover everything you think is important to your case."

With that lead, Reese launched into a long explanation of the angles of Angela Knoll's dead body, the knife wounds, the defensive wounds, and a half dozen other clues he deemed important to the conclusions he'd drawn about how her client's ex-wife had died. She let him drone on, certain the jury was being lulled deeper and deeper into their already comatose state, and she flipped through the pages in her file to signal she was barely listening.

Reese was still talking when she felt a tap on her shoulder. She glanced to her left, almost surprised to find her client, Peter Knoll, sitting beside her, wearing an anxious expression. He opened his mouth to speak, but she shook her head and pointed at the legal pad in front of him. She'd been meticulous in her instructions prior to the start of trial. No talking in the presence of the jury. If he had something important to say he was supposed to write her a note on the pad and pass it to her. She would be the final arbiter about what to do with the information. She watched him pick up a pen and furiously scribble on the pad. She turned her attention back to her file, but the scratching of the pen against the paper was an unwelcome distraction, and she willed him to finish quickly.

Ask him about the rope. It wasn't in the room. NOT MINE!

The last two words were underlined with bold, deep strokes of emphasis. Tiresome. Clients who chose to go to trial almost always professed their innocence with fervor. She didn't really blame them.

Either they were full of the indignation that came with actually being innocent, or projecting the appearance of innocence was their only refuge against the court of public opinion. She really didn't care either way as long as they could pay her exorbitant fee. Cases like this, where she suspected law enforcement had made missteps in investigating their case, were a bonus for her.

Knoll jabbed the pen against the paper again, and she deftly snatched it from his hand and wrote two words underneath his. *My rules*. She didn't capitalize the words, underline them, or over-punctuate, but she did give him a withering look, her head carefully turned away from the jury box. Satisfied he was under control, she returned her attention back to the witness.

"Thank you, Detective. It sounds as if your investigation was extremely thorough. Certainly, you and your colleagues combed every inch of the crime scene as well as my client's apartment as part of your work."

Detective Reese shifted in his seat again, while he tried to decide if the compliment was a trap. "We do our best."

She reached into the file box under the table and pulled out an oversized envelope. "Permission to approach the witness, Your Honor," she said, not waiting for the judge to respond before she was in motion. By the time the judge agreed, she was standing next to the detective, dangling the envelope like a tempting treat. She could see Starr inch to the edge of her seat, waiting to pounce. She knew she should've shared what was in the envelope with her before showing it to her witness, but then she'd lose the effect of the reveal. Besides, she was certain there was plenty about this case that Starr had not shared with her and this was her way of drawing that to the attention of everyone in the room. She tore off the top of the envelope instead of merely unfastening the clasp, and slowly withdrew a thick cord of rope, letting it dangle from her hand, the end moving back and forth in front of Detective Reese's face like a pendulum of portent. She barely resisted smiling as the blood drained from his face.

"Do you recognize this?" she asked.

He cast a furtive glance at Starr, but Catherine knew Starr would know better than to coach him now. She let a few beats of silence pass before she eased the pressure. "Let me help you out. This is a piece of rope that I brought with me to court today. There's no reason you should know this particular piece of rope, but I do believe that it's extremely similar to another piece of rope that you claim to have come across in the course of your investigation. Isn't. That. Right?" she asked in slow staccato.

She turned and walked back to counsel table as she asked the question so that her back was to him as he muttered his response. She waited until she'd returned to her seat and was once again facing the front of the courtroom before speaking. "I'm not sure the jury heard you. Would you repeat what you just said or should I have the court reporter read it back?"

He cleared his throat. "I was confused for a moment. Yes, we did find a length of rope at the defendant's house. It looked similar to the one you just showed me, but as you pointed out, it can't be the same one since you brought that one with you and the other one was booked into evidence."

"And you know the other one is in the evidence room because you're the one who checked it in, correct?"

"Yes."

"Would it surprise you to know that I purchased this rope, which happens to match the exact specifications of the rope described in the medical examiner's report, at Home Depot?"

"I guess not," he said, his narrowed eyes, a signal he was trying to figure out where she was going with her questions.

Catherine moved quickly to a new subject. "In your report, you stated that you were the first officer on the scene."

"Yes."

"And you found the front door slightly ajar, so you entered the house. Upon entering, you found Mrs. Knoll lying on the floor with a rope around her neck."

"Yes."

Catherine made a show of picking up an official looking binder and flipping through the pages, settling on a spot somewhere in the middle. She stared across the room until Reese was squirming in his seat. "What did procedure dictate that you do next?"

She saw his surprise at the open-ended question. Normally, it would be a risk for her to deviate from the tight yes or no line of inquiry, but whether he realized it or not, she was giving him a noose and hoping he would hang on it.

"Glove up, cordon off the scene, call for backup and a crime scene unit."

"Let's start with the gloves. You stated that you removed the rope from Angela Knoll's neck before anyone else arrived at the scene."

"That's correct. I thought she might still be alive, and I wanted to—"

Catherine cut him off. "Please just answer the question, Detective." She looked back down at her notes, pretending to read something very important, but all she'd written was *he's lying*.

"Did you put gloves on before you touched Angela Knoll's neck, before you removed the noose?"

"No. As I explained before, I was in a hurry to try and save her life."

She resisted smiling at the opportunity he'd just given her. "Let's talk about that for a moment. You've read the ME's report, correct?"

"I have."

"And you've seen the part where he states unequivocally that Angela Knoll died as a result of the knife wounds inflicted to her chest."

"Yes, but I didn't know she was dead at the time I entered."

Catherine started to caution him to answer only the question she'd posed but decided his tendency to fill in the gaps would only serve her purpose here. "So, your testimony is that you'd received a distressed phone call from Angela Knoll. You happened to be nearby, so instead of calling it in, you rushed to the house. The door was ajar, and you burst in, found Mrs. Knoll on the floor, rushed to her side, and removed the rope around her neck. You didn't take time to put on gloves or take any other steps to make sure the scene wasn't compromised, in an effort to save her life?"

He barely waited until she finished her question before he slammed his palm on the rail of the witness stand. "Exactly!"

Catherine wanted to smile, to gloat at his careless response, certain that Starr Rio, who'd risen to make an objection to her overly long and detailed question, was now fuming that her witness hadn't allowed her time to stop him from responding. Instead, Catherine kept up appearances for the jury and merely raised her eyebrows in an incredulous expression. "Thank you for clarifying that. I have just a few more questions."

Step by step, she took him through his history with her client. Reese had shown up at the Knolls' house on several other occasions, investigating domestic disputes called in by both Peter and Angela before they'd separated, and he'd always taken Angela's side. When he'd gone to question Peter about Angela's death, he'd claimed he found rope matching the rope from Angela's neck at the crime scene. Through careful questions, she crafted a scenario she could use in closing to paint him as the would-be hero who would do whatever it took to save the damsel in distress even if it meant taking matters into his own hands to frame her client.

After she'd laid a strong foundation, she looped her inquiry back to the scene of the crime. "You enter the house and see a bloody crime scene." She reached for a piece of paper and read his testimony under direct word for word. "'Blood was everywhere.'" She looked up and waited until he agreed before moving on to the next point. "You ran to Mrs. Knoll, felt for a pulse, removed the rope, set it to the side, and continued to try and revive her, but she never regained consciousness. Correct?"

"Yes."

Catherine stood, walked over to Starr, and asked for State's exhibits K and J. Starr reluctantly handed her a large envelope with a clear glass window that contained the rope Reese had testified he'd removed from Angela Knoll's neck, and an eight-by-ten photo of a coil of rope found at her client's apartment. Although the jury had already seen both items during Starr's direct examination of Reese, Catherine held both items away from their view as she returned to the witness stand. She set them both on the rail.

"Detective Reese, you've already testified about both of these items, the rope found at the scene and the rope you testified you found at my client's apartment. My question to you is do you see any difference between the two?"

He immediately shook his head. "No. I mean one is longer, which just means that he cut off a portion to use when he committed the murder, but otherwise, no, I agree with the crime scene investigator. The rope is exactly the same."

She watched his smug face and fought to keep her cool. "I agree. Would you like to know why?" She watched him spend a moment trying to figure out if hers was a trick question, but as she predicted, he was unable to resist.

"Sure."

She picked up the envelope and the photo and held them side by side in full view of the jury. "Because neither one of these pieces of rope has blood on it." She let the comment hang in the air for a moment, watching the jurors' faces until she was certain they got the point. They'd seen the photos. Angela Knoll had been covered in blood. There was no way a piece of rope around her neck would have escaped the bloodbath. Unless it hadn't been part of the crime. Unless it had been placed there afterward by an overzealous detective looking for a way to conclusively pin this crime on her client. Her theory was that when Reese didn't immediately see any evidence that would tie Peter to the crime, he had used some rope he had in his car to make it look like Peter had topped off a stabbing spree with a bit of strangulation. Since Reese had led the team that searched Peter's apartment, it would've been simple for him to plant the rest of the rope there to link the evidence.

But Catherine resisted tying up all the loose ends now, when Starr still had the opportunity to try to punch holes in her theory. She'd save her arguments for closing, certain she could raise enough questions for the jury to find reasonable doubt. Instead, she picked up the exhibits and returned to the defense table. "Your Honor, I have no further questions for this witness."

❖

Starr paced the short length of the DA workroom, her impatience growing. When the door opened, her number two, Matt

Abbott, barely hid his wince of surprise at finding her here rather than in the courtroom. "Get in here," she snapped. She waited until Matt closed the door behind him before she unraveled. "We need to decide if we're going to address what just happened or move on."

Matt shook his head. "It's a problem. I mean Landauer made her point. There's no way that rope was there with all that blood around and didn't get a drop on it. Your guess is as good as mine about how to handle it."

Starr bit back a sharp retort about how guessing didn't win cases and stood in place. This case was going downhill fast, and she didn't have the time or energy to waste on licking her wounds. She'd known, going into trial, that the rope was going to be an issue, but there was plenty of evidence to support the charge even without the rope. She had a fifteen-minute break to figure out how to rehabilitate her witness, and try to get the jury to focus on the evidence he hadn't messed with. No matter what Catherine Landauer thought about how Reese had handled the case, Starr was convinced Peter Knoll was guilty as sin, and she wasn't about to give up until he spent the rest of his life behind bars.

"Go talk to Reese. He needs a thrashing, but don't beat him up so bad that he sounds like he's whipped when he gets back on the stand. I'll go over my notes for redirect and I'll meet you in there."

Matt opened the door to the workroom and ran smack into the towering form of Fred Nelson, her immediate supervisor and the first assistant to the district attorney, Patrick Murphy. Starr wanted to groan at the interruption, but instead she mustered half a smile. "Matt, head on out," she said. "Nelson, what can I do for you?"

"You can kick this case to the curb as fast as possible," Nelson said, sliding into one of the chairs in the crowded room. "I saw the reporter from the *Statesman* typing up a damn blog like she has the story of the decade. What the hell kind of show are you running in there?"

Starr mentally calculated how much time she could expect to do if she punched her boss in the face and decided he wasn't worth it. Nelson loved to drop in on his prosecutors and stir up shit, claiming victory when they were winning and crowing they'd gone off the rails when they weren't. God forbid he ever offered any assistance, although it had been so long since he'd been in a courtroom, she doubted he would have anything to offer. She summoned whatever Zen she could find. "We're having some trouble with Detective Reese's testimony, but I'm working on redirect right now. I'm confident we can get the jury to see things our way."

"Well, I'm not. Cut a deal."

"No fucking way." She spat the words out, not caring about the shocked look on his face. "If the jury wants to cut him loose, then that's their call. Peter Knoll killed his wife, and probably others that we'll find out about later while he's waiting for the needle in Huntsville. The guy's a freak. I refuse to participate in giving him a pass."

"Twenty years isn't a pass."

"It is to me, and if you think Catherine Landauer is going to tell her client to take twenty, you're crazy. Did you hear her on the news last week, spouting off about how he was the real victim? That clip has been running nonstop, and making a deal now only vindicates her theory." Starr gathered up her notes. She was done trying to reason with her boss, and it was time to get back to work. She took two steps before his chilling voice stopped her in her tracks.

"You'll make a deal, or I will report you to the bar for what just happened in there."

She swung around and crossed her arms—a show of strength to hide the chill creeping up her spine. "I didn't do anything."

"Maybe, but you have a reputation for taking shortcuts when you think it will help you win. It's not a far reach for the state bar ethics committee to believe you contributed to the detective's misguided sense of justice."

She narrowed her eyes, appraising his words. Their boss, the DA, was retiring in a year and it was well known around the courthouse that Nelson planned to run for the position, a spot she'd been gunning for since she started at the office as an intern fourteen years ago. If Nelson was trying to undermine her with this case, the next year of battle between them was going to be hell.

He wasn't wrong. She was always prepared to do whatever it took to win, but she'd never actually committed an ethics violation even if she'd come close. An investigation by the state bar would derail her campaign before it even got started. Still, she wasn't going to win anything by backing down to threats.

"Report whatever you want," she said, calling his bluff. "I need to get back in there."

He shook his head. "I've asked Landauer to meet us in here. You can offer her the deal, or I will, but it's happening. I've already spoken with the victim's family and they see the value in closure."

A knock on the door cut short any retort on Starr's part, and she was certain Catherine was standing on the other side. May as well get this over with. She swung the door wide and invited her in. Catherine Landauer was an enigma. She fought hard for her clients and she was a shark when it came to cross-examining anyone from law enforcement, but unlike most of the defense bar who left the adversarial nature of their jobs at the courthouse and joined police and prosecutors for drinks after hours at the local bar, she'd never spotted Catherine outside of the courthouse. In her mind, Catherine spirited away after each case like a genie in a bottle until it was time to come out and grant the wish of some other defendant who needed her skills. And from what Starr knew of her reputation, Catherine granted their wishes with incredible consistency. They hadn't gone up against each other before, but Starr had checked Catherine's win record against hers and found they were neck and neck. Now that they were in trial, Starr could tell that Catherine's reputation as a cop ball buster and top-notch litigator was well earned, which would make this deal sting even more.

Nelson cleared his throat and Starr met his eyes. He wasn't going to give in. She could try to reach Murphy and plead her case directly to him, but she knew it was pointless. While Murphy could be counted on not to take sides in next year's election, as long as Nelson was his top lieutenant, he would defer to him on pending cases. *You offer her the deal, or I will.* Nelson's words rang like a gong between her ears, pushing her to a decision. What she wanted to do was stalk out of the room and tell the first reporter she could find that Nelson was stealing the case from the jury and offering a deal to a murderer. Let him be straddled with the bad press that would come from such a deal when it came time to start campaigning. But respect for the office held her back. This was her case. Reese had fucked it up and she hadn't done her due diligence. Time to make the tough call and take the consequences.

"Catherine," Starr said, "We'd like to offer your client a deal."

Catherine nodded slowly, her face impassive. "I thought you might. Dismissal?"

Starr started to laugh, but there was absolutely nothing about Catherine's expression to indicate she might be kidding, and sarcasm would defeat the purpose at this point. "Let's start with twenty years."

"You're wasting my time."

Catherine turned to go, and Starr glanced at Nelson who raised his eyebrows and shook his head. "I'm not actually," Starr said, sensing Catherine would respond better to a show of strength than weak supplication. "Detective Reese was a bit of a train wreck, but his testimony isn't our whole case. We have other cops who can testify about being called out to the house and seeing evidence of your client's treachery. The jury will take all of this into consideration, and when they find your client guilty, they'll get to hear about how he treated his ex-wife, the first one. He'll be begging for twenty at that point."

"Five."

"The minimum wasn't meant for repeat offenders. Fifteen." Starr could sense Nelson shuffling in place behind her, but she wasn't about to consult with him before she negotiated downward. If he wanted a deal, he'd get one, but he might not like the terms.

"Seven."

"Fifteen is generous. He'll do ten and be out on parole. Maybe he'll even hire you again when he gets back in trouble, because we both know he will." Starr immediately regretted her words as Catherine's face turned to iron, but she didn't walk out. "Fifteen or we take this to a jury. I will get a guilty and the jury will have no mercy by the time I've put on my sentencing evidence. You can be certain about that."

"Do you like breaking the law, Ms. Rio?" Catherine's voice was smooth and icy. "By sponsoring Detective Reese's testimony, that's exactly what you're doing. Although I suppose it's certainly in keeping with your usual methods."

Starr focused hard on keeping her face fixed in a neutral expression, but she could feel Nelson's eyes boring into her from across the room while Catherine's fierce blue-gray eyes flashed like steel swords ready to do battle. They were stunningly gorgeous, even in anger.

She shook away the distraction. "My only 'method' is winning justice for the citizens of Travis County, and offering your client the minimum would be a travesty that I cannot abide."

"Then we're done here. Good luck rehabilitating your witness."

Catherine turned and started walking toward the door, and Starr imagined a dramatic whoosh of air following her. Winning this case would be hard, but it would be worth it to wipe the smug sense of satisfaction off Catherine's face.

"What about ten?"

Starr jerked her head and stared at Nelson, but he was focused on Catherine who'd stopped walking when he'd lowered the offer. Catherine slowly turned.

"I'm listening."

"Ten years," Nelson said, "But it's still an aggravated offense, so he'll do most of that."

Starr watched in disbelief as they hashed out additional terms of the deal, but she was no longer focused on the specifics, only the general knowledge that Nelson was effectively stealing her case and dismissing months of hard work.

"Are you good with this?"

Starr looked into Catherine's eyes and she was taken aback by the question. Her gut response was to remark that she had little choice, but she'd already had her power stripped away. Admitting it was only more torture. Instead she turned it back on Catherine. "Are you?"

Catherine's eyes flickered slightly before shuttering back to their normal nonchalance. She turned back to Nelson. "I'll talk to my client and have an answer for you before the jury gets back."

The minute she was out of the room, Starr let loose on Nelson. "If you want to try my cases, then try them, but don't undercut me and expect me to sell your decision to the victim's family. You can explain to them why their daughter's killer will be out before she would've turned forty."

"Practicing the talking points for your campaign?"

"Hardly seems necessary. Actions like these speak for themselves, but if you try to pin this decision on me, mark my words, it will backfire." Nelson raised his hands and mimicked shaking in fear while wearing a condescending smile. Starr wanted to punch him. "Maybe you should wait to celebrate," she said. "Judge Westin may not accept the plea."

"He will, trust me."

Starr opened her mouth to tell him that if that was the case then he could just do the plea himself, but prudence stopped her. If Nelson took over her case mid-trial, he'd find a way to spin the plea and make her look weak in the process. She didn't care what he thought of her, but she did care how potential voters would view how this case was handled. Better she handle the plea and engage in spin of her own. "Great. I just need a minute to talk to the family. Why don't you start filling out the paperwork?"

She didn't wait for an answer before smacking the file into his hand and striding out the door. She'd been bested from both within and without today, and she wasn't used to losing.

Chapter Two

Catherine balanced a file box on her hip and pushed open the door to her office building. As the door opened, the box started to slide, but Doris Beechum, her assistant/office manager, rushed over to help. "You're back early," Doris said. "Judge Westin have a fire he needed to get to?"

Catherine let Doris take control of the heavy box, knowing it was useless to protest. "Trial's over. Mr. Knoll is doing ten years."

Doris gave a low whistle. "Ten years. How did he take it?"

"Like the gift it was." Catherine pointed at her office door. "I need a few minutes. Anything urgent before I go into lockdown?"

Doris hesitated for a moment, and then shook her head. "Nothing that can't wait." Catherine started to walk away, but Doris called out after her. "That woman phoned again. The one whose son is charged with online solicitation of a child. I keep telling her you're not interested, but she insists if she could just talk to you, woman to woman, you would change your mind."

Catherine rubbed her forehead. "Block her if you have to. Just make her go away." She made her way to her office, ignoring Doris who stared after her. Catherine was well aware she was the only attorney in Travis regularly handling felony cases who wouldn't accept any cases involving child abuse, a fact Doris had never pretended to understand. The truth was most practices couldn't afford to turn them down as they often garnered lucrative fees and were more common than one would hope. But she couldn't afford *to* take them, even if it meant her staff thought she was crazy for turning away the business. For her part, she wondered why the calls continued to come in considering the rest of the bar knew her rule and didn't refer these cases to her, but idle curiosity about how these defendants found her wasn't strong enough to compel her to actually meet with the accused.

In her office, Catherine typed out a closing memo to the Knoll file. She followed this same practice with every case, meticulously detailing the entire proceeding, from intake to resolution, while it was all fresh in her mind. She recalled with vivid memory her first meeting with Peter Knoll. She'd suspected his guilt at the time, but she'd also relished the opportunity to best Detective Reese on the stand. Knoll had gotten less than he'd deserved and Detective Reese would likely escape with a slap on the wrist, but she'd done her part to make sure the system worked—her singular goal.

When she finally finished the memo, it was dark outside. Conscious that Doris would still be waiting, she closed the file on Knoll and gathered some work to take home. "Let's go," she called out as she neared the door, slowing just enough to allow Doris time to follow. She'd stopped telling Doris that she didn't have to stay late years ago when she figured out Doris Beechum was going to do what she wanted no matter what Catherine said. She shouldn't have been surprised. Doris had spent years in the employ of the attorney who'd previously owned this practice, and when Catherine had inherited the business, she'd kept Doris on precisely because of her strong will and no-nonsense attitude. Doris was at once fiercely loyal, but extremely professional and circumspect—a combination that assured Catherine her personal privacy would never be violated.

Secretly, she was grateful for the company as they walked toward the back of the building in the still quiet of the night to where her vehicle was parked. The area was well lit—she'd overseen the installation of the floodlights herself—but she wasn't in the habit of relying on others to keep her secure. She mentally counted the steps to her parking space by tapping her fingers on the keys in her pocket. She waved good-bye to Doris who peeled off toward her own car, but waited until she was inches from the door of her sedan before clicking the button on the key fob. She cracked the door and stared inside, taking in every detail, before climbing behind the wheel. She pulled the door firmly to and engaged the locks.

She was only a few blocks away from the office when she realized she was starving. She ran through a mental inventory of her fridge which didn't take long since she hadn't shopped during the trial. Spotting Guero's up ahead on the left, she made a snap decision to grab dinner out, a celebration of sorts. She could work over dinner.

"How many in your party?" the perky hostess asked, making Catherine wish she'd gone through a drive-thru. She looked over at the bar. "I can order over there, right?"

"Sure," Perky replied, handing her a menu.

The bartender was much more laid-back. He took her order for a Tecate and delivered it without any embellishment. Deciding to indulge, she placed an order for fajita nachos, and while she waited for her food, she glanced through the long list of emails that had gathered in her inbox. She was barely through the first page of messages, when someone settled into the seat beside her.

"Celebrating?"

Starr Rio looked like a completely different person with her dark hair cascading around her shoulders instead of pulled back into a French twist. She'd shed her suit jacket, and her royal blue blouse was less buttoned up than it had been in the courtroom, not to mention the color made her blue eyes pop. The entire effect was sexy, and Catherine was momentarily without words. She recovered quickly. "Are you?"

"Why can't you just answer the question, counselor?" Starr said with an edge in her voice. She swallowed a draught from a glass of amber liquid and set it down hard on the bar. "I will. No, I don't have anything to celebrate."

Catherine looked around the room, wishing she'd chosen to sit in the dining room where it wouldn't be socially acceptable for someone to plunk down next to her. Doing battle in the courtroom was one thing, but she had no desire to rehash the confrontation in public. Yet Starr's inability to see that she'd deserved the loss nagged and she couldn't quite let it go. "You were lucky to get a plea."

"Really? I stuck around to talk to the jury. They weren't as impressed with your cross-examination of Detective Reese as you and Nelson. I think if we'd let this go all the way, they might've sent Knoll away for a very long time."

Catherine shrugged. Jurors often liked to pontificate when they were no longer bound to follow the rules of evidence, which was why she rarely bothered to talk to them after a trial. "Maybe, but your victory would've been short-lived." She started to say more, but the bartender appeared with her nachos.

"Those look amazing," Starr said.

Catherine resisted the urge to pull her plate closer. "I'm sure they have more."

Starr leaned back in her chair, obviously reading the rebuke. "I'm sure they do, but I couldn't possibly eat all that." She grimaced. "Sorry, I didn't mean that the way it sounded. There's nothing wrong with eating a full plate of nachos. I've done it many times, it's just—"

"Stop." Catherine pushed the plate so it was centered between them. "I couldn't possibly eat all these either. Have some."

"If you're sure."

Catherine nodded unable to keep from matching Starr's grin. She filled Starr's plate and watched while she dug in. "You must really like nachos."

"I like food of all kinds, but nachos are definitely high on the list. These are especially good."

"I know, right?"

Starr wiped her mouth with the napkin. "Okay, you were schooling me when the food arrived. Care to continue?"

Catherine did a quick rewind and remembered what she'd been about to say. It felt kind of petty now since they were sharing food, but she didn't want Starr to get the impression just because they were breaking bread they were no longer adversaries, although the way that Starr scrunched her eyes every time she took a bite of nachos was way more endearing than she'd like to admit. "We were talking about the trial. If the jury had found my client guilty, you and I both know an appellate court wouldn't uphold the conviction."

Starr crunched on a chip. "Not necessarily."

"Did you know about the rope?" Catherine lobbed the question and held her breath. She wasn't sure what she expected Starr to say. If she admitted she'd known Reese was lying, she'd be complicit as well.

"I knew the evidence wasn't conclusive."

"That's a fancy way of saying you knew your star witness was a liar."

"Reese isn't a bad cop. Besides, we both know Knoll was guilty or he wouldn't have taken the plea."

Starr punctuated her remark by taking another bite of nachos, stoking Catherine's anger. "Some day your methods are going to bite you in the ass."

"You don't know what you're talking about," Starr said.

"I do, actually. Everyone knows you like to bend the rules to get your way."

"'My way'? I think what you really mean to say is that I will do whatever it takes to make sure that bad guys like your client don't go free so they can commit new crimes."

Catherine took a drink from her beer and appraised Starr. She was passionate, for sure, but it wasn't the kind of passionate protest that came from being overly defensive. She seemed to really believe she was doing the right thing. Catherine wasn't sure if that made her more dangerous or less, but she was tired of talking about it. "Let's agree to disagree. There'll be plenty more cases to haggle over in the future."

The frown fell away from Starr's expression and she tilted her glass toward Catherine's beer. "Truth. Here's to future fights."

Catherine barely met the toast. She set her glass down and picked up her phone, hoping Starr would take the hint, finish her food, and leave. No such luck.

"Why have we never been up against each other before?"

Catherine didn't look up from her phone screen. "I have no idea."

"Rumor has it you don't take child abuse cases. Is that true?"

"Is there something you want to know?"

"Pardon?"

Catherine flicked her hand in the air between them. "We're not friends and I'm not in the habit of engaging in idle conversation with strangers. I have work to do, so perhaps you could find someone else to chat with. Take the nachos. I've lost my appetite." She saw Starr work to quickly cover her shocked expression, but she didn't care. Starr was just one more in a string of people who wanted to know the real story behind attorney Catherine Landauer, but Catherine wasn't falling for the casual good ole girl conversation. She reached into her bag and pulled out some papers just as the bartender reappeared.

"How is everything? Do you want to order more food?" He'd directed his question to both of them, but Catherine rushed to answer first. "I'm good." She pulled her plate closer and huddled around it, using her papers as a shield.

Starr pushed her plate away and swallowed the contents of her glass. She set it on the bar with a thud. "Like the lady said, we're good. Real good," she said. She reached into her pocket and pulled out a tip and set it on the bar. "Enjoy your dinner, Catherine." She was on the move as she delivered the farewell, and Catherine tried hard not to watch her depart, but she failed. Starr intrigued her, despite her bravado, and a tiny part of her wanted to engage further, but she knew better than to risk casual conversation, especially with anyone who worked at the courthouse. When the bartender returned to ask her if she'd like another drink, she pointed at Starr's empty glass. "What was she drinking?"

"Bourbon. Balcones, it's a local brand."

"Pour me a glass, please," she asked before she could rethink the decision. She doubted Starr would ever talk to her again, and she doubted if she'd ever want to, but if the occasion arose, they could swap whiskey stories. Catherine was used to inventing details to discuss that would keep her from having to disclose truths about her life.

❖

Starr spent the drive home with Catherine Landauer's accusation weighing heavily on her mind. She didn't have any regrets about the way she'd handled the Knoll case, so she wasn't sure why she'd let Catherine's comments get under her skin. She had no proof Reese had planted evidence. Certainly, he'd mishandled it, but that was up to a jury to decide. If anything, she wished Nelson hadn't forced a plea because she was confident she could've delivered a closing argument strong enough to blow past any doubts about Reese's sloppy evidence handling, leaving the jury with no choice but to put Knoll away for much longer than the seven years he'd gotten. Catherine had to know the guy was a total creep and society was better off with him behind bars.

Starr shook her head. She'd expected she and Catherine could put their work aside and share a friendly drink outside the courthouse like she did with other defense attorneys, but the rumors about Catherine were true—she was all work and no play. Too bad, because she was smart and gorgeous, the perfect package. Given the opportunity, Starr would've liked to share more than nachos with her, but clearly that was never going to happen.

She drove up to her house and pulled in the driveway. It wasn't late, but it was pitch-black outside and she was grateful for the motion-sensitive light over the garage. As she drew closer, she spotted someone lurking in the shadows. She reached into the console between the seats to make sure her gun was where she'd left it, and she grabbed her phone, ready to dial 911. She cracked the car window and shouted. "You have five seconds to get the hell away from my front door." She let hang the "or what" part of her statement, not interested in signaling she had her own firepower. She reached a silent count of three before a hulking form stepped out of the shadows.

"Pearson, is that you?" She shut the car off and lowered the window all the way down. "I almost shot your ass," she said as he strode up to her car window. "What are you doing here?"

"Need to talk to you about a warrant, Starr. Can I come in?"

Detective Jack Pearson worked the child abuse unit for the Austin Police Department, and they'd become good friends during the time Starr had led the unit at the DA's office. She missed seeing him on the daily, but as relieved as she was to see him instead of a burglar, she couldn't help him out. "I can't be grabbing warrants for you, Jack. Nelson will have my hide if he finds out I'm stepping on Pam's toes," she said, referring to the current head of the child abuse unit.

"I doubt Nelson will have anything to say about it. Murphy himself sent me to you. We've got a brewing situation and I need your help right now. Sorry, I know you probably didn't plan on working tonight."

She hadn't planned on working tonight, but it wasn't like she was celebrating either. Her "win" in the courtroom today wasn't a victory for anyone but Knoll, and it still galled her, especially since Catherine Landauer didn't even have the decency to be gracious about the generous plea offer. Maybe work was what she needed to cool the sting of Catherine's rebuff. "Come on in. Least I can do is make you a cup of coffee since you came all the way out here."

She led the way to the door. Pearson lived in the northern Austin suburb of Georgetown, a fact she'd needled him about plenty of times before. He'd protested that the housing prices were high in Austin proper, but she suspected that he enjoyed the more laid-back vibe and law-and-order feel of the smaller town. Either way, he'd have a long drive home at the end of the night, and she could offer him the courtesy of hearing him out. "Have a seat." She pointed at the kitchen table. "How are Liza and the kids?"

Jack rubbed his eyes. "Liza's great. Just got a promotion at the hospital. But the kids are growing up too fast. I don't know how to stop it though."

"Nothing you can do," Starr said. She pressed the button on the electric kettle and spooned coffee into the French press. While she waited for the water to boil, she slid into the seat across from him. "You look worried. Is it the kids?"

"Yes and no. I mean Jack Jr. and Macy are great now, but if I could lock them away until they turn thirty, I'm pretty sure I would do it." He leaned in, his brow furrowed. "A kid went missing this afternoon. On her way home from school. One minute she was walking down the street, talking to one of her friends. They get to her friend's house and the friend goes inside, while the girl keeps walking. Friend looks out the window and sees the girl talking to someone in a pickup, and she hasn't been seen since."

"White pickup?"

Pearson looked surprised. "Yes, how did you know?"

"Amber alert. Saw it on the way home."

Pearson nodded. "I didn't know it was posted yet, but it doesn't surprise me. Yes, it was a medium-sized, white pickup, and that's about all we have as far as a description goes. When she didn't show up at home, the girl's mother called the friend, who told her what she'd seen, and here we are."

"Any leads?"

"Not many. Girl's cell phone is a dead end. Find feature and cell phone towers place it last in the vicinity of her friend's house, but nothing after that. We've searched her parents' house and didn't find anything helpful, but there's a formerly estranged uncle in town who's got a record and who happens to have a white Ford pickup registered in his name."

"What's his record?"

"Nothing big time, but he slammed the door shut when we tried to talk to him. We're thinking if we can get a judge to grant a warrant to search his truck we can use that to get him to open up. In the meantime, we've got folks talking to all her friends and teachers, and search teams are already in motion."

Starr nodded as he talked. She totally got the urgency of the situation, but still wasn't sure why he was here. "As much as I'd like to help, you're going to have to go to Pam on this. I can give her a call if you want."

"Murphy's giving this one to you."

"What? Why?"

"I may have forgotten to mention who the girl is. She's Hannah Turner."

Starr jerked at the familiar name. "Mayor Turner's daughter? No fucking way."

"Yep, which is why we have to put every resource we have in motion right fucking now. In fact, I was hoping that after we get the warrant, you would go with me to talk to the mayor and give her an update."

Holy shit. A tumble of thoughts cascaded through her brain. Horror at how the mayor must be feeling knowing her daughter was missing, angst at the idea of being sucked back into the gruesome world of child abuse cases, but both of these emotions were tangled up with a sense of excitement that she was being tasked to lead this investigation. She was born for this and it was her chance to prove she was ready to head the office.

The electric kettle whistled loudly, tearing her back to the reality of Pearson's request. She looked wistfully at the kettle, and then back at Pearson. "I know you love my coffee, but if we're going to get ahead of this, we don't have time for my special brew." She stood and grabbed her keys. "Let's go."

CHAPTER THREE

Catherine had been at her desk for an hour when Doris came in with a steaming mug of coffee. She accepted it with thanks, having long since given up telling Doris she could get her own coffee. "Do you have the file for the Stevens plea?"

Doris set the mug down and pulled a file from under her arm. "Here you go. Anything else you need before you leave?"

Catherine shook her head, constantly amazed that Doris was able to anticipate her every need, especially since she was well aware she didn't communicate her desires very well. "Why don't you take off early today? I'm not coming back to the office after court, and since the Rockland trial got postponed, we can put off organizing the witness files until next week." She looked back down at her work before Doris could answer to make it clear that her suggestion was actually an order.

"Sounds great. I'll take a late lunch and close up shop for the afternoon. Have a great weekend."

Catherine waited until she was alone again and then closed her eyes and rubbed her temples. She'd been out of sorts all morning and she wasn't sure why. The Knoll case was over, and her looming federal trial had been postponed for a month. She was caught up on the rest of her cases, and business was good, but an unrelenting sense of doom pervaded her thoughts and she didn't think it was going away on its own. She knew what she should do, but she resisted, choosing instead to stuff her feelings and hope they would go away.

The courthouse was humming for a Friday. Usually the end of the week was calmer with pleas having been worked out and trials coming to a close, but today attorneys were hanging out in the halls talking to each other rather than rushing off to golf games and lunchtime happy hours. She passed several small groups, nodding to each, but not joining in. Joining in wasn't something she did. Her peers knew this, and most no longer even tried to get her to take part in courthouse gossip, but she couldn't help but hear snippets of their conversation as she passed.

"The mayor's daughter," "She's beside herself," "I heard she wants to do a press conference," "No good can come of that," "Maybe she'll turn up. It's only been a day," "You know what they say…"

Curiosity claimed Catherine's attention and she slowed her pace. She hadn't listened to the news in the car, but now she was almost desperate to know what was going on. She pulled out her phone and opened the app for the local news, gasping when the lead story loaded. *Mayor Turner's twelve-year-old daughter presumed kidnapped. Law enforcement has few leads.*

She sank against the wall, the power of the digital words fierce and wounding and personal. She wanted to read them again, will them to form into another headline, one that didn't strike at her heart and threaten to take her down.

"Catherine, are you okay?"

Catherine looked up at the familiar face of Judge Lisa Tatum, who'd been a friend in law school. She waved a hand. "Sure. Just slightly dizzy, but I'll be fine." She saw Lisa glance at the screen of her phone, and she winced. "Do you know if there's any word on the mayor's daughter?"

"Not yet, but they're pursuing some leads. Between us, they came to me last night for a warrant. They're doing that delicate balancing act between keeping the press informed enough to stay interested in the case and keeping things under wraps. I've gone through one of these before. I bet there'll be a press conference soon if we don't hear anything."

"Pam's going to have her hands full." Catherine knew the chief of child abuse from years ago, when she, Pam, and Lisa had been in law school together. Now that Pam was in child abuse, they no longer went head-to-head on cases, and Pam's all-consuming job meant they rarely saw each other. Now it would get even worse. She made a mental note to drop by and say hello.

"Oh, I don't think Pam's working this one. Starr Rio brought me the warrant affidavit with Detective Pearson. I got the impression Starr is taking the lead."

"What?" Catherine's stomach flipped and she felt the blood drain from her face. She wanted to ask if this was some kind of cruel joke, but her throat closed, and she choked on the words.

"Seriously, are you okay?" Lisa's brow was furrowed, and she reached out a hand, but Catherine instinctively jerked away at the touch. She knew her reaction was irrational, but the roar in her ears brought with it a wave of emotion, exponentially stronger now than when she'd just learned about the missing girl moments ago. Her skin felt tight, and she strained against the urge to drop her bag and run as fast as she could toward the exit, far away from this news, this situation.

Reaching deep into reserves she'd carefully cultivated over time, she took a deep breath and mustered a smile. "I must be feeling a bit under the weather today. Nothing serious, I'm sure." She edged away. "I'll talk to you later." She moved quickly before Lisa could say more, suggest they get together, or any of the other overtures she usually made when they ran into each other. Overtures that Catherine routinely ignored. Seeing each other at the courthouse was one thing, but connecting outside made it too easy to let someone get close to her, and she studiously avoided such interactions.

But there was one person she wanted to see right now. She strode to the stairwell and climbed the stairs to her destination. She resisted screaming at the woman at the desk who asked if she had an appointment, instead forcing her mind to remain calm as she waited impatiently for the county employee to take her sweet time fetching the prosecutor she was there to see. Finally, the woman handed her a badge. "She said you can go on back. I'll buzz you in."

Catherine ignored the dull roar in her ears and wound her way through the long hallway until she reached her destination. Pam was waiting in the doorway.

"Hey, girl, it's great to see you." Pam stepped back and appraised her. "But you don't look so hot. Are you okay?"

"Are you working on the mayor's daughter's case?" Catherine blurted the words, unwilling and unable to apologize for her abrupt greeting.

Pam glanced down the hallway before pulling her into the room and shutting the door. "Have a seat." She waited until Catherine sank into the chair across from her desk. "What's going on?"

"Pam, I need to know. Lisa said Starr Rio brought her a search warrant last night. Is she working the case with you?"

Pam shook her head. "Looks like I've been benched for this one. Of course, I'll lend a hand if asked, but Murphy put Starr in charge of the task force. Doesn't bother me personally since I've got more than I can handle going on right now, but Nelson came unglued when he found out. Probably thinks it will give Starr a leg up in the race for Murphy's job."

Catherine heard the words, but they barely registered. She had to do something. Someone like Starr Rio shouldn't be working this case. It was unconscionable and the results would be catastrophic. "You have to talk to him."

"Nelson?"

"No, Murphy. Starr just blew a case because she put a witness on the stand who manufactured evidence. In a case like this, with so much pressure, she'll do whatever it takes to get a conviction even if it means whoever did it goes free because of her shoddy work."

Pam stared at her like she'd grown a second head. "Starr used to run this department, and she's got a ton more experience than me. I know she can be a bit overzealous at times, but if I thought for one second she was a bad seed, I'd be the first one at Murphy's door to report her. Look at it this way—she'll have the entire city of Austin watching every move she makes. If she takes a wrong turn, there's no way it'll get past the press."

Catherine sat silently, processing Pam's words in the context of another case she knew where an entire city had been watching. She knew Pam believed what she was saying, but Pam was blithely dismissing the very real threat that pressure from all the scrutiny would tempt Starr to cut corners, especially since she was predisposed to shortcuts in the first place. She wanted to press the issue, but she didn't want Pam to think she was losing her mind. She'd have to find another way to get her point across, one that didn't expose her own vulnerabilities.

"You're right, of course." Catherine stood. "I should get going. I've got a plea in Richards's court and you know how he hates waiting."

Pam came out from behind her desk and gave her a light hug. "I'm glad you came by, even if it was to talk business. Don't be a stranger."

"I won't," Catherine said, well aware that Pam knew she was lying. She left the office and headed back to the stairwell, but before she entered, she reached for her phone and pulled up a number she hadn't called in months. When the voice on the other end answered, she didn't waste any time. "I need an appointment and I need it today."

Starr rubbed her eyes, took another sip of the now cold coffee, and avoided looking at herself in Pearson's rearview mirror. She figured she probably looked like hell, but now was not the time to let up. "I can go for the rest of the day as long as you get me a hot coffee." She pointed at Jo's up ahead on the right.

"There's no parking."

She admired the fact he wouldn't use his badge to skirt the rules, but she was more concerned about her dipping energy. "Let me out and I'll buy. Two times around the block should do it."

He pulled close to the curb, and she hopped out and merged with the variety of SoCo java junkies lined up to get the best brew in Austin. This place had been her go-to when she'd lived close by, but now that she lived on the north edge of town, she rarely fought the traffic and crowds to satisfy her cravings. Pretty much summed up her entire life. All cravings took a back seat to the job and her ambition, but she told herself that would all change as soon as she achieved her pinnacle of success as the newly-elected district attorney of Travis County. For now, she'd have to be satisfied with an Americano and a breakfast burrito, and she ordered two of each from the redhead at the window who greeted her with a smile.

"Haven't seen you around before," the girl said as she handed back Starr's credit card.

"My loss," Starr said, trying to decide if she was being flirted with.

"If you say so," the redhead said with a slight smile. She handed over a bag. "The croissant's on me. Have a great day."

Starr spotted Pearson a moment later and waved to a spot away from the breakfast crowd. On her way back to the car, she replayed the encounter with the girl and smiled. She probably flirted with most of the customers, but the attention still felt nice. Starr couldn't remember the last time she had been on a date. Oh wait, there had been that setup her brother Davis had arranged last month that had taken a bad turn when the woman launched into a diatribe about police brutality before they'd even ordered drinks. Starr was all for an open discussion of current events, but Erica had made it pretty clear she had an agenda, and she wasn't interested in debating the topic, only ramrodding her viewpoint home. Starr had left a twenty on the bar and told Erica she didn't think they were meant for each other. She'd called Davis on the way home to ask him what the hell he'd been thinking. He'd laughed and told her she was too rigid, which was hilarious coming from a cop. Part of her had been relieved it hadn't worked out, since her job and the upcoming election would put a serious strain on her schedule.

She climbed into Pearson's car and shoved the bag toward him. "I bought you a burrito."

"There's a croissant in here."

"That's mine."

"What the fuck, you didn't think I would want one?"

"It was a gift. Besides since when do you eat pastry?"

"Since Liza doesn't allow carbs in the house. She's hangry all the time, and now that she's Lady Keto, I'm constantly craving pasta and baked goods, which I never did before. Split it with me?"

Starr laughed and tore the croissant in half. "Now you know why I'm not married."

He grinned. "The list of reasons why you're not married goes way beyond this croissant."

She play punched him in the shoulder. She knew he was teasing, but like most teases there was a strain of truth running through his words. She told herself she shouldn't care, but she did—a fact to examine later when they weren't deep in the middle of trying to find the mayor's daughter. "I think we should go back to the Turners' house."

Pearson groaned, but he took the next turn to take them back toward the wealthy Austin neighborhood where the Honorable Linda Turner and her husband lived. The hardest part of any case was dealing with the victim or the victim's family. They craved reassurance, answers, insights, and frustration quickly turned to anger when none of those things were forthcoming. Early on in the case was the worst, but it was the most important time to establish a foundation of trust because a family that didn't trust law enforcement was more likely to engage in risky behavior that could compromise the investigation.

The mayor's house was a sprawling two-story ranch style home on a large lot at the center of a cul-de-sac. Starr spotted one patrol car in the drive and another farther down the street, both in place at the request of the police chief, a perfect example of locking the barn door after the horse went missing. After Pearson parked his car, she followed him up the drive, lingering behind while he stopped to talk to the officers in the patrol unit parked in the drive.

"Everyone home?" he asked.

The officer shook his head. "Mr. Turner left a little while ago with one of ours. Picking up some work from the office. He wanted to go on his own, but we insisted on accompanying him."

"Good call," Pearson replied. "Let me know when he shows back up. We're going inside. Anything we need to know?"

"Family attorney showed up a little while ago and he's been huddled inside with the mayor, but other than that everything has been quiet."

Starr braced for resistance, wondering who the family attorney was and why he was here. She pulled Pearson aside before they reached the front door. "Don't you think it's a little weird that Dad is headed to the office when his daughter is missing?"

"I do, but can't say as I'm surprised. Tell me you didn't pick up on the tension between them last night."

"I did, but tension is one thing and optics are another. Brace yourself. I have a feeling that Mama Bear is not going to be very happy."

The atmosphere inside the house was thick with angst. Mayor Turner pushed past the officer in the foyer to get to them, but her hopeful expression fell away the moment she spotted Pearson's grim face. "Oh," she said.

"Good morning, ma'am," Pearson said. "We don't have any updates, but Ms. Rio would like to talk to you again."

The mayor looked puzzled for a second before her features settled into what Starr recognized as her public face. "Of course."

Starr reached out a hand. "You'll likely be seeing a lot of me until your daughter is home, safe and sound. Mr. Murphy has taken a personal interest in your daughter's case and assigned me to work with Detective Pearson's team to ensure we maximize our resources so that we can return your daughter home safe and sound."

Turner nodded. "Tell me what you need."

Starr glanced around. "I was hoping to talk to you and your husband at the same time, but I understand he had to leave. Will he be back soon?"

"I believe so, but we don't need to wait. I can fill him in later."

Starr asked the question only to gauge her reaction, and the flicker of annoyance was quick and telling. It was perfectly normal for families facing tragedy to start to fall apart at the seams, but usually the fraying started later, after frustration at the lack of answers began to wear. It had been less than forty-eight hours and already the cracks were beginning to show, which signaled a deeper issue divided them. Starr was determined to discover the source and figure out whether it had anything to do with their daughter's disappearance. "Perhaps we could sit down?"

Turner shook her head like she was trying to wake up. "Certainly. Forgive my manners. Follow me."

Starr shot a look at Pearson who shrugged. They both followed the mayor down the hall to a large room lined with bookshelves. Starr didn't recognize the man sitting in the room, but he had lawyer written all over him, from his expensive suit to the pompous expression with which he regarded them. He rose to greet them.

"Linda, is everything okay?"

"Nothing will be okay until Hannah is back," she said, but her tone wasn't chastising, it was forlorn. "William, this is Starr Rio from the DA's office and Detective Pearson who is taking the lead on the investigation. William is a long time family friend. He's also a lawyer. Perhaps you know each other," Turner said, looking at Starr.

Starr stuck out her hand and tried not to squirm at the half-assed handshake William delivered. "I don't believe we've met." She saw William cut his eyes toward Pearson like he wanted to wish him out of the room, but Pearson merely nodded and smiled.

Turner motioned for them to sit down, and the moment they were settled, William launched in. "I was thinking perhaps I could act as a liaison. Understandably, the Turners are overwrought, but you could let me know what's going on and any information you need and I'll facilitate the communications."

What the hell? Starr resisted saying the words out loud, but just barely. Instead she crossed her hands in her lap and looked at him, letting silence work for her. It didn't take long.

"We could proceed a different way too. We want to be flexible and work with you on all aspects of the investigation."

Starr felt Pearson getting restless behind her. She wanted to stop this cat and mouse game and set him loose on this joker, but if there was something else going on that would help them solve this case, they weren't going to figure it out by pushing. "We appreciate your help. I was just saying to the mayor that we thought it would be a good idea to talk when Mr. Turner returns. What do you think?"

"That sounds like a good plan, but in the meantime, Linda could tell you what she knows in the interest of efficiency."

He said "interest of efficiency" like he was talking about a corporate merger, and Starr cringed inwardly, but on the outside, she maintained a steady smile. "That would be perfect. Don't you agree, Detective Pearson?" The question was rhetorical. Mostly she just wanted to make eye contact with Pearson to make sure they were on the same page—find out what had prompted the Turners to feel like they needed to have an attorney present while they talked to the police about what had to be the most devastating thing that could happen to a parent.

"Absolutely," Pearson said. "I'd like to start by going over Hannah's daily routine."

Turner cast a quick look at William whose nod was almost imperceptible. "My husband usually drops Hannah off at school around seven forty-five. She has private lessons with her clarinet teacher, Mr. Gordon, before band practice. But yesterday, Keith had an early meeting, so Hannah rode in with one of her friends' parents, Rochelle Delson."

Starr made a note that they'd need to talk to the Delsons but didn't interrupt the flow of the account. Pearson merely nodded. "We've talked to Mr. Gordon, so we know that she made it there on time. Her other teachers say that she was in all of her scheduled classes. What did she usually do for lunch?"

"It varied. Like most kids, she hated taking a lunch even to the point she would use her own allowance to pay for lunch when we wouldn't give in…"

The mayor's voice trailed off, and she coughed to cover her throat choking up. Starr could only imagine how painful it must be to rerun every interaction in her mind, knowing it might be the last conversation she'd ever have with her missing daughter.

"How about we get a list of her friends?" Starr said. "People she hung out with at school. We can fill in details from what they remember."

Mayor Turner reached for a Kleenex, dabbed at her eyes, and cleared her throat. "Yes, that sounds good. We'll do that as soon as we're done here."

"Did you get the warrant?" William interjected in a complete non sequitur.

Starr stared at him for a moment, contemplating her approach. She could feel Pearson bristling at the question, but of course the mayor's office would have the resources to find out more about a pending investigation than the average citizen, so she wasn't sure why they were surprised. What did surprise her was that they didn't know what had happened. "We don't have sufficient grounds to obtain a warrant yet. We need more information. I know you told Detective Pearson about your brother-in-law's record, but I ran his criminal history and he's never been accused of any crimes against people, only financial crimes. Without something to tie him to your daughter's disappearance, no judge is going to give us a warrant to search his car or his home."

"Is that so? There are a lot of judges in this town." Mayor Turner's implication was clear, and William reached over and placed a hand on her arm.

"What the mayor means," he said, "is that surely you can find someone open to the possibility the child's uncle has some knowledge of Hannah's whereabouts?"

Starr turned away from him and focused her attention on the mayor. "Do you think your brother-in-law took your daughter or knows where she is?"

"I don't know. Maybe. He asked us for a loan last week. He could be trying to ransom her. I know no one has asked for a ransom yet, but maybe they are waiting for the right moment."

Starr wanted to brush away the hypothetical as pure speculation, but she'd seen too many other crazy things in her career to ignore the accusation completely. "I think it would be helpful to speak to your husband about this. Did he say when he'd be back?"

Again the subtle exchange of looks between the mayor and William. Starr was about to call them on it when they were interrupted by a man's voice from the doorway.

"I'm here."

Starr had never met the mayor's husband. Professor Keith Turner rarely appeared with his wife at public functions, and generally kept a low profile. She watched him carefully as he rushed across the room to his wife's side. He was trim, athletic, and good-looking. He taught economics at the University of Texas and, based on what Starr had found on the internet the night before, he was well liked by his students, especially the female ones. Bookish wasn't her thing, so she didn't get it, but she could imagine how the handsome professor might make the coeds swoon.

"Do you have an update?"

Pearson responded quickly, likely to dispel the look of hopefulness on his face. "Not yet."

Starr watched his face fall, and he reached for his wife's hand. The pause lasted a second too long before she clasped his outstretched hand, and Starr seized on the obvious discord between them. "Your wife just told us about your brother. Would you like to fill us in about his record?"

CHAPTER FOUR

Catherine pressed the buzzer and stared at the door, willing it to open. She was already annoyed that she'd had to wait all day for this appointment. She'd barely been able to concentrate on any of her work and had finally abandoned all pretense at productive activity, choosing to spend the balance of the day buried in the internet, hungrily devouring every bit of information she could find about Mayor Turner's missing daughter. The details were scarce. The day she'd gone missing, Hannah Turner had gone to school. According to her teachers and classmates, it had been a normal day. She'd walked home in the company of one of her friends. When they'd arrived at the friend's house, Hannah had continued on her own, but her friend spotted her talking to someone in a white pickup, and she hadn't been seen since. The police were circulating photos of Hannah, and as much information as they had, but it wasn't much. Search and rescue teams were forming to hunt for her, starting with the wooded area a few blocks from the school, but Catherine knew more intimately than any of them that she could be anywhere, and she might very well be missing for a very long time.

Her gut clenched and she reached for the buzzer again, her finger wavering while she fought for control. *Keep it together.* She lowered her hand and paced the room, silently repeating the mantra until she thought she'd calmed down, but when the door finally opened, she nearly jumped out of her skin. Dr. Wanda Marsh stood in the doorway wearing a purple dress that billowed around her tall, willowy frame.

"You're late," Catherine said. "I almost left," she lied.

Dr. M looked at her watch. "I'm exactly on time, but I'm glad you didn't leave. Would you like to come in?"

Catherine hesitated, the familiar push and pull tearing her apart. Staying was necessary, but she longed to be far away from this office and the reason why she was here in the first place. But the truth was she didn't have a choice. She never would. "I'll stay."

"Excellent. Come on in."

Catherine followed her into the room. She hadn't been back here in over six months, but nothing about the office had changed, from the homey collection of outdated furniture to the funky collection of folk art adorning the walls and every available surface. Catherine spotted her favorite brown corduroy chair but lingered in the middle of the room until Dr. M said, "have a seat," before settling in, telling herself it would be impolite not to. Once she was seated, Dr. M plunked into the chair across from her, her legs tucked up into the cushion and her hands outstretched and welcoming. Her casualness had bothered Catherine at first. She'd taken the unprofessional clothing and the mismatched furnishings as a sign of disrespect, minimizing her issues, but at some point, Catherine had started to realize Dr. M's approach was a subtle way of breaking down any barriers between them. If she'd shown up in a suit and ushered Catherine into a sterile office atmosphere, there would have always been a wall between them—two professionals vying for who could be the smartest person in the room. Dr. M's laid-back demeanor caused Catherine to stand down. These meetings weren't a contest; they were a fight for survival, and she took deep comfort in knowing they were on the same side.

"It's good to see you," Dr. M said with genuine warmth. "Is there something particular on your mind today?"

Catherine wanted to yell "Of course there is. This is the first time I've been here in months," but she knew that just because she'd been slammed by the news of Hannah Turner's disappearance didn't mean it was on everyone else's radar. Instead she focused on clearing up unsettled business. "Thanks for seeing me. I know it's been a while."

"You're always welcome here."

Catherine felt a tinge of annoyance that Dr. M wasn't angrier that she'd stopped these sessions, against her advice, only to abruptly insist on being seen at once months later. Catherine knew her anger wasn't rational, but she didn't care. "Why am I always welcome? Are you so desperate for clients, you'd take back one that ran out before she was done?"

Dr. M's facial expression didn't change, but Catherine caught a flicker in her eyes that signaled sympathy, and she struggled to keep that from sending her into a rage.

"If you want to talk about why you left, we can do that, but I got the impression on the phone that something new had become an urgent matter. We can start with whichever subject you'd like."

Catherine had a choice. She could keep trying to push Dr. M away or she could tell her the reason she'd come in the first place. She took a deep breath and took the plunge. "Have you seen the news?"

"I read the paper this morning."

"Then you must know about the mayor's daughter."

Dr. M nodded. "There weren't a lot of details in the story I saw, but I gather everyone is really worried."

"And they should be. They should be way more worried than they are. They have absolutely no idea what they're dealing with."

"And you do?"

"She was taken."

"Maybe. I heard the police are looking into several possibilities."

"That's what they tell the press to keep it from becoming a feeding frenzy. She's been taken. I know from a very reliable source that the police know this, and they are following up on leads."

"That's good that the police are on it. Right?"

Catherine shook her head. "Please."

"You disagree?"

"I absolutely disagree. All they are likely to do is fuck things up." Catherine's voice rose with the declaration and she saw Dr. M's face scrunch slightly, but she didn't care. She was paying her, after all, and if she wanted to shout to get her point across, that was her prerogative.

"And you know this?"

"Without a doubt."

"Because of what happened to you."

Catherine bit back a sarcastic response and sat silent, wondering why she had come here today. Yesterday, in the panic of hearing about Hannah's disappearance, she had been desperate for the familiar comfort of Dr. M's office, but it had been too long since she'd been here and now everything was awkward and unfamiliar. "I think I should go."

"That's one choice."

"You act like I have a choice about anything," Catherine snapped as the powerlessness of her past nipped at her present. Intellectually, she knew she wasn't without power. She'd spent years working to make sure she had choices, that her past would not confine her to living her life in the shadow of what had happened to her, letting it define everything about her. But right now it felt like all her hard work had been in vain. All the money, all the time, all the angst of regurgitating every sordid detail, every rotten feeling, every memory that for years had jarred her from sleep, screaming in the night, and here she was, weak and vulnerable because of a news story about a little girl she didn't even know. "I just can't."

"Give me two minutes, and if you decide you want to leave after that, I won't try to stop you."

Catherine suspected the two-minute promise was a trick, but she let herself fall for it. She sat back down but stayed on the edge of her seat. "Time starts now."

"You say you can't, but you underestimate your abilities. You heard about Hannah Turner and you called me. How long did you wait? Not even a day?"

"For all the good it did. You made me wait a day to see you."

"You assured me on the phone you weren't in immediate danger. Another choice. You make choices all the time, and most of them are about surviving. You changed your name. You put yourself through law school. You run a successful practice. For five years, you came to see me every week. These are choices you have made. Important choices. Choices that say you care about taking care of yourself, but the truth is you will probably have to keep making these choices the rest of your life because what happened to you was horrible and traumatic, and while we can give you tools to cope with it, I can't make it go away. So, the question is, are you going to choose to deal with how this is affecting you or are you going to choose to bury your feelings so that they can resurface in some random way that will likely bite you in the ass when you least expect it?"

Catherine smiled and shook her head. "You sounded all professional until you said 'ass.'"

Dr. M grinned. "Well, none of us is perfect."

Catherine wanted to tell her that what she said *was* perfect. It was exactly what she needed to hear to shake her out of her head, and she needed to get out of her head because her brain was conjuring up all kinds of crazy nightmares right now. But instead she settled on a simple, "I'll stay."

"Sounds good. Let's start with how you heard."

"At the courthouse. Everyone was talking about it."

"Did you join in?"

"No. I mean not generally. I talked to a friend of mine who's a judge, and she told me a little more detail and the name of the prosecutor working the case." Catherine's voice shook as she said the last words and she struggled to steady her voice. "She didn't tell me anything that's not public."

"Okay, but she did tell you something that triggered your reaction."

"What are you implying? Don't you think it's natural for me to react this way, simply based on the facts?"

"Sure, but there's something else going on. Surely you can feel it too. Why is this particular case affecting you so strongly?"

"Why do you think?"

"I know why in general, but I guess I mean as compared to other cases. You're at the courthouse all the time. I imagine you hear about all kinds of missing children cases, and perhaps much worse."

Catherine knew the answer, so why was it so hard to admit it? Especially here in this safe place. Nothing she said here would ever be repeated, but the act of saying something out loud had a power she wasn't sure she wanted to unleash, especially here where the next step was to examine her feelings around it. She struggled with her emotions for a few minutes before blurting out the reason for her angst. "The prosecutor they assigned to the case is a fraud. She's going to blow the whole thing, and even if they make an arrest, they will never bring the defendant to justice."

Dr. M set her notebook down and nodded. "That sounds horrible."

"It is."

"What do you think motivates her?"

"What?"

"This prosecutor, what's her name?"

"Starr. Starr Rio."

"It sounds like you've had experience with her before."

"I have."

"In the courtroom?"

"Yes, recently."

"And she screwed you over?"

"Tried to."

"Back to my original question. What motivates her?"

Catherine knew what motivated people like Starr—the desire to win, power—but that didn't justify their behavior. "It doesn't matter. If she's not following the law, if she's cutting corners, then she shouldn't be working this case."

"Have you considered that they assigned her to work this case for that very reason? It's possible that finding this child as quickly as possible is more important than bringing her abductor to justice. There are different kinds of incompetence."

"I know that." Catherine bristled even though she recognized the truth in Dr. M's words.

"Of course you do, but this is personal. Is it possible you wish you'd had someone like Starr working on your case? Someone who was more concerned about finding you than building an airtight case?"

Catherine's head started to swim and her eyes were filled with spots of light. This hadn't happened in so long, it took her a moment to recognize the signs, but once she did she fought the mist falling down around her. She couldn't afford to relinquish control, not when she'd fought so hard to regain it. She gripped the arms of the chair.

"Are you with me?"

The firm, quiet voice penetrated the veil, and Catherine struggled to form words. "Need a minute."

She felt a hard object being pressed into her hand, and she knew without looking it was one of the quarter-sized, royal blue hunks of sodalite Dr. M kept in a wooden bowl on the table next to her chair. Catherine squeezed tightly and ran her thumb along the smooth surface of the rock until the mist started to fade. It had been so very long since she'd needed this particular ritual, she'd thought she was past it. She wanted to let the stone drop to the ground and tumble far away, but she couldn't bear to let it go. Not when her feelings were still so raw. She gripped it hard. "I'm okay now."

"Did you go all the way back?"

"No," Catherine said, pleased with the realization she hadn't totally backslid. "Just got foggy. I managed to kick my way out of it."

"That's a big deal." She waited a beat. "Why don't you tell me more about this prosecutor?"

Catherine started to say she didn't know much, but the truth was she'd spent last night on the internet filling in all the pieces she could find. She didn't want to talk about Starr, but she figured it couldn't hurt to have a safe place to disclose all her concerns, for all the good it would do Hannah Turner. "You've probably heard of her. She's planning to run for district attorney."

"Pretend I don't follow the news and fill me in."

Catherine hated pretending, but she knew from experience protesting wasn't going to get her anywhere. "Starr Rio. The heir apparent to the district attorney, Patrick Murphy. Everyone at the

DA's office thinks she's wonderful, but she cuts corners to win, and sometimes those corners are the defendant's civil rights."

"You've had a few run-ins with her?"

"Just one, but it was enough. The rest I've learned from research. Starr is the absolute worst person to be working this case." She could hear the desperation in her own voice, bordering on craziness. She wished she knew a way to convey to everyone that she knew what she was talking about without having to rehash painful details.

As if she could read her mind, Dr. M said, "I trust that you know that, but tell me, is it because of what you do now or because of your past experience?"

"Does it matter?"

"Maybe."

Catherine considered the question, but it was hard to balance the scared girl she'd been with the fierce attorney she'd become. As a child, she'd spent weeks in captivity because the task force assigned to find her had taken shortcuts and focused on the wrong suspect. As an adult, she fought to make sure law enforcement paid for sloppy mistakes. When they'd first started these sessions, Dr. M had questioned her many times about why she hadn't used her power to advocate to help victims instead of those accused of a crime, and it had taken her years to verbalize her reasoning. It boiled down to the fact she couldn't handle the grief that came with working with victims, but she relished holding cops accountable. Simply put, if they did their job, they would win, but if they didn't, they would remember how she'd torn them apart, and hopefully, it would make them do better in the future.

But that didn't really answer Dr. M's question. Would she have wanted someone like Starr Rio on her case? Someone whose overzealous advocacy meant she'd place a priority on finding the missing girl over convicting the person who'd taken her? A ruthless prosecutor who cared more about winning than the rights of the accused.

Probably. No, make that yes, absolutely. But she wasn't Hannah Turner with a rich, well-known mother equipped with bottomless resources to put to work to find her daughter. She'd never have the opportunity to know how it felt to choose between her own freedom and the revenge of justice since her kidnapper had never been caught, a fact that still stung. Maybe Starr was the perfect match for this case and Catherine knew in her core, the best thing she could do was let it go. Her past had nothing to do with this case, and the sooner she stopped trying to make this personal, the sooner her nightmares would stop.

CHAPTER FIVE

Starr studied Professor Keith Turner carefully. Nothing about his visage signaled her question about his brother provoked nerves on his part, but she was certain she detected a wall falling into place, shuddering his demeanor into neutral.

"What would you like to know?" he asked. He motioned to a chair next to the mayor. "Do you mind if I sit down? It's been a particularly trying couple of days."

His reference to their daughter's disappearance was designed to evoke sympathy, but Starr sensed he was only saying what he thought they wanted to hear and it reeked of insincerity. "Of course, please do," she said. "We were just talking to your wife and your family lawyer about various aspects of the investigation. Both of them mentioned your brother, so I'd like to follow up on that. How long has he lived in Austin?"

"He doesn't," Professor Turner said. "I mean, he's only here temporarily, while he's waiting on a job to open in California."

"The mayor mentioned he has a record. Is he currently on probation or parole?"

For the first time, Professor Turner showed some sign of discomfort and shifted in his seat. "Not that I'm aware of. We're not particularly close. You know how it is. Siblings living in different parts of the country. You fall out of touch."

Starr couldn't relate. Her oldest brother lived in New York, but they still managed to see each other several times a year, and the rest of her siblings and their kids gathered at her parents' house in nearby Georgetown at least once a month to catch up with one another and share a meal. She plastered on a fake smile and lied. "Sure, I get it. When's the last time you talked to him?"

Professor Turner looked at the mayor who returned his glance with a frozen stare. He shrugged. "Not long ago. Probably this past weekend."

"Where was that?" Pearson asked.

"We had an early birthday party for Hannah at the zoo. Nothing fancy. Just some friends and their parents. I invited Ricky to come." Again, the flicker of a glance at his wife, like he was looking for her approval. "I didn't think he'd actually show up, but he dropped by for a little while. He even brought Hannah a gift."

"What did he give her?" Pearson's tone was casual, but Starr felt him tense and she did too.

Keith scrunched his face like he was trying to remember. "It was a necklace. A heart with a little diamond. Probably a little extravagant for a twelve-year-old, but it was nice, and she liked it a lot."

Pearson shot Starr a look and tried not to show his reaction. Pretty memorable gift, and definitely not appropriate. The scenario started to play out: convicted felon uncle who barely knows the kid comes to her birthday party, gives her an extravagant present, and a few days later she goes missing. There was more here. A lot more, but Starr didn't want to spook either Keith or his brother with an over-the-top reaction. "He must really care about her."

"Likely making up for lost time."

Pearson pulled out his flip book. "We'll want to talk to anyone who has seen Hannah in the last week, so I'll add your brother to the list. Can you give me his contact info?"

Starr stood. "While he's doing that, do you mind if I use the restroom? Mayor Turner, do you mind showing me the way?"

Turner looked at William, but Starr couldn't read the signals they exchanged. After a few seconds, Turner smiled her public smile. "Certainly. Come with me."

Starr waited until they were down the hall from the study to speak. "Mayor, may I be frank with you?"

"Yes, I expect you to be straightforward with me."

"I know you have the family attorney in there with you, and as an attorney myself, I'm all for protecting your rights and having legal counsel to help you do so, but I'm sensing some serious tension between you and your husband, and if it has anything at all to do with this case, I need to know. Right now, access to information outweighs anyone's rights. The clock is ticking, and if we don't have some serious leads in the next twenty-four hours, we may never see your daughter again."

The mayor sighed. "I'd like to tell you that my differences with Keith are because of Hannah's disappearance, but the truth is, we've been having trouble for a while and the acrimony escalated since last weekend." She pointed to a door on the right. "Let's go in here. We won't be disturbed."

Starr followed her through the door into another study, but this one had lighter colors and more modern furniture. Turner didn't invite her to sit.

"Ricky asked us for money when he got to town to tide him over until his 'job' comes through." The mayor added air quotes around the word job. "I don't know if Keith gave him money, but I made it clear I didn't want to extend a loan. Next thing I know, Ricky shows up at Hannah's birthday party with a gift that had to have cost at least a few hundred dollars. I pointed out the irony to Keith, and he shrugged it off, but it's definitely caused a rift in what was an already rocky road between us." She folded her arms. "I'm telling you this because I want my daughter back. If I see anything about my marital issues in the press, I'll know it came from you and I will ruin you. Do you understand me?"

Starr stepped into the mayor's personal space. "You don't know me very well, but I'm going to be the next district attorney of this county. As DA I won't take kindly to threats, and I'm starting now. We will do everything in our power to find your daughter, and if foul play was involved, we will bring the perpetrator to justice. Despite the fact that you just threatened me. Do you understand?"

Starr stayed in the mayor's personal space until she nodded, and then she slowly stepped back, pulled out her card, and handed it over. "Send me everything you can about Ricky or have William do it." She turned to walk away. "And, Mayor?"

"Yes?"

"Tell William not to stand so close when you're in public. People will start to think something's going on between you." Starr turned before she could respond and went back to collect Pearson. On their way back to the station, she told him about her conversation with the mayor.

Pearson grunted. "Why did you have to go and piss her off?"

"I didn't mean to, but I needed to rock her back a bit. She's going to micromanage this entire investigation if we don't watch out, and she needs to know right off the bat that she's not in charge."

"I agree, but there are more subtle ways to get that point across without threatening to tell the press she's having an affair with her lawyer, even if it is true."

Starr knew he was right, but she didn't regret the maneuver. It was a pissing match that she hadn't started, but one she needed to win. Round one—law enforcement. But they hadn't really won anything since Hannah was still missing. "Let's go pay a visit to Ricky Turner. And I promise I'll let you take the lead on this one."

"Okay, but when we're done, you're buying me lunch to make up for the croissant."

Starr's phone buzzed and she reached for it and read the display. "Uh-oh. Change of plans."

"What's up?"

"Murphy just summoned me and Nelson to the office."

"If he assigns Nelson to this case, I'm quitting."

"Not going to happen." Starr spoke with confidence, but the truth was she had no idea what this meeting could be about. Had the mayor called her boss immediately after they left? Would Murphy really yank the case and give it to Nelson? Her stomach lurched at the idea. "Come with me, and I promise I'll buy you lunch after."

❖

Catherine strode through the courthouse with purpose, repeating the words of her therapist in her head. She was a citizen of Travis County, and she had just as much right to inquire about the status of the Turner case as anyone else. She was going to march right into Starr's office and ask her how things were going. She didn't have any scheduled court appearances today, so she weaved her way swiftly through the crowd of people without having to worry about connecting with waiting clients. She didn't get far.

"Hey, Catherine, do you have a sec to talk about the trial setting next month?"

She turned toward the sound of the voice to see Fred Nelson, Murphy's first assistant, and Starr's nemesis. She hadn't seen him since the day they pled the Knoll case, and it was unusual for him to be taking point in a trial, but she had only one trial on the docket next month, so he must be talking about it. "What about it? Are you trying the Paulson case with Jane?"

"Matter of fact I am," Nelson said. "She's pretty swamped so I'm helping out. I miss the courtroom. It'll be good to flex my muscles again."

Catherine nodded, but she was certain his reasons ran deeper than that. The Paulson case had garnered a lot of press attention, and it was more likely he was trying to hog the spotlight from Starr, but that wasn't any of her business. "What do you want to talk about?"

He motioned to a workroom off to the right and they ducked in. There were a couple of other attorneys meeting with ADAs inside, but he led them to Jane Wagner's desk and perched on the edge of it. "You filed a motion to continue," he said.

"I did," she replied, hiding her annoyance that he appeared to be cutting Jane out of the loop. "I still don't have all the discovery I was promised, and after last week's trial, I would think this office would want to be especially careful about making sure I get the information I'm entitled to receive in order to properly represent my client. Besides, Mr. Paulson's out on bail." She cocked her head. "The continuance was filed as an agreed motion. Jane didn't have any objection. Are you telling me you have a problem with putting off the case?"

"Jane might not have any objections at first, but word is your client might be planning a new scheme. The fact that he's out on bond means he's a potential risk to the citizens of Travis County. We'd really like to resolve this case as soon as possible to minimize that risk."

Catherine recognized the posturing for what it was and called him on it. "Are you filing a motion to revoke bail?"

"I don't have any plans to do so at this time, but my concerns might solidify the longer we have to wait to try this case."

"Here's what I'm hearing. You want to go to trial next month despite the fact your lead attorney has agreed to a motion to continue. If I don't rescind the motion, you plan to file a motion to have my client's bail revoked despite the fact he has done nothing to violate the terms of his release. Do I have that right?"

Nelson held up his hands. "Look, I'm just doing my job. Your client was spotted near his wife's office last week. He didn't directly contact her, but he's obviously thinking about it. Makes me wonder if this was the first time he's gotten close in the lead-up to the trial. Makes me think he's trying to collude with her. You know how strict Judge Mallory is when it comes to witness tampering. If we're forced to wait to have this trial, then I'll be forced to go to the judge and do whatever is necessary to make sure my star witness isn't intimidated in advance of her testimony."

"Bullshit." Catherine sputtered the word. Paulson and his wife had been accused of an extensive scheme to defraud investors in their home-based business enterprise, and the wife had agreed to cooperate with the DA's office in exchange for probation, while her client was facing a lengthy prison term if he was convicted. If it was true that Paulson had been near his wife's office in contravention of the court's order, she would deal with him, but what pissed her off more was being threatened.

"If you have evidence my client is interfering with a witness," she said, "take it to the judge, but remember that Mallory doesn't like when people waste her time." She shook her head and turned to go but stopped before she reached the door. "And don't forget to get me the discovery. Mallory will ask about the status of it when she hears this motion, which I'm going to ask her to fast-track. Good luck with the campaign," she added as she left the office, infusing her voice with a healthy dose of sarcasm.

As she strode through the halls, she reflected on how fast things could change. Last week, anyone would have pegged Nelson as her ally after the way he pushed Starr to offer a deal on the Knoll case, but today he was a contentious adversary, if not a worthy one. Nelson might be good at administration, but he was no star litigator. Not like Starr.

Speaking of Starr, it was time to accomplish what she'd come to do. Catherine rode the elevator to the fifth floor. As she approached the reception desk, she ran into Matt, the prosecutor who'd tried the Knoll case with Starr.

"Hi, Catherine," he said with a curious expression. "Do we have something going on together?"

"No, but I'm looking for Starr. Have you seen her?"

"Actually, she was here a few minutes ago. You might still be able to catch her." He motioned to the receptionist to buzz the door open and led Catherine back into the suite of offices. "You have good timing. She hasn't been working out of her office much since the Turner girl went missing. She teamed up with Detective Pearson and the task force on the case, and they've set up shop at police headquarters. She asked me to cover a hearing this afternoon, and I don't expect to see her in the office on a regular basis until they find Hannah."

"Any news?" she asked, bracing for his response.

"I heard they have a lead on someone close to the family, but if you repeat that, I'll deny I told you." He pointed at the screensaver on his phone that featured a picture of a little girl in a polka-dotted dress. "I tell you what though, I'm hugging the hell out of my kid and keeping her close. I know this is probably a one-off thing, but it really makes you think. Do you have kids?"

"No, but I—" She stopped before sharing anything personal and finished with, "I can only imagine what the mayor's family must be going through."

"Here you go," he said, stopping in front of a door bearing Starr's name engraved on a plaque.

"Thanks." She waited outside the cracked door until he was most of the way down the hall, and then pushed her way in, her practiced speech at the ready. But no one was there. Damn. She looked around, taking in the various commendations on the wall and a few framed photos of Starr with various other people, some she recognized as local dignitaries. One featured Starr on a white-water raft, looking like she was having the time of her life. Catherine shuddered at the prospect of facing death-defying waterfalls with nothing but a rubber boat and paddle between her and certain death. Besides she'd had plenty of wilderness experience when—

Catherine brushed away the thought. She wasn't here to spy on Starr's personal life or revisit her own. She considered her options. She couldn't very well traipse down to the police station and insist on speaking to Starr. People would think she was crazy. The words of her therapist echoed in her head. *Don't let it fester when you can do something about it.* But what was the something?

"Catherine Landauer, are you looking for me?"

She looked up into Starr's face. Haggard eyes replaced the fiery demeanor she usually wore, and Starr looked like she hadn't slept since Catherine had seen her at Guero's earlier in the week. "I am actually, but I was told you wouldn't be in today." She realized her tone was overly harsh the minute the words came out, and she tried to strike a balance between being annoyed Starr wasn't out working on the case and being glad she had this opportunity to talk to her. "Can we talk for a minute?"

"Sure, if you don't mind talking while I look something up. I'm only here for a few minutes."

Catherine followed Starr into her office. Starr sat down at her desk and fired up her computer, while Catherine stood in the center of the room, unsure if she should sit or stand. She started to equivocate. "This can probably wait. I don't want to keep you from your work."

Starr faced her. "Actually, I could use a few minutes away from my current status, which is pure frustration. What's on your mind?"

This was it. Blurt it out or go away. "What are you doing to find Hannah Turner?"

A few beats of silence passed, and Catherine watched Starr's expression go from confused to what could only be interpreted as brewing anger. "Really?"

"Really." Catherine folded her arms. She was angry too, and her vision blurred for a second as her eyes started to blink rapidly—a childhood tic that hadn't reappeared until this week. She fought to gain control and felt the movement slow and her vision clear. "I have every right to ask the question. I'm a tax-paying citizen of this county. Do you have a suspect?"

"I'm not going to talk to you or anyone else about an ongoing investigation. You, more than anyone else, should be able to respect that."

Starr had a point. She and any other defense attorney would have a heyday at trial if they could prove the police had fixated early on a particular target. But she had a right to know at least what the press knew. "The news says that you're holding a press conference this afternoon. Surely you can tell me what you plan to say."

"I'm not holding a press conference, Murphy is. If you want to talk to him and see if he wants to share what he plans to say, feel free, but if all you came here to do was tell me I'm not doing a good enough job, then get in line. There's a little girl who's either lost or has been taken, and until she's found, safe and sound, there is nothing you or anyone else can say that will make me feel worse than I already do."

Catherine heard the frustration in her voice, but there was something else behind it. Compassion, empathy. Starr truly cared about Hannah Turner and what happened to her. Could she have misjudged Starr? Could she trust her enough to share her own experience in the hope what she'd gone through could help the task force find Hannah faster?

A litany of choices sprang to mind, pointing toward a single conclusion, but the innate distrust she'd carried most of her life held her back. Besides, all she had were vague offerings, based on her own experience, unlikely to be of use in this particular case anyway. She'd been silly to come here, thinking she could help.

"Did you want anything else?" Starr asked, her voice weary.

A knock on the door kept Catherine from answering, and the receptionist poked her head in the door. "He's ready for you."

Starr thanked her and stood. "I have to go."

"Okay."

"If you need something else, talk to Matt Abbott. He's covering for me while I'm working on this case."

Catherine stood and Starr followed her to the door. They were both still in the office and inches from each other. In the close proximity, Catherine could see the dark circles and swollen bags under Starr's bloodshot eyes. Had she slept? There was a slight shake in her hand as she reached to open the door. She wasn't eating, or she wasn't eating well anyway. Starr did care about this child and was making it her mission to find her. Catherine felt a sudden urge to reach for her arm, to clasp it, and tell Starr to hang in there. Not to give up, no matter what. And to explore every option, even the ones that seemed completely random and illogical.

"I have to go."

Catherine shook out of her trance and realized Starr was in the hallway and she was standing alone in Starr's office. "Sorry." Embarrassed that she'd zoned out in the middle of their conversation, Catherine edged away from the door. "If I think of anything, I will let you know."

She left before Starr could respond, but not before she saw the puzzled look on Starr's face. Why had she said that? Of course, it didn't make any sense, and now Starr probably thought she was as crazy as the tipsters who came out of the woodwork whenever a case like this became public. Too late now to change this impression, but she had to think of a way to help without exposing herself to the same level of scrutiny. It was a serious challenge.

Starr entered the room, not surprised to find Nelson already seated in Murphy's office. She resisted the urge to check her watch, instead plastering a fake smile on her face. "Good morning," she said even though it was no longer morning and there was nothing good about it. She resented being called in when there was important work to do, but showing her annoyance wasn't going to do any good, especially not with suck-face Nelson sitting in the room.

Murphy motioned for her to have a seat before he jumped directly to the point. "We have a press conference scheduled for this afternoon. Is it going to be a cluster fuck, or do we have some actual news we can share?"

Both of them stared at her, and she wanted to ask them who the "we" was since they were clearly relying on her for information. "We may have some news, but I'm not sure yet when we will have something you want to share."

"Spill."

She ran through the details about where Hannah Turner had last been seen, including the description of the pickup truck. "We've run cameras in commercial areas nearby, but come up with nothing, and we've canvassed as well." The cops had done all that, but if he could use "we" in a broad sense then so could she. "The friend who saw her get in the truck didn't see anything to make her think Hannah was forced, so we're covering that angle as well by talking to her friends to find out if Hannah mentioned anything to them about where she might be going, and we've covered most of them so far."

"What's the holdup?" Nelson asked. "Do you need more resources?"

She took a breath to keep from snapping at him. "Two of Hannah's close friends are on an out of town trip. They don't have cell phone access, but we're working on reaching them and I should have more information before the press conference." This morning, she'd told Pearson to do whatever it took, and they'd contacted the other jurisdiction to get their cooperation. Frankly, it was doubtful that Hannah's friends knew anything, but in these early stages, it was just as important to look like they were doing everything they could as it was to actually do something productive. When the victim's mother was the mayor, the need escalated.

"What else do you have?"

Starr knew she had to tell him about the mayor's brother-in-law, but she could at least control the narrative before it got out of hand. "Professor Turner's brother recently moved to town. He came to Hannah's birthday party last week and is having some financial troubles after a recent fraud conviction. He asked the Turners for money, and not a small amount."

"Did they give it to him?"

"I'm not sure yet. Mayor Turner made it pretty clear she thinks he's shiftless, but I'm not certain that the professor wouldn't slip his brother funds on the side just to keep the peace, although he showed solidarity with his wife when we were there. If he didn't, then perhaps there's a motive there, but we've received no contact about a ransom, so this may be complete conjecture. We're getting bank records now."

"Holy shit," Nelson said. "You're pulling bank records on the mayor? No way you're going to keep a lid on that. When the press gets wind, they are going to go crazy with conclusions. Do you think you might have checked with us first?"

That was it. Starr stared him into silence before turning to Murphy. "You put me on this case because I have experience and you trust me. I've worked plenty of high profile cases and am perfectly capable of handling myself with the victim's families and the press. Requesting records is standard operating procedure in cases like this, and this office will not proceed differently because of the parties involved lest we give the appearance of impropriety. If you do not have confidence in my abilities and my strategic decisions, say so now and I'll hand over the reins."

Murphy cleared his throat and shot Nelson a look that told him to stand down. "Let's dial this back a bit. There's going to be plenty of finger-pointing if this girl isn't found soon, but it's not going to happen inside my office. And keep in mind, both of you, that it's still my office. Next year, when one of you is sitting here, you can make the hard calls, but for now, it's up to me. Starr, have we brought the brother in for questioning?"

"We were headed there when I got the call to come in here. Pearson is pulling all his records now."

"Then let's not waste any more time here. Go talk to him. I want updates as soon as you're done. And I want you both here for the press conference. If we don't have something solid soon, the chief is calling in the feds."

Pearson was going to love that. Starr nodded and left the room. She was at the elevator when Nelson jogged up beside her. "Maybe I'll come with you."

"No," she said, irrationally punching the button again even though it was still lit.

"No?"

"You heard me. This isn't about getting glory. It's about getting information that can help us find this girl. Too many of us show up, and this guy is going to clam up even if he doesn't have something to hide."

He held up his hands in surrender. "I'm just trying to help."

He wasn't, and they both knew it, but Starr wasn't interested in debating with him on the point in public. They'd have plenty of time to debate later about all kinds of issues, but for now she needed to focus on this case, because if they didn't find this girl and her abductor, then Starr's chance at becoming the next DA would be dead on arrival.

Chapter Six

Catherine drew the covers over her head. She should spend the entire day in bed, which would be much easier than facing anything the outside world had to bring. It was Saturday, so it wasn't like she *had* to be anywhere, but her desk at the office was loaded with work, and if Doris showed up on Monday morning and saw the files still there, she'd wonder what was wrong since Catherine had worked weekends ever since she'd gone into practice. The real question was, if she didn't go to the office, how would she keep herself occupied until Monday morning?

She lasted all of a minute before the nagging need to know if there was any news about Hannah Turner urged her out of bed. She sat up, puffed the pillows, reached for her phone, and started scrolling through the news sites, quickly becoming frustrated when every page she viewed appeared to be a repetition of the one before, consisting of replay after replay of the press conference from yesterday and quotes from Murphy's canned speech to the press. Starr Rio stood at Murphy's side, her face fixed with determination, but the fact that neither Murphy nor the police chief shared any substantial specific information was telling.

Catherine knew what they were thinking. The clock was ticking for this girl, and if they didn't find her in the next twenty-four hours, she'd probably turn up dead or never be seen again. Eventually, the missing person signs that had been plastered around town would begin to fade, and the search teams would return to whatever they'd been doing before Hannah Turner's life became entwined with theirs.

She growled with exasperation and tossed her phone toward the foot of the bed. She felt helpless, and the feeling brought back so many memories that it paralyzed her. Very few people had her perspective, but what good did it do? She had no idea what had really happened to Hannah, and for all she knew the girl was already dead. But what if she wasn't? What if she was alive somewhere, a prisoner whose only hope was that there were people in the world still trying to find her, longing for her safe return?

Her gut clenched, and she closed her eyes. *Not my problem.* There were plenty of people focused on Hannah Turner—police, the search and rescue crews, her parents. Catherine needed to direct her attention elsewhere, or risk reopening wounds she'd worked her whole life to heal.

She crawled out of bed, dragged on sweats, and made her way to the kitchen, determined to get her mind off this case. First order of business was coffee to jog her brain out of its fog, but a quick search of the cabinets revealed she'd forgotten to buy any. A more in-depth inspection revealed she'd forgotten to buy pretty much anything, and the only item in the fridge was a single container of cottage cheese that had expired. Damn. She hadn't been hungry until she realized she didn't have any food. She made a list of a few essentials, put her hair up, slipped on a pair of Nikes, and grabbed her keys to head to the store.

But first coffee. She turned onto South Congress and circled around the block, looking for parking, mentally planning where she would pick up groceries as soon as she was caffeinated. There weren't a lot of grocery stores in her neighborhood, and Doris was always encouraging her to use a delivery service, but she'd rather have the slight inconvenience of stopping by the store than have strangers show up at her door. Besides it wasn't like shopping for one, which was all she'd ever done, was a burden. Yogurt, eggs, bread, salad mix, cream for coffee, and a few other ingredients to vary her meals were all she needed to fuel her work. More often than not, she'd grab food to go and eat it standing at the kitchen counter.

Jo's was super busy as usual for a Saturday morning. Catherine liked the crowd because it allowed her to blend in and go unnoticed.

She took a place in line and breathed in the scent of the cold morning air. It had taken years for her to enjoy the outside again after having lived a month outside under absolutely deplorable conditions. She closed her eyes and took a moment to remember she was no longer that timid, lonely little girl. She was an adult, free to go wherever she wanted, whenever she wanted. She was strong and capable, and no one would ever be able to force her to do something against her will. Most importantly, she was alive—a fact for which she was grateful, even if she hadn't always been.

"Guess we have something in common after all."

Catherine opened her eyes, but she didn't have to see the face to recognize Starr Rio's crisp, distinctive voice. Damn. Her peaceful meditation faded into frustration. "What are you doing here?"

"Same as you, I guess."

Catherine focused on her breathing and dug deep. She wanted to be mad at Starr for taking time to stand in line for coffee when Hannah was still missing, but maybe Starr needed caffeine to fuel her work, and didn't she want the people who were on the case to be at their very best? Or maybe Hannah had been found? "Did you find her?" she blurted out the question before she could think.

Starr put a finger to her lips and shook her head. At that moment the guy behind the window said, "Can I help you?"

"Let's talk in a minute," Starr said, gesturing toward the waiting employee. "I'll buy your coffee."

Catherine hesitated. It sounded like an innocent offer, but she suspected Starr had some ulterior motive. But if she said no, she'd look like a jerk. The chance to get some information was too tempting. "I'll buy." She motioned for Starr to join her at the counter. "Whatever you want. This is probably the most generous offer you'll ever get from me, so feel free to take advantage."

Starr ordered a large Americano with an extra shot, and Catherine told the guy to make it two. She paid, and they stepped to the side to wait for their drinks.

"I thought I was the one who made offers," Starr said.

"I guess that's true," Catherine said. "But from what I hear, they're never good ones."

"I suppose that's a matter of perspective."

"True, but there are prosecutors who genuinely want to work things out and there are those who toss out some token offer just to be able to say they gave it a go," Catherine said.

"And I fall into the latter category."

"Granted I don't have a lot of experience doing deals with you, but I'm betting that if Nelson hadn't pushed you, you never would've offered ten years on Peter Knoll's case."

"You're right about that. I wouldn't have offered you anything." Starr inclined her head. "They're calling your name."

Catherine honed in to the sound of a male voice calling out "Catherine," followed closely by another name "Jill," and she shuddered. There was a time when the sound would've made the blood drain from her head, but she'd moved past that to barely disguised revulsion.

"Is something wrong?" Starr asked.

Annoyed at Starr's ability to zero in on her emotions, Catherine pushed past her. "Be right back." She took the few steps to the pickup window slowly. She needed time to think, time to compose her feelings, and time to think of a way to get away from Starr as quickly as possible. But a quick escape would mean she wouldn't find out whatever crumbs of information Starr was willing to share. She pulled on the steely reserves she'd learned to rely on so many times before and returned to Starr's side and handed her a cup. "Shall we sit or walk?"

Starr glanced around, probably taking in the crowd and the possibility of being overheard. "Let's walk."

They strolled down South Congress, walking in awkward silence for a few moments until a tiny furball puppy ran across their path. Catherine scooped him up in her arms and hugged into his squirmy body and playful nips until the embarrassed young woman chasing him caught up to her.

"Stay safe, little guy," she said as she reluctantly handed him over.

"Do you have pets?" Starr asked after the woman left.

"No, but I've always wanted a puppy." Catherine realized her comment begged more questions, and she quickly followed up with "But it's too hard with my work schedule."

"Same here," Starr said. "Someday, though."

They slipped back into silence, but something had shifted between them. Anyone watching would probably think they were two friends out enjoying the sunny morning. Catherine wondered what that would be like. She had plenty of acquaintances, but Doris was the closest thing she had to a close friend, and even she didn't know her biggest secrets. She pretended for a moment that Starr was someone she liked. The scenario wasn't that far-fetched. They were intellectually compatible. Starr had graduated in the top of her class, a few years ahead of Catherine, and there was no arguing that she was a smart and capable attorney. If Catherine wasn't hiding so much, would she choose to be with someone like Starr?

"Let's start with a simple topic," Starr said. "Are you a runner?"

"What?" Catherine stopped and looked down at her attire. She laughed. "Not hardly. I was out of coffee at the house and threw on the first thing I could find. I'm not much of an outdoors person." She bit her lip, wishing she could take back the overshare. Starr didn't need to know her likes and dislikes, and she didn't want her to. Did she?

"Thank goodness," Starr said with an exaggerated sigh. "About the running. I was going to have to hate you if you said yes."

"Uh-huh." Catherine recognized Starr's attempt at teasing her, but she looked straight ahead and kept walking, bent on keeping the conversation from turning personal.

"Why don't you like me?"

Startled out of her reverie, Catherine stopped walking. "What?"

"I'm a likable person." Starr grinned. "Early polling says so. Sure, I'm kind of a bully when I'm trying to get my way, but my way is usually right, so there's that. Besides, I only pull out the big guns when I'm fighting for justice and all. But people generally like me, except you, and I'd like to know why."

Catherine considered the question carefully, turning it in every direction in search of a trick, but she saw none. She started walking again. "It's not that I don't like you. You're an adversary. We don't have any other relationship. There's no need to like or dislike. It just is."

"You're not telling the truth. You actively do not like me, and I'd like to know why."

"You play fast and loose with the truth." Catherine raised a hand to stop Starr from interrupting. "I know, I know, you think it's okay to do whatever it takes to put away the bad guys, but you don't stop to consider you might have the wrong suspect or that even if you have the right one, by cutting corners in the rush to justice, you might get overturned on appeal."

This time it was Starr who stopped in her tracks. "Wow. Been holding that back for long?"

"You have a reputation. There are some people who think it's a good thing. I just don't happen to be one of them and not just because I work on the other side."

"Why then?"

"What?" Catherine was taken aback by the question. It should be obvious why Starr's approach was a problem in general. She wasn't prepared to share how it affected her personally.

"Take this case for instance," Starr said, pressing the point. "If I had a chance to find Hannah, but doing so meant compromising a conviction, wouldn't you want me to do that?"

"That's a trick question because it assumes that you would sacrifice one for the other. What I think you would be more likely to do is take the risk and then hide it from the defense attorney to get your conviction." Catherine regretted the words immediately, not just because they were overly harsh, but for the look they evoked on Starr's face. Their détente was ending quickly.

"We don't know each other very well," Starr said, "so I'm not sure how you draw that conclusion. I'm not ashamed of my reputation or my results. If you're concerned about Hannah Turner's well-being, then rest assured there is no better person to be on the case." Like a closing bell, Starr's phone rang, punctuating the uncomfortable air between them. She glanced at the screen. "I have to go. Thanks for the coffee. Maybe someday I'll return the favor and give you an opportunity to get to know the real me."

Catherine watched as Starr rushed off, unable to help feeling empty at the vacuum Starr's large presence left behind. She shook away the feeling. Starr Rio was a politician, gifted at saying exactly the right thing at the right time to leave people questioning their preconceived notions, especially if those notions didn't already lean in her favor. Catherine only hoped that Starr's strong motivation to win the hearts and minds of voters would fuel her motivation to find Hannah. And fast.

❖

Starr drove like a madwoman, wishing she had lights and sirens to clear the traffic in front of her. Pearson's text was simple and to the point. *We found something. Hurry.* His cryptic text was followed by a Google Maps link.

She knew that if they'd found Hannah, he would've said "her" not "something." She visualized the area where he'd directed her to go. It was a park near Barton Springs. The area was fairly well trekked on a regular basis, but there were some hidden coves where it would be possible to hide out. It was miles from Hannah's house, and the spot where she'd last been seen. What had they found? Was it some sign that Hannah had been there? If so, what was she doing so far from home? How had she gotten there?

Starr resisted the urge to fall further into the spiral of what-ifs and focused on getting to the location in one piece. When she arrived, she spotted Pearson standing by the side of the road next to an unmarked van. She threw her car in park and rushed to his side. "Talk to me."

Pearson pointed at the van. "Crime scene techs. Made them come out here in a plain van to keep the press out of this. We got an anonymous call saying they'd seen something suspicious out here. This way." He led the way down the trail and Starr followed, grateful she wasn't wearing a suit. Pebbles gave way under their feet and tumbled ahead of them down the path, and she couldn't help but think that a person pushed down this hill wouldn't fare well from the fall.

When they reached the bottom of the trail, they were standing on the sandbar next to the water's edge. Two analysts had already blocked off the area with tape and were busy taking photos and gathering samples of the sand. Pearson led her closer to their work, and they both backed away to give him and her space to see the centerpiece of their display. Starr looked down and zeroed in on a large white satin hair bow. She leaned closer, and Pearson motioned to one of the techs who turned it over with his gloved hand. It was pretty and girly, and even lying in the dirt, it looked sweet and feminine and innocent. And absolutely nothing like what she'd seen in any of the things she'd seen in Hannah's room which tended to fall into tomboy territory.

"I don't get it," she said. "Do you really think this bow is connected to Hannah? It doesn't look like anything I've seen in the pictures her parents showed us. She didn't strike me as a girly girl."

"Kinda like you, I guess," Pearson said. He directed the crime scene techs to resume their work and motioned for her to join him a few feet away. "No, I don't think it's hers, but someone called this in to 911 and hung up before the operator could get a line on the caller." He looked down at his flip book. "Here's what the caller said. 'I'm calling about Hannah Turner. I think she was here. Good girls shouldn't be without their bows.' He gave the address and hung up."

"He?"

"We can listen to the tape ourselves, but the operator said it sounded like a male voice."

"'Good girls shouldn't be without their bows'?" Starr repeated the words, letting them rock around in her head. "What the hell does that mean?"

"Your guess is as good as mine, but it's a clue. Whoever called wanted us to come out here, and they wanted us to find this bow and make something of it. I think after these guys are finished, we should take it to the Turners and see what they make of it."

Starr sighed. She'd been hoping a few more hours would go by before she had to face the Turners again. At least this time they had something to show for their efforts, and she hoped it would be fruitful. "Okay." She glanced back up the trail. "We've got to keep this under wraps until we know if it's a real clue or some kook sending us on a wild goose chase. How long has that van been parked there?"

"Too long. I'll get the guys to move it. They're almost done here."

"And we need the 911 call log and swear the operator to silence. Let's get a check on dear uncle's cell phone records and get the cell tower info for the time of the call. Even if he didn't make the call from his own phone, the records should be able to tell us where he was when the call came through. And we'll need to pin him down on what he says he was doing this morning."

"You're pretty focused on him, are you?"

Starr remembered her conversation with Catherine from earlier and wondered if she was jumping to conclusions. "He's all we've got right now. If something comes up to point us in another direction, I'm happy to follow any reliable leads, but I don't want to be the person who ignores a clue right in front of her for the sake of keeping an open mind. Do you?"

Pearson shook his head. "You're right. But after meeting Ricky Turner, I'm just not feeling it. I've been wrong before, though, so we'll do this your way."

No pressure there. Starr checked her phone while they waited for the crime scene guys to finish up, relieved to see that Murphy hadn't called yet this morning. A call from him meant he was getting pressure from the mayor, and pressure was going to cause them to make mistakes. And jump to conclusions if Catherine Landauer was to be believed.

The thought of Catherine led her mind back to before Pearson's call. For a few rare moments, as she and Catherine had walked along South Congress, Starr had managed to pretend she led a normal, carefree life where weekend brunches and leisurely strolls with a pretty woman by her side were the norm rather than the exception. She'd liked that feeling, and she found she liked Catherine, or at least her passion for her work, even if the feeling wasn't mutual. Driving here to meet Pearson, Starr had allowed herself to hope that this strange clue would be a quick fuse to blow the case wide open and that Hannah would be found and safely returned to her parents soon, leaving her with the opportunity to have more than a glimpse at a personal life before she entered a campaign that was certain to eat up all her time.

An hour later, they were at the Turners' house. This time, instead of just the patrol car out front, two large black SUVs blocked the drive, accompanied by several armed security guards. The press was camped out across the street, but Starr avoided looking at them as she accompanied Pearson to the door, not wanting to get trapped into answering questions about the status of the investigation. Pearson pulled the patrol cop aside at the door and whispered to him for a second, and then they entered the house. The mayor was waiting in the entry, her eyes frantic.

"You found her? Is she alive?"

Starr took the mayor's arm and led her back toward the study where they'd met yesterday. She hated this part of any case, where the victim's loved ones vacillated between hope and despair, but fortunately she didn't have to deal with it often since she usually didn't meet the family this early in a case. But from the time a defendant was arrested and the case file landed on her desk, part of her job was to shepherd the victim, if they were alive, and their family through the criminal justice system and deal with their reactions to the uncertainty of the process. Recognizing the worry that came with not knowing, she didn't wait to deliver the biggest blow. "We didn't find her, but we have something to show you." She pulled out her phone and held up a photo of the bow, purposefully set against an objectively plain background, because the bow lying in the dirt had looked so forlorn and foreboding. "Do you recognize this?"

Mayor Turner grabbed the phone and pinched the screen to enlarge the photo, taking time to examine it from all angles. Pearson, who was standing behind her, scrunched his forehead as the seconds ticked by. Starr resisted the urge to push for a response and pondered instead what the mayor's silence was telling them. After what seemed like forever, the mayor handed the phone back to her.

"Hannah doesn't wear bows."

Starr nodded, choosing her next words carefully. "I didn't think so. Is it possible she had this bow for some other reason? Maybe it was something she carried around to remind her of something?"

"Why do you think this belongs to her?"

Fair question. "We set up a tip line, and one of the calls this morning directed us to this. They were specific about the location and that we would find a clue there."

"The caller was the kidnapper, right?"

"It's possible." Starr knew she sounded cagey, but she didn't want to share anything more at this time, not when they had no idea who was involved in Hannah's disappearance. For all they knew this bow was the result of a cruel prank. Tip lines had a tendency to bring out the worst in human behavior even as they were a valuable tool to gather potential clues. "Is your husband home?"

"I haven't seen him this morning." Turner twisted her hands in her lap. "Things between us are even worse than I led you to believe yesterday. Keith moved into the guest room several weeks ago, and we don't really keep track of each other's comings and goings. William advised me not to share that information with you, but I think you deserve to know in case it affects your investigation."

Starr took the revelation with a grain of salt. More likely William had proposed that the mayor share the information in the event it helped her divorce case. If the mayor could be direct, then so could she. "Is there a custody dispute?"

"Keith loves his daughter."

Starr ignored the non sequitur. "I'm sure you both do love your daughter very much, but I imagine it's hard to sort out how to handle things in such a unique power dynamic." She folded her arms. "Here's the big question. Does your daughter know about your marital troubles?"

"I don't think so. I mean, she may have sensed we haven't been getting along, but I doubt she thinks it's serious. Hannah is a very optimistic girl. Why?"

"Because it wouldn't be the first time a kid ran away when there's trouble brewing at home."

"You're kidding, right?" Mayor Turner gestured at the ceiling. "You've seen this place. We've worked hard to make sure she has everything she could ever want. Private school, a pool, horseback riding lessons, you name it."

Starr wanted to point out that material things didn't always cut it, but she figured the mayor already knew that on some level, and her driving home the point would be cruel. "We have to explore every angle. If she were to go somewhere to get away from it all, where would she go?"

"We've been asked that a thousand times," Mayor Turner said. "I gave Detective Pearson a list of her friends, and as far as I know they've all been contacted."

"I know, but I'm asking you to dig a little deeper for me. Is there a particular place that Hannah likes to go? A park, the library, anything you can think of?"

Turner looked annoyed at being asked to try harder, but she could hardly deny the request, so Starr was surprised when she stood up and walked across the room. "I wouldn't ask you if it wasn't important."

Turner stopped at the bookshelf closest to the door and pulled a five-by-seven frame from the shelf. She handed it to Starr. "Besides the zoo, that's her favorite place in Austin. She's fascinated with the bats. Can't get enough of them. Even when they aren't in season, she likes to stop at the bridge, convinced she can connect with them. Says she wants to be a chiropterologist when she grows up. Of course, kids say stuff like that all the time."

Starr stared at the picture of the Congress Street Bridge where crowds flocked at sundown from spring to fall to watch the nightly bat flight across Lady Bird Lake. She'd driven over the bridge just a few hours ago on her way to Jo's Coffee and then back again after she'd shared coffee with Catherine. When she was a kid she'd been fascinated with the bats too. Was Catherine?

Where did that thought come from? She spent a second entertaining it and decided she doubted Catherine was a bat watcher. She wasn't sure why. Could be because Catherine had remarked about how she wasn't much of an outdoor person. Made it hard to imagine her hanging over the rail of the bridge, trying to spot the first dark cluster of flying mammals heading out for their evening meal.

"I don't think it will be helpful, but that's all I can think of," Turner said, holding open the door to signal their private meeting was over.

"Thank you," Starr said, but as she started to leave an idea struck her. "I'd like to look at Hannah's room one more time. That would be okay, wouldn't it?"

"Uh, sure." Turner motioned to the stairs. "If it's okay with you, I'll stay down here."

"Of course."

Hannah's bedroom was as she remembered it, but Starr's perspective had changed. Now she was looking for some sign that Hannah was aware of and troubled by her parents' marital strife. She seriously doubted Hannah had run away from home. If she had, then she was either completely out of touch with media or she was the most heartless twelve-year-old that had ever lived, considering the massive amounts of coverage about her disappearance and pleas for her safe return. Starr wasn't sure why she wanted to dig deeper into Hannah's psyche, but something told her she should, that maybe a deeper understanding would give her a clue about who had taken her away from her sheltered, privileged life with no discernible explanation.

She entered Hannah's room and looked around, starting with Hannah's desk. Hannah was a doodler and the desk pad was a collage of drawings, some completed and some half-finished. Everything from horses to ladybugs, and lots of bats sprinkled in. Starr traced one of the drawings with her forefinger as if she could capture some connection to Hannah by doing so, but all she got for her efforts was pencil lead on her skin. *Where are you?* The words ran on repeat like a steady drumbeat in the back of her head but getting louder and louder with each refrain. Time was running out.

Chapter Seven

Catherine held the remote in her hand, but she didn't click the on button. She felt like someone who was trying to incrementally give up cigarettes by holding an unlit one as the first step. It wasn't working. She didn't need to click the button to know what she'd see on any of the local news channels. Or on the radio. Or in the newspaper. With no new information on the case, there would only be endless speculation by fact-starved reporters and news anchors charged with keeping viewers tuned in at all costs.

She got it. The people who had kids were glued to the television, hanging on the hope that Hannah would be found as some universal reassurance this would never happen to them. Everyone else had their reasons, and it wasn't for her to judge although she wanted to. She wanted to tell them all to stop sitting in front of their televisions and get out of the house and start looking for Hannah because, if she was alive, she was probably close by. And if she wasn't alive, then…

Catherine shuddered as she remembered a time she thought dying would be preferable to being held against her will, being groomed to face a future that would be unbearable and from which she would have no escape. Her own experience both motivated and held her back from getting more involved, but that was a cop out. She should be out there with the rest of the volunteers, helping put up signs, manning the hotlines, walking the neighborhoods. Did she have the strength to do so?

Her phone buzzed with a text and she grabbed it, happy for the distraction. It was Doris. *Sorry to bug you on a Saturday, but the office vm had a message from a potential new client who wants to meet today. Let me know what you want me to tell them.*

Catherine wasted no time responding. *I can meet them at four pm at the office. Send me the initial info. Thanks.* Relieved for the distraction, she sprang to her feet and headed to the shower. When she emerged, she checked her phone again and made a few notes about the new case. A nice, nonviolent, federal white-collar case. Exactly what she needed. Hopefully there would be lots of documents and accounting to review—plenty to keep her mind occupied while she and the rest of the city waited for news of the missing girl. She made a mental promise to join the volunteers if Hannah wasn't found by the time her appointment was over.

She looked through her closet and settled on a suit. Federal court was more formal than state court, and white-collar clients tended to consider appearance more closely in determining which attorneys were the most successful. She did a quick Google search of the name Doris had texted her and found the case involved Medicare fraud with no associated violence or other sordid details. She sighed, relieved to have something to focus on other than Hannah's case, something impersonal and bland.

The drive was quiet and quick. She actually liked working on Saturdays—less traffic and no ringing phones. When she arrived, she unlocked the office door and wandered through the house turned law office. She'd loved this place since the first day she'd started working with Neil Daniels, Doris's old boss, and one of the few people who'd known about her past when she'd relocated to Texas. Neil had helped her change her last name and facilitate her application to law school and the state bar in a way that allowed her to retain her privacy while avoiding the questions that would naturally come up with the required background checks. He'd been her mentor and her friend, and ultimately her benefactor, having left his practice to her when he dropped dead of a heart attack five years before in this very office.

Her therapist had questioned her about her decision to keep the building after the trauma of Neil's death, but selling it felt like a betrayal. Neil had loved this space and she took comfort in its familiarity. The house/office included a reception area, a large open kitchen and living room/conference room, and three good-sized rooms, two of which comprised her office and a library. About once a year, Doris pointed out that they could lease out the extra room to another lawyer, but Catherine brushed her off. She would never invite strangers to share this space. She put on a pot of coffee, and while it was brewing, she made sure the conference room was picked up. The coffee pot had just beeped when she heard the bell on the front door jingle.

"Hello?"

Catherine turned toward the sound of the voice. Dr. M often asked her if she ever felt vulnerable working alone in the office or dealing with people who'd been accused of committing crimes. The short answer was yes, but there was a part of her that enjoyed testing that vulnerability, because unlike when she was a child facing the terror of a man who was holding her captive, she was a strong, powerful adult who knew how to exercise her power. And fire a gun. For a second, her attention pulled to the SIG Sauer P238 tucked under her desk. Truth was the gun probably wouldn't do much good unless she was sitting at her desk during an attack, but Catherine felt better knowing it was there. Once a month, she took it to the range, used it to shoot up a target, cleaned it, and put it back where it belonged.

The young couple standing in the doorway surprised her. She'd expected her potential client to be older, more established, but this guy looked to be in his late twenties. She stuck out a hand. "I'm Catherine Landauer."

They introduced themselves as Clive and Violet Burson, and she led them to the conference room. "Thanks for meeting us on such short notice," Violet said. "Clive's been frantic since the FBI showed up at the house."

"I imagine that was scary for both of you." Catherine looked down at her notes. "I did a little research since you talked to Doris. Clive, you worked for Haltech Medical for six years?"

"You sound surprised," he said.

"I am, a little. Don't take this the wrong way, but you look pretty young. Both of you."

"I started working for a smaller medical billing provider when I was in college. My dad got me the job. The owner was an old friend of his. About a year after I started, the company sold out to Haltech, but I stayed on. I was never crazy about the new owners, but they seemed to know what they were doing. Guess I was wrong about that."

Catherine made a note to ask him if they'd offered to get him his own attorney and focused on his impressions of the owners. "Tell me more about your gut feelings about the owners."

"It's hard to explain. They're nice and they treat me well, but I've always gotten the sense that they're on the verge of busting out of this business. The guy before had it forever, and I think if he'd had kids who wanted to follow in his footsteps, he never would've sold, but these guys seemed like they were trying to leverage the business for something else. Doesn't give the rest of the staff a lot of confidence in their career futures."

Catherine nodded, but she wasn't sure what to make of his description. "The FBI arrested you for Medicare fraud. I checked the online court system and you haven't been indicted yet and the arrest warrant is sealed. I might be able to get a copy of it when the courts reopen on Monday, but in the meantime, did they tell you anything about why you were arrested?"

"Sure. They came to the office a few times, trying to talk to employees when the owners weren't there. All I ever told them was that I wasn't in charge and that I hadn't done anything illegal."

"And you talked to them each time they came?" He nodded. "And how many times was that?"

"Three. No, wait. It was four. This one agent would hang out outside and wait for us to go to lunch."

Catherine wanted to pound her head against the table. There should be a class in high school with the theme "call your lawyer when..." She forced her expression into neutral and asked him several questions about the length and content of each conversation.

"When did you first suspect the agent was focused on you as part of his investigation?"

"I never thought he was focused on me. He said he wanted to help me out of this situation. That he knew I probably didn't know my employer was breaking the law, but it could spill over onto me unless I helped him out."

"And you declined to help?"

"I told them I'd have to think about it. In the meantime, they started talking to my boss, and then I never heard from them again. What do you make of that?"

Catherine folded her hands on the table. "I think that your boss took their offer faster than you did, so instead of directing them to the problem, you're now part of it. It's likely that your boss, what's his name?"

"Jerry Randolf."

"Jerry, by virtue of his position, probably has more usable information than you did, which would make him more credible on the witness stand. He's probably going to testify before the grand jury."

"So, I've missed my opportunity?"

"Not necessarily, but if you want to try and work something out, we'll need to give the agents some information that they either can't get from Jerry or that bolsters whatever he's telling them."

"And how will we know?"

"I'll ask them. If you hire me to represent you, the first step is for me to find out everything I can about the case, including pinning down their goals so we can figure out if you can assist. But there will be no guarantees up front about outcomes, either from me or the FBI. The process can be brutal. If you decide to cooperate, you will go through numerous debriefings which may seem like interrogations before they decide they can trust you. If you contradict yourself at all, all bets are off and you're back where you started, and they can use your statements against you if you go to trial and attempt to say something different. Even if they believe you, they might decide your information was not substantial enough and might not agree to recommend that your sentence be reduced. It's happened many times."

She paused to let her admonitions sink in. There were plenty of attorneys who wouldn't go to these lengths to give all the cons about cooperating, who would instead cast cooperation as the be-all end-all of getting out of doing federal time. It was true that cooperation was the key to staying out of prison, but she wasn't going to be the one who gave false hope just to sign a client. "But at the end of the day, you'll still have to decide which risk you want to take, jury trial or helping the prosecutor and hoping the judge gives you a decent sentence."

Clive's phone lit up and buzzed on the table. He apologized and turned it over. "Sorry about that." He glanced at his wife. "Do you have any questions?"

Violet pulled a piece of paper out of her purse and spread it out in front of her. Catherine braced for the interrogation, but Clive's phone buzzed again. He picked it up with a sheepish look. "Sorry, I'll make sure it's off." Before he could do so, there were two more buzzes in quick succession. "Oh wow," he said, staring at the screen.

"Is everything okay?" Catherine asked while Violet looked over his shoulder.

"We've been following the news about that missing girl," he said. "You know, the mayor's kid. Our little girl is the same age, and I—we—can't even imagine what it would be like if she disappeared. We've been glued to the news ever since the story first broke..."

He kept talking, but all Catherine heard was a dull roar that built to a loud pitch. She half stood. "Did they find her?"

He pointed at his phone. "They're about to have a press conference. KVUE says they found something."

Catherine wanted to shoo them from her office and bolt for home where she could stare at the TV until the news appeared. She caught Clive looking up at the TV on the wall. "When's the press conference?"

"Right now." He shifted in his seat. "I know we have a lot to cover, but do you mind if we check it out?"

Catherine grabbed the remote and clicked the TV on, bracing for whatever news would appear once the screen awoke. The startup time seemed to take longer than usual, and she tried hard not to resort to her usual pacing while she waited. After what seemed like forever, the picture came into view, and Catherine realized she was looking at the lobby of police headquarters. A podium had been placed in the center of the room, and the camera zoomed in as Starr Rio approached it, her face grim and her eyes tired. She looked even more haggard than she had this morning, and Catherine feared the worst, but when Starr held up a tagged evidence bag containing a large white bow, cold chills ran through her body, and she grabbed her throat with fear. Her knees buckled and the room went black.

CHAPTER EIGHT

Starr had reservations about the press conference. Once they shared that they'd found a clue and what it was, crazies would start to come out of the woodwork. In her opinion, they should keep looking at Professor Turner's brother, Ricky, since he was their only viable suspect so far and stats said the most likely culprit was someone close to the family. But ultimately, she agreed with Murphy and the police chief that a deluge of leads was better than not enough of them.

Murphy had asked her to be the one on camera today. It was a big deal, but she knew he'd likely picked her to give a feminine face to the investigation. She should be happy for the free press. She'd be featured on all the networks, interrupting the early evening news, but right now she didn't care how this exposure would benefit her future campaign. The only thing she cared about was getting Hannah back, and today's press conference was designed to spook the abductor into thinking they were very close to finding him. To that end, Pearson had a patrol unit watching Ricky Turner's apartment in case the press conference prompted him to make a move.

The police chief introduced her and she stepped to the microphone. "Good evening. I'd like to jump right in and let you know that the entire Austin Police Force and the Travis County Sheriff's Office is hard at work on this case, but we need your help. Today, we received an anonymous tip about a clue in the case, which led us to this item." She held up a glassine bag containing the white bow and took a breath before delivering the lie she'd practiced. "We've verified that this bow contains physical evidence linking it to Hannah Turner."

She leaned forward and stared hard into the cameras in what she hoped was a strong but pleading way. "If you know anything about this bow or have any information at all about Hannah's disappearance, please call the hotline number that's running across your screen. I'm not going to disclose the location where this clue was found or the attendant circumstances. If you know that information, that would certainly lend some credibility to any information you have to offer. Basically, we are looking for anything that can lead to the recovery of Hannah Turner as quickly as possible, and we need your help. This must be a community effort. The phone line is open and you can elect to remain anonymous, but it's imperative we hear from you today. The sun set twenty minutes ago, and the temperature is dropping. If you have children of your own, you would want them inside right now so they can eat a hot meal before you tuck them into their warm bed. Let's bring Hannah Turner home."

She moved quickly from the podium despite the many raised hands and a loud chorus of shouted questions. She and Murphy had decided in advance she shouldn't take any questions in order to keep their messaging on point and to manage the flow of information. All it would take was one reporter who'd dug up Ricky Turner's criminal record and the entire conference would spin out into an indictment of the mayor's family instead of a means to try to get the public to come forward with any information they might have.

Pearson met her off stage. He jabbed at his cell phone. "The calls are already starting to come in. They'll text me the ones that appear to be actual clues instead of lookie-loos." He shoved the phone in his pocket. "You did good."

"We'll see. I'm still not sure this was the right decision, but if it brings her back, I'm not going to argue with the result. Any movement at our favorite suspect's house?"

"No. You ready to roll?"

"Absolutely."

They were almost there when Starr's phone rang. She stared at the phone. The number on the screen was vaguely familiar but she couldn't place it. Deciding to err on the side of caution, she answered. "Rio here."

"It's Catherine Landauer. I need to see you. Right now."

Right. She'd given Catherine her cell during the Knoll trial, but Catherine had never used it, seeming to prefer email instead of calls or texts. "I'm on my way to an appointment. I don't know if you saw the news conference, but we have a lead, and we need to follow up."

"That's why I'm calling. I need to see you right now. Are you still at police headquarters?"

Starr paused before answering. Catherine sounded out of breath and oddly panicked. "Are you okay?"

"What? Of course. Can you just tell me where you are? It's important or believe me I wouldn't ask."

"I'm on the way somewhere. Can you just tell me what it is?"

"No. What time will you be done with whatever it is you're doing?"

Catherine's voice was infused with anxiety, and Starr wondered what the hell was going on. "I can meet you in an hour. How about Guero's," she said, naming the only place she could think of off the top of her head, knowing it would be familiar to Catherine.

"Fine. I'll be there."

Silence filled the line and Starr stared at the phone in disbelief.

"Everything okay?" Pearson asked.

"I guess so." She shoved her phone into her pocket. "Do you know Catherine Landauer?"

He chuckled. "Barracuda? Sure, I know her. You have a case with her?"

"Had a trial with her a week ago, you know the one where she kicked Reese's ass, and the defendant wound up pleading out to next to nothing. But she's not calling about that case. She has some strange interest in this one."

"That so. What's the deal?"

"I don't know, but she's kind of obsessed about it. You have any reason to think she's off balance in any way?"

"Never struck me that way. Does seem strange though considering how she has a reputation for taking out law enforcement on the stand. Plus, she doesn't take any cases involving child victims. Only criminal defense attorney I know of that doesn't besides the ones with DWI-only practices."

Why did Catherine have an aversion to child abuse cases? Starr filed the question away to reexamine later. "She wants to meet with me. Something about the press conference set her off. I told her I'd show up after we're done here."

"You want me to come with you?"

The obvious answer was yes. If Catherine really did have some useful information about the case, then it made sense to have the lead detective present if for no other reason than to be a witness to whatever Catherine had to say. But Starr hesitated. "I'll take this one on my own. She sounds a little skittish, and I don't want to scare her off in case she really does have something that can help."

"Sounds good." Pearson's tone was neutral. "We're here." He pointed at Ricky's house. "How do you want to play this?"

"You take the lead. I'm here to show you have direct access to get a warrant, an indictment, whatever we need to get him to start talking." Starr followed him to the door and stepped to the side when he rang the bell. They heard some rustling inside and then the slow clomp of footsteps growing closer. When the door swung wide, Starr held back her surprise. Ricky looked so much like his brother, he could be his twin.

"What are you doing back here?" Ricky said to Pearson.

"Just doing our job. You want us to find your niece, don't you?" Pearson raised his shoulders as he asked the question, not a trace of defensiveness in his tone. "I brought help and some information. Invite us in and we'll share what we have so far."

Ricky looked over at Starr, and then back at Pearson. Despite the grim frown, Starr could tell he was wavering, but she resisted saying anything for fear of scaring him into shutting down. Whether he was the concerned uncle or the psychotic kidnapper, the promise of an inside scoop should be enough to get him to invite them in.

He turned away from the door, but left it open, a tacit invitation to follow. Starr let Pearson take the lead, and she focused on taking in as much detail as she could as Ricky led them down the hall to the kitchen. No photos, no personal items, the two doors they passed were both shut. She detected no sounds other than their footfalls.

"Coffee?"

Starr took one look at the grimy surface of the coffee maker and smiled. "A little late in the day for me, but thanks."

Pearson also declined. "Sorry I forgot to introduce you. Ricky, this is Starr Rio. She's the prosecutor assigned to the task force. She's worked with me many times before, and we've been very successful at prosecuting dozens of perpetrators."

"I know who she is. I saw the press conference."

"Excellent," Pearson said. "Then you saw the evidence we've collected."

"That bow doesn't look like anything my niece would wear."

Starr couldn't resist chiming in. "You've gotten to know her well since you moved to town?"

Ricky hunched his shoulders. "Well enough."

"I must admit I agree with you. First time I saw it, I thought, this can't be Hannah's."

"Right. So you're no closer now than you were the day she was taken, are you?"

"Well, I wouldn't say that." Pearson pulled out his phone, scrolled to a picture of the bow, and set it on the table. "I think we can all agree this wasn't hers, but that doesn't mean she didn't have it on at some point." He lowered his voice to a conspiratorial whisper. "Our working theory is that the kidnapper gave it to her, and then left it behind as a clue. He probably called in the tip himself."

"Interesting theory."

"Won't stay a theory for long. We were able to get several pieces of evidence from this little bow."

"What is it you want from me?"

Starr stepped closer as if to intervene in the grilling. "We could use your help. Look, we know you've been in prison. Is it possible that you made enemies there that might want to get back at you by kidnapping someone close to you?"

He shook his head vigorously. "I did my time with my head down. I don't have any enemies other than the people who are constantly reminding me that my past means I will never have a chance at a future."

His voice was laced with bitterness, and Starr pounced on that. "I get it. I see people every day who write off their lives for a payoff in the moment. You made a mistake. I don't think you should have to pay for it for the rest of your life, but is it possible that you don't know any other way to get ahead?"

"Are you implying that I'm somehow involved in kidnapping my niece to make a buck? If so, where's the ransom note, the demand for a payoff? What do you have to say about that?"

"How do you know there's not been a ransom note?"

"Because my brother would've told me if there were."

"When's the last time you spoke with him?" Pearson asked. They'd specifically asked Keith not to talk to his brother or anyone else for that matter about the case.

"Am I under arrest?"

"No," Starr said.

"Then I'm done answering questions. I'd like you both to leave."

Pearson stood and Starr followed him back out of the house, waiting until they were back in the car before saying anything. "I didn't expect him to confess, but what do you make of him?" she asked.

"My gut says there's something off about him, but I don't know how or if it relates to his niece." He scrunched his face in a classic something smells but I can't put my finger on it expression. "He didn't flinch when we mentioned the bow was being tested."

"Which either means he knows there's nothing on it because he was super careful, or he isn't involved. He's all we have right now, so let's keep a car on this block and monitor his movements."

"Fair enough." Pearson pulled away from the curb. "Where to now?"

Starr remembered her scheduled rendezvous with Catherine and realized she hadn't allowed enough time to get there. If she had

Pearson take her back to her car, she was going to be late. "I need to take care of something. It won't take long. Can you drop me off at Guero's? I'll catch an Uber back to headquarters as soon as I'm done."

She had him drop her off down the block from the restaurant to give her a few moments to collect her thoughts. It had been a long freaking day, and it was hard to believe it had only been this morning since she'd last seen Catherine. As she approached, she spotted Catherine on the patio of the restaurant. Unlike this morning, she was dressed in a suit, and this was the put together woman Starr was used to seeing around the courthouse, but as she drew closer, Starr noticed Catherine didn't look as composed as she usually did. She was glancing around furtively, and she looked like her world could come crashing down at any moment. "Sorry to keep you waiting. Traffic was awful. I don't have a lot of time. Do you want to grab a table?"

Catherine shook her head. "Do you have a picture of the bow with you?"

Starr hesitated. "What's going on?"

"The bow. Show it to me, please."

Catherine's voice was commanding, but it carried an undercurrent of anxiety that immediately put Starr on edge. Deciding there was no harm in showing Catherine something that had been aired for all the world to see, she pulled out her phone and thumbed her way to the photograph. She held it out to Catherine who took the phone and held the edges in a fierce grip. Starr watched her study the photo, turning the phone several times to catch all the angles, but instead of handing it back, Catherine held it like it was a lifeline. "What is it?"

"Have you done a database search yet?" Catherine shook her head. "You haven't. If you had, you would know that this clue means you're dealing with a known child abuser."

"What are you talking about?"

Catherine bit her bottom lip, a sign Starr took to mean she wanted to say something more, but didn't for some reason. Starr wanted to prompt her but sensed it would only spook her away.

Finally, Catherine spoke. "I'll tell you some things, but you'll have to find the rest out on your own. Before I say anything, promise me you will follow up on what I'm about to tell you. And I don't want to be involved."

"Okay."

"Say you promise."

"I promise." Starr made a show of crossing her heart, but she grinned like it was a joke.

"It's not funny."

"I know, sorry. You just sound so serious and I don't have a clue what to expect."

"You've heard of Jill Winfield?"

Starr thought for a second. The name certainly sounded familiar. She searched her mind and landed on a childhood memory. "Yes, of course. She was abducted from her home when she was twelve. Her mother was killed by the abductor as I recall, and they never caught him. Wait a minute. Do you think that the same person was involved in this case? He'd have to be like sixty years old."

"Actually, more like fifty. He was younger than most people thought."

Starr made a mental note to ask her why she had that fact memorized. "Tell me why you think it's the same guy."

"You have the answer right in front of you if you'd bothered to be more thorough."

Catherine's know-it-all tone rankled. "Since you seem to know so much, why don't you tell me?" Starr asked. Silence followed while she tried to read the troubled expression on Catherine's face. She was just about to walk away, when Catherine finally spoke.

"The bow. It's your biggest clue. The kidnapper left it behind for a reason. He wants us to know he's back in action. He's teasing us because he got away the first time and he thinks he'll always be above the law."

"Us?"

"What?" Catherine asked.

"You've said 'us' twice. He wants 'us' to know he's back in action. He's teasing 'us.'" Starr stared intently into her eyes. "What aren't you telling me?"

Catherine stared back, her expression blank for a few seconds, and then her eyes started blinking rapidly. She shook her head and the blinking stopped, but her voice was laced with angry impatience. "I've told you everything I can. The bow is the key. Run a search with the FBI and it will connect you to the kidnapper. Everything you need to know will be in the original file." She edged away. "I have to go."

Starr called out. "Wait."

Catherine stopped but she didn't turn around.

"Can I call you later if I have more questions?" Starr didn't bother trying to hide the desperate tone in her voice. Catherine knew something. Something vital about this case, and whatever it was caused her pain, pain that Starr felt compelled to erase.

The pause was interminably long and seemed longer because Catherine never turned back to face her. Noise from the restaurant filled the air with a party atmosphere completely incongruent to the urgency Starr felt as she waited for Catherine to respond. Finally, Catherine started walking again, but her voice carried over the boisterous sounds of the Saturday night crowd. "Contact the FBI. Do it now."

CHAPTER NINE

Catherine paced the waiting room of her therapist and punched in another text on her phone. She knew Dr. M was here because the lights were on and a car was parked outside the small building. She also knew Dr. M saw clients on the weekends because she'd often accommodated her schedule when she was in trial.

Hell, she should be an investigator. She'd be a helluva lot better one than the team that was trying to find Hannah Turner. She'd scoured the news since her meeting with Starr last night but had seen nothing to indicate the task force had made any progress. She'd resisted the strong urge to contact Starr again and ask if she'd followed up on the connection to her own case. Of course, Starr had no idea that she had any personal connection to the bow. Jill Winfield hadn't been in the public eye in years, and Catherine had taken many carefully calculated steps to ensure the public couldn't connect the powerful attorney she'd become with the little girl whose face had been plastered on news channels around the country after she'd been snatched from her bed and held captive.

She sent another text, her agitation growing at Dr. M's lack of a response while her meeting with Starr replayed on an endless loop. She should've sent an anonymous note, left a message on the tip line, anything to avoid the risk her true identity might be found out. If all she'd wanted was to tip off the task force that the crimes were connected, she could've done so without potentially exposing herself to the lead prosecutor on the case. What was it about Starr that made her take that risk?

Maybe it was the very thing that she professed to hate about her. Starr's take no prisoners type of justice was infuriating for Catherine the defense attorney, but for Jill Winfield, who'd spend her life looking over her shoulder for the man who'd never had to answer for his crimes, it was refreshing. She was drawn to Starr, but acting on the impulse to trust her would only draw her back into a past she'd managed to bury.

The door to the inner sanctum opened, and Dr. M appeared. She looked surprised to see Catherine standing in her waiting room.

"Finally," Catherine said. "I've been texting you for hours."

"Catherine, we don't have an appointment."

"I know that."

"Would you like to make an appointment?"

The exchange was infuriating, but Catherine recognized Dr. M's efforts to school her about boundaries. "Look, I know I'm not supposed to just show up here, but this is an emergency and I didn't know where else to go." Damn. Her voice was cracking. She cleared her throat, struggling to hide the depth of her desperation even while she knew she had to show she was frantic for help. "I know I've pushed your buttons before, but you have to admit this is over-the-top, even for me. I promise I wouldn't bother you if it wasn't important. Is there any chance you can talk to me now?"

Dr. M looked back toward her office. "I suppose I can spare a little time, but if you're in immediate danger of—"

"I'm not going to harm myself or others," Catherine said, finishing the portion of Dr. M's outgoing message that cautioned patients to call 911 under those circumstances. She stepped closer to the office door. "I'll take whatever time you can spare."

Dr. M held open the door. "Come on in."

Catherine followed her into the office and took her usual seat on the couch. Now that she was here, she felt silly for having barged in, and she wasn't entirely sure where to start. Dr. M settled into her chair, her familiar notepad in hand.

"Is this about the Turner girl?"

The Turner girl. The phrase grated against Catherine's already raw nerves. How many people had once referred to her as the Winfield girl? Newspapers, newscasters, police, lawyers. Both before and after she'd been found, she'd been a commodity to be examined and exposed for maximum gain, her identity secondary to the prurient interest of the prying public. "Please don't call her that."

Dr. M leaned forward. "Okay. What would you like me to call her?"

"Her name is Hannah. Let's call her that."

"Sounds good. Are you here to talk about Hannah?"

"Yes. No. I mean, I'm here to talk about me, but she and I are connected now, and I don't know what to do about it."

"Would you care to expound on that?"

"He's back."

Dr. M nodded knowingly. "I can certainly see how this case has affected you, and it's pretty normal for memories to come flooding back."

Catherine nearly growled at the misperception, but it was her own fault for not being clear. "No, my memories aren't stressing me out. Russell Pratt is back. He's here in Austin, or at least he was, and he's taken Hannah. I don't know why, but I'm certain it's not a coincidence."

Dr. M set her notebook down. "Tell me how you know."

Catherine had a choice. She could take offense that Dr. M didn't take her at her word, or she could take this opportunity to confide her fears to the only person currently in her life who knew for certain who she really was, including all the sordid details of her past. She relayed the information about the news conference and the bow, including her meeting with Starr the night before.

"Talk to me about the bow. I remember you mentioning it, but it's been a while since we talked specifics. Pretend I'm hearing this for the first time."

Catherine cleared her throat and fixed on a spot on the far wall. "The bow was for the ceremony. He would bring it out every day and tell me that when I was ready, I would wear the bow in my hair and walk down the aisle to marry him for all eternity."

"When you were ready?"

"That's what he said, but what he really meant was when he was ready. He was waiting for me to get a little bit older, have my first period so I'd be able to bear children. We weren't supposed to have sex except to make babies, so marrying me aka raping me had to wait until there was a religiously justifiable reason to do so. He was such a prude about it, he wouldn't even look at me when I was changing clothes or using the bathroom." She heard the bitterness in her own voice, but she embraced it. She'd earned the right to be angry, and as much as she wished she could push it all away in the back of her head, never to be thought of again, she knew that wasn't realistic. So she owned it.

"You sound awfully matter-of-fact about it all. Is that a factor of how many times you've had to tell the story or is it because you're shutting down the emotional side of it all?"

"Why do you ask questions when you already know the answer?" Catherine didn't bother trying to hide the edge in her voice. "It's annoying."

Dr. M smiled. "And yet you keep coming back. Even without an appointment."

Catherine half rose. "I can leave."

"You can, but you shouldn't unless you want to. You may not realize this on a conscious level, but you're reliving your own experience through this case. You were already feeling the similarities before, but now that the bow has come to light, it's clear this case is directly related to what happened to you." Dr. M paused and stared intently at her. "What are you thinking right now?"

"I'm wondering what his next move will be. Did he leave the bow on purpose? Was he the one who called the police? He had to be. No one else would find anything significant about the clue. But why would he risk exposure when he clearly has Hannah hidden away where none of us can find her? It doesn't make sense. Unless…"

"Unless?"

"Could he know I'm here? Did he leave the clue for me, knowing that even if no one else remembered, I would know it meant he was back?"

"What would his goal be?"

"I don't know. Deal with unfinished business?" Catherine shook her head. "It still doesn't make sense that he would risk exposure after all these years just to taunt me." She tried to let the thought go, but it lingered, digging its claws into her subconscious.

"Okay, now that we've talked about what you think, let's talk about how this makes you feel, you know, because that's my specialty."

Catherine shifted in her chair and wondered if she would ever be okay talking about her feelings. Probably not, but she knew firsthand the consequences of ignoring them. Still. "I'm okay."

"What does that mean? Describe it to me."

She sighed. "I can function. I'm not shutting down." She looked down at her hands which were frenetically twisting a pen, and then back up at Dr. M whose expression was knowing. "Okay, so I'm a little agitated, but I think that's pretty normal under the circumstances."

"Definitely." Dr. M looked down at her notes. "It's been a while since you stopped taking the Celexa. Do you think you might need some to get through this patch?"

"No." Catherine wasn't averse to medication. She'd spent years on various medication regimes trying to find the best method of staving off the side effects of having been kidnapped, losing her only parent, and being thrust into the spotlight of a world starved for the intimate details of the crime that had been perpetrated against her. At first, the medicine had helped her deal with her new reality—she wasn't sure she could've gotten through life without it—but it came with its own set of issues in the form of side effects, and after carefully easing off it, she had no desire to go back. "I want to try to get through this without meds, but I promise I'll let you know if I need some extra help."

"Fair enough. I won't press, but I am going to ask you to tell me more about your feelings. I've got agitated. What else?"

Damn. Catherine knew there was no getting anything by her, but she didn't feel like sorting through the swirl of emotions churning in her mind. What do you call the feeling for not wanting to talk about your feelings? She suppressed a laugh at the thought and focused on what she was indeed feeling because Dr. M was unlikely to let up. Breathing was difficult, her limbs were leaden, and her usually sharp mind was dulled by the onslaught of too many thoughts coming at her from all directions. These feelings were undeniably familiar, but she feared speaking them out loud would give them more power despite the fact that years of therapy had taught her the reverse was true.

"I feel trapped," she blurted out. "It's the same as when I wake up from a nightmare. I can't breathe. I can't move. I'm paralyzed and I feel like I'll never break free." She met Dr. M's steady gaze. "All these years, I've known he was out there somewhere, but I let myself assume he'd gone into hiding or died. I assumed he would never be able to have power over me again. But he's here. I know it with every fiber of my being." She clenched her fists so tightly her nails dug into her skin. "And I'm not that little girl anymore, but that doesn't change the fact I feel as powerless as she did, which means I'm back where I started, and I cannot begin to tell you how much that frustrates me."

"What are you going to do about it?"

"There's nothing I can do except show up here and pour my heart out to you on a regular basis. And pray the task force follows up on the lead."

"Have you thought about telling this prosecutor, what was her name?"

"Starr. Starr Rio." Catherine braced for what Dr. M was about to say.

"Have you thought about telling Starr who you are?"

"No."

"Would you like to talk about it?"

"No." Catherine didn't elaborate, not wanting to provide an opening. She stood. "I should go. Thanks for meeting me. I know you didn't have to and I appreciate it. I feel much better now," she lied. What she felt was a strong desire to flee as quickly as possible.

Dr. M mercifully refrained from mentioning her abrupt departure. Until she'd almost escaped. "Your personal safety is my greatest concern. Here." Dr. M pointed at her head. "And here." She pointed to her heart. "Whatever we need to do to support you. Okay?"

"Okay." Catherine ducked her head to hide her pain and hurried out, wishing she could as easily run away from her feelings and the terror of confronting them.

Starr paced in front of the whiteboard in the conference room they'd set up at police headquarters, her mind reviewing the evidence over and over. For the first time since the task force had been convened, she was alone in the room and she'd hoped the peace would give her added clarity, but all it did was stir up thoughts of inadequacy. Somewhere a little girl was frightened, separated from her family and friends, being subjected to God knows what, and they were no closer to finding her than they had been when she'd first gone missing.

Ricky Turner hadn't left his apartment. The unit below his was vacant, and they'd gotten permission from the landlord to station someone there, but they hadn't heard any strange noises or even a second set of footfalls to indicate there was anyone else in his apartment. Her gut told her Ricky was a dead end, but they didn't have anyone else to focus on yet and they needed a lead, or they'd start to lose hope. The online and phone tip lines were a train wreck comprised of half-truths and lots of lies. Everyone claimed to know something, but nothing was verifiable. The cops assigned to the task force had spoken to everyone who'd had an opportunity to see Hannah before she disappeared, and they'd followed up on every lead, no matter how weak, and they had nothing to show for it.

And then Catherine had shown up with her vague claims about the bow. Starr didn't hold out much hope that a simple white satin bow could be traced to a child abductor from over twenty years ago. If there really was a connection, why had Catherine been the one to make it and not any of the dozen officers they had working on this case? As improbable as it seemed, Catherine's clue was all they had to go on right now, and Pearson was on the phone with the FBI right now. Would the connection be clear to them?

Starr wondered again if Catherine had some personal connection to the Winfield case. She'd spent some time on the internet last night running searches to familiarize herself with the facts. Jill Winfield had been taken from her home by a young man, likely early twenties. Jill didn't know it at the time, but Russell Pratt had broken in to her home and smothered her mother with a pillow allowing him to take Jill with little fuss. Because the abduction had happened on the weekend, several days passed before anyone even noticed Jill was missing. The school had sent a counselor to check on her after a few missed days and no returned calls and found Jill's mother's dead body and no sign of Jill.

Jill had been held by Pratt for just over a month before she escaped. During that time, he had groomed her for a future as his wife. The grooming had taken place only five miles from Jill's home in a trailer in the woods. The local sheriff's office had been out to the trailer, but they professed they'd seen nothing during their visit to make them suspicious that Pratt might be holding Jill captive, although further investigation conducted after the case was over proved they simply hadn't looked hard enough.

Starr recalled, and the internet backed her up, that Jill was the hero in the story. She'd managed to squirrel away a fork and used it to pick the lock of her chains, choosing to make her escape on one of the rare occasions that Pratt left her alone to get provisions in town. She'd wandered through the woods, hungry and alone, for over forty-eight hours before she finally stumbled on a campsite of some hunters who took her into town. No one was more surprised than the local sheriff and FBI who'd centered their focus on a teacher at the school who'd had a prior arrest he hadn't disclosed to the administration.

With Jill's only parent dead, she was placed into the custody of her estranged aunt and her family. The family made a show of asking for time alone to deal with this situation, but they trotted Jill out on the regular morning show circuit, presumably collecting the large payouts associated with such appearances. Starr had played back some of the archived video and found that the family looked way more engaged in the interviews than Jill. From her time as a child abuse prosecutor, she recognized the familiar signs of withdrawal and mistrust in Jill's mannerisms. She looked like she would rather be anyplace but where she was, and Starr couldn't blame her. There was no benefit to this public display for anyone.

While she was online, Starr had done a little digging on Catherine Landauer, but the information was shallow. She'd gone to both undergraduate and law school at UT. She'd graduated near the top of her class, and, after a brief internship at the DA's office, had immediately started working for Neil Daniels, who'd been a fairly prominent criminal defense attorney before he'd died of a heart attack about seven years ago. Catherine now owned the practice, and according to the county records, she also owned the building where her law firm was located, free and clear. A quick search showed the building was now prime real estate, which meant she must be doing well.

Starr pushed a little further to see if Catherine came from a rich family, but she found nothing referencing a family of any kind or even where Catherine was from. All her online professional bios merely listed her education and career accomplishments, including no personal details. No family, no hobbies, nothing to tell her more than Catherine was a hard-working lawyer with a singular focus on her career.

The door to the conference room burst open, and Pearson strode through with a sheaf of papers in one hand. "I got something. FBI coughed up their file on the Winfield case, and I printed out a copy for us to review."

Starr minimized the screen before he could see what she'd been researching. Catherine Landauer was a mystery, but one that she didn't have the time to solve right now, and she didn't want to have to explain her obsessive interest in her because she couldn't even explain it to herself. She reached out a hand for the file. "Have you looked at it yet?"

"Barely. Figured you'd bite my head off if you didn't get equal time with it. But there was a bow, and based on the picture in here, it's identical to the one we found."

"Holy shit."

"Holy shit is right," he said. "You okay with releasing the one we found to them for analysis?"

Starr considered the question carefully. Too many horror stories of evidence being lost or compromised were fresh in her mind, but the feds had access to labs they could only dream about. And they'd be quick, and quick was essential. "What's your gut say?"

"I say we do it. We're running out of options."

"Okay, but make sure we get lots of photos. And I want it hand-delivered, no courier service or mail service. I'll find the money in our budget if we have to. Send someone you trust."

"On it."

Pearson shoved the file at her while he made a call to make the arrangements. Starr tuned him out and started reading. Each word she took in stirred memories of the case. She'd been just a few years older than Jill had when she'd been kidnapped, and she and every other child in the country had lived through the stress of their parents' collective nightmare that the same fate could befall them. Obsessive warnings not to talk to strangers and early curfews abounded despite the fact neither would have made a difference in this particular case. Jill's captor had crept into her house in the dead of night and smothered her mother with a pillow before abducting Jill and holding her captive at his trailer only five miles away. It wasn't until Jill escaped that she learned her mother had died. The news hailed Jill as a hero, but Starr had seen enough crime victims to know that she might have physically escaped, but she was not unscathed. The fact that Pratt had never been apprehended likely only added to the trauma.

Starr remembered her parents talking to her about what she should do if a stranger approached her and how to call 911 if someone entered the house who didn't belong there. It had been and still was surreal, but Starr had seen so many horrible things in her career as a prosecutor, she was sad to say the facts of this case didn't shock her. But they would have then, back when abductions and sexual abuse weren't regular features in the daily news. She didn't know if these crimes were more prevalent now or if they just were highlighted by the constant barrage of news and information as a result of the internet.

Pearson hung up the phone. "See anything helpful yet?"

Starr pushed the papers aside. "Let's talk about this for a sec. Even if the bow is substantially the same, what's to say Hannah's kidnapping is not a copycat? I mean don't you think that's more realistic than thinking that Russell Pratt, who has eluded capture for all these years suddenly decided to emerge in another state to snatch the mayor's daughter? What would his motive be to come out of hiding now and risk arrest? I don't see anything in here about other connected crimes. Do you think there's some connection between him and the mayor? Why Austin? It just doesn't make sense."

Pearson grunted. "Don't ask me about the connection. I'm not the one who insisted that these crimes are connected, but if someone was going to do a copycat, why pick this one? It's been years. Usually the copycats are trying to bank off the notoriety of the original crime. Hell, we've all forgotten about this case."

"Except for Catherine," Starr muttered.

"What?"

"Catherine Landauer. Why was this case on her radar?"

"*Dateline* junkie? She wouldn't be the first attorney who practices criminal law to use it as a hobby too."

"Sure, but don't you think it's a weird coincidence that it was this particular case she remembered?"

"I guess."

Despite Pearson's uncommitted response, Starr was convinced she was on to something. She did a quick mental run through all of her interactions with Catherine the last few days about this case. Catherine had been overbearing, anxious, and insistent, none of which were signs of a news junkie high on the familiarity of stumbling on a copycat case. No, something about this particular case had burrowed under Catherine's skin, and the desire to know what it was nagged at Starr as well. The desire pressed her to ask Pearson if he would run a background check on Catherine.

"You're kidding right?"

"No," she said. "If you had someone else on the outside who was this interested in the case and wasn't an attorney, you'd have no problem running a check on them to make sure there was nothing strange about their obsession. Why is this any different?"

"Because if she ever finds out, there will be hell to pay. She'll claim the cops and the DA's office are out to get her, and that will be the main point she raises in every motion hearing, every bond decision, every trial from here on out."

"Since when do you care what a defense attorney says about you?" Starr considered all angles, but she ultimately decided to stick with her gut. "I can get someone else to do it if you're not comfortable."

"Nice try. You can't manipulate me. I'll do it for you, but if someone asks about it, I'm going to send them your way. You better be prepared to answer why."

Starr nodded, but her mind was whirring. She wasn't at all sure what she'd say about the why, but she had no choice but to follow her gut and her gut told her Catherine Landauer had something to hide.

CHAPTER TEN

Catherine heard a noise and looked up from her desk to see Doris standing in the doorway, a frown on her face. "What's wrong?"

"Clive Burson called to say they hired someone else."

It took Catherine a moment to remember who Clive Burson was, but she hid her memory loss behind a nonchalant hand wave. "It happens."

"Not to you. I can't believe he would be so quick to hire someone else after you came in on a Saturday night to meet with him and his wife."

Ah, the potential client. It had only been two days since she'd had a blackout during her meeting with the Bursons, and she barely remembered it. She was going to have to get control of her thoughts if she wanted to stay in business. Thankfully, Doris didn't seem to have the whole story about how she'd run out of the meeting without any plausible explanation. "It's okay. I don't think we were a good fit."

Doris pursed her lips like she was mulling over the assessment. Catherine knew her well enough to know that Doris didn't believe her, but loyalty would prevent her from asking more questions. "Anything else?"

"No, your afternoon is clear. I'll let you know if anything new comes in, but I left the Paulson case file on your desk in case you want to get caught up on trial prep."

"Thanks," Catherine called out as Doris retreated back to her desk. She pulled the Paulson file toward her. She hadn't noticed it sitting there, a fact that should be surprising, but wasn't. The list of things that had fallen off her radar since Hannah had gone missing were long, and they were stacking up to be a huge impediment to her normally ordered life. She had two big trials coming up in the next couple of months, and it was time to focus. She turned back to her computer and dove into the files of electronic discovery she needed to review. She was deep into a set of dense financial statements when she heard a knock on the door. Damn. Just when she'd found her rhythm. She kept her eyes on the computer and called out, "Come in."

The door opened and she heard footsteps behind her. "I'm really focused here," Catherine said. "If it can wait, I'd really appreciate it."

"I'm not sure." Doris cleared her throat. "I know you said you didn't want to be bothered, but it's kind of strange and I thought you'd want to see it right away."

"It?" Catherine reluctantly pushed away her keyboard and turned around to see Doris standing in front of her desk holding a large flower arrangement away from her body. Carnations. Loads of white carnations. A sour tinge filled Catherine's mouth and it went dry. It couldn't be. No. It was just flowers. They didn't mean anything.

"Ugly, right?" Doris said. As she spoke, she twirled the arrangement in her hand, letting it rest on the edge of Catherine's desk. Catherine stared, transfixed at the sickening garden of white flowers, but it wasn't the flowers that captured her attention now. It was the half dozen large white satin bows protruding from the flowers. They looked exactly like the one Starr had displayed at the press conference.

Catherine gripped the edge of her desk. "Where did you get those?"

Doris flinched at the growl in her voice. "Are you okay? You look a little pale."

"Where. Did. Those. Come. From." Catherine enunciated each word carefully, hoping the edge of authority in her voice would convey exactly how strongly she felt about getting an answer.

"A delivery guy brought them. Like three minutes ago. If I hurry, I might be able to catch him."

Catherine was out of her chair and running toward the door before Doris finished speaking. She burst into the lobby, and finding it empty, rushed out the door. She scanned the parking lot while she tried to catch her breath. Her burst of energy had been in vain. No strange vehicles, no strange people. Everything she saw was a regular component of her usual everyday life, but with every cell in her body, she knew her everyday life was on the verge of drastic change. When she returned to her office, her mind was whirring with possibilities.

"There's a note." Doris pointed at the envelope protruding from the gross array of bows and flowers. Doris started to grasp the edges, but Catherine shouted, "Don't." At Doris's surprised look, she softened her voice. "I'll open it later. Can I have a moment alone, please?"

She waited until she heard the door click shut before digging through her desk for a pair of tweezers she often used to pop the stubborn lock on her file cabinet. Using the tweezers, she carefully pulled the envelope from the bouquet and shook out the card inside. It landed faceup on her desk, and the broad strokes of the block letters glared back up at her.

SHE'S NOT YOU, BUT SHE'LL HAVE TO DO.

Catherine dropped the tweezers and the metal clanged against the hard surface of her desk, echoing in the silence of the room. She wanted to wail, to bang her fists against the desk, to kick the walls—anything to stave off the agony coursing through her body, but she'd spent a lifetime tamping down her emotions, and now was no different. She opened her office door in time to catch Doris spying. Who could blame her? She'd been acting like a crazy person lately, but it was time for all of this to stop. "Call Starr Rio on her cell and tell her to get over here right now. Don't take no for an answer."

Catherine didn't wait for a response. She stalked back into her office and sat in one of the chairs across from her desk. No point working now. Her life was about to be turned completely upside down, and she didn't have a clue what the future would hold, but the thing she'd feared the most had happened. Her past had come back to haunt her.

❖

Starr pointed at the last piece of pizza in the box on the conference room table. "Dibs."

Pearson, who'd just slid into the seat next to her, shook his head. "How do you eat like that?"

"First rule of litigation and politics. Eat what you can, when you can. If I waited until it was convenient and nutritious, I would starve to death."

Pearson pointed as she jammed a slice of pepperoni in her mouth. "No danger of that. Seriously, Starr. It wouldn't kill you to have a real meal."

"Don't worry about me. I promised my mother I'd come by tonight, which she'll take for an excuse to fatten me up so I have the energy to do God's work."

"Is she still teaching cooking classes?"

"Yes, but she's taken on a million other projects too. When the election goes full swing, she and Dad will be my number one volunteers."

"You're lucky."

"I know." Starr did know. Her mother's constant reminders that she didn't visit enough notwithstanding, she was well aware she was fortunate to have a large family that actually loved and liked each other. "You're welcome to come with me. Mom loves you."

"And I love your mother, but my wife is going to disown me if I don't show my face at home one night this week."

Neither of them would say it, but both of them knew that the case was getting bleak. With every hour that went by without new clues, the chances Hannah would ever show up were growing thin.

Pearson shoved a folder at her. "Here's that stuff you wanted. I'm not sure what you're looking for, but I don't think this is going to be helpful."

Starr glanced around to make sure no one else was around, before she twisted the clasp and pulled out the few papers inside. She held them up. "Is this it?"

Pearson nodded. "I couldn't find much about Landauer before college, and there's not a lot even after that. She keeps a really low profile."

Starr skimmed the pages and found nothing she wasn't able to access via the web. She wasn't sure what she'd expected, but she was disappointed nonetheless. She zoomed to the last page. "Don't these usually have some info about birth date and place? Why are those fields blank?"

Pearson looked over her shoulder. "They aren't blank." He pointed. "See that code. It means findings inconclusive."

"How can a person's date of birth and birthplace be inconclusive?"

He hunched his shoulders. "Never seen that on a report before." He rocked back on his heels. "Wait, I did see that once, but it was a different kind of deal."

"What do you mean?"

"It was for a guy that was in WITSEC."

"Witness protection?" Starr felt a sense of urgency torquing up inside her.

"Yeah, they don't always bother making up stuff that goes all the way back into a person's past unless it's absolutely necessary. Most folks don't look back before college, and especially not before high school."

"Are you suggesting that Catherine Landauer is in the witness protection program?"

Pearson raised his hands in surrender. "I'm not suggesting anything. You're the one who wanted me to run a background check." He pointed at the papers in her hands. "That's it. I make no promises about what it contains."

Starr took a deep breath. He was right of course. She'd just expected to find something definitive to connect Catherine to Jill

Winfield or Russell Pratt or anything related to the case Catherine seemed obsessed about. Her mind ran through the possibilities. Based on her appearance and when she'd graduated from law school, she and Catherine were probably around the same age, which meant Catherine would've been around the same age as Jill when Pratt had kidnapped her. Maybe Catherine had known Jill, or maybe she was a relative. Maybe something similar had happened to someone she knew and it had affected her to this day.

Maybe, maybe, maybe. The conjecture was wearing her out. Thankfully, one of the patrol officers stuck his head in the door.

"Sorry to bother you, but a call just came in, and it sounds important."

Starr pointed at Pearson. "You take it." She held up the papers. "I'm going to read through this again."

The cop cleared his throat. "Actually, ma'am, it was for you, and I didn't know you were still here so they left a message. It was Catherine Landauer's office. They want you to head over there now." He paused and looked at Pearson. "And they asked us to send a CSI unit."

Starr dropped the papers she was holding onto the desk. Whatever was in Catherine's past paled in comparison to whatever the hell was happening right now.

"What do you want to do?" asked Pearson.

"I want to get over there right now."

"I'll go get my car and pull around front."

"New plan—I'm parked right by the front door. Are you going to vouch for me if we get stopped for speeding?"

"Count on it." Pearson barked at the officer while striding toward the door. "Call CSU. Give them the address and tell them to meet us there." The officer ducked back out and sprinted away, leaving Pearson to hold the door. "You coming?" he said.

Starr nodded. She looked around the room at the evidence they'd compiled so far, wondering if she should bring anything, but she knew in her gut nothing in this room was as important as what they were about to see. A few minutes later as she and Pearson were speeding across town, it occurred to her for the first time that the officer had been vague when he referenced who had wanted them to come out there. Not "Catherine wants you to head over there now," but they. And send a crime scene unit. Was Catherine okay?

The drive was indeed fast. It wasn't long until they turned onto the quiet block where Catherine's office building was located. From the outside everything looked perfectly normal. A quaint house with a large porch. Based on the location, this piece of real estate would command a lot of cash, and again Starr wondered how Catherine had come to own it.

She was out of the car before Pearson, ignoring his call for her to wait. She rushed up the steps and had her hand on the door handle when he ran up behind her and slipped between her and the door.

"Uh, crime scene? Let's go in slow in case there's a reason to protect evidence. What's your hurry?"

Starr looked down at the ground like the answer would be in the wood planks of the porch. She was anxious, but she couldn't tell if it was the prospect of getting a clue about Hannah or if it was something more personal. She shook away the anxiety and focused. "Sorry." She stepped back. "You go first."

Pearson gently turned the knob and eased the door open. After a moment of looking around, he walked through and held the door open behind him. Starr waited a second and then followed close behind. They were only a few steps in before a tall, striking, silver-haired woman stepped out from behind a desk in what served as the lobby. She held out her hand to Starr.

"You must be Ms. Rio. I'm Doris Beechum, Catherine Landauer's assistant. Ms. Landauer is waiting in her office for you."

Starr shook the well-manicured hand and introduced Pearson, brushing over the niceties in her hurry to see Catherine. She followed Doris closely down the hall, their footsteps echoing on the hardwood floor. The wall was lined with the usual lawyer stuff, diplomas, framed certificates of admission. Doris stopped in front of the door at the end of the hall and rapped on the wood frame.

"Come in."

When the door swung wide, Starr took in every detail quickly and methodically. Other than the bookshelves, there was lots of open wall space—no knickknacks or artwork, nothing personal except the enormous and tacky-looking bouquet of flowers centered in the middle of her desk. Her gaze settled on Catherine who was pale and drawn, and then flicked back to the flower arrangement. And then she saw them. Bows. Giant, white satin bows dotted throughout the crowd of ugly carnations. The room was sick with the smell of the flowers, but the bows were the star of the show, a bright white message and Starr got it full-on. She met Catherine's eyes, and the deep pain and fear she saw reflected reminded her of a picture of a little girl she'd been staring at less than an hour ago. Instantly she knew exactly what was going on. Careful to keep her voice calm, lest she spook Catherine back into her shell, she said, "You're Jill Winfield."

Catherine knew the moment she'd instructed Doris to make the call that she wouldn't be able to keep her identity hidden any longer, but she hadn't expected Starr to reach the conclusion on her own. But should she really be surprised? She'd been dropping hints like crazy. She could almost hear Dr. M saying, "You wanted her to know."

Was she right? She'd gone to such lengths to prevent anyone in her life from knowing her past, and the isolation was sometimes paralyzing. Relationships, whether friendships or more, were always cut short when they reached the point of reciprocal sharing. Sometimes she was the one to sever the ties, but often it was the other person who believed she was keeping secrets. And she was. She'd always imagined that someday she'd find someone with whom she felt like she could share the story of her past, but as time passed the probability faded, and she'd learned to embrace her career as her only refuge. But the moment this wretched bouquet showed up in her office, she knew that part of her world was no longer safe either. When Starr blurted out her question, she had no choice but to tell the truth.

"Yes, I am."

Starr sank into the chair across from the desk, and for the first time, Catherine realized she was not alone. The detective working on the case, Pearson, was standing in the doorway, looking at the two of them like he was watching a suspense flick and he wasn't sure if he should be there. Catherine waved toward him. "You may as well join us. Is the crime scene unit on the way?"

Pearson pointed at the bouquet. "Do you mind if I take a closer look?" he asked.

"Be my guest. I haven't touched it other than to read the card and I used tweezers." She pointed to the tweezers still sitting on her desk. "I took a photo of the message." She handed him her phone.

Starr leaned over to look, and they both scanned the image. Starr looked up at her. "So it is him."

"It appears so." It was easiest to keep the conversation short to avoid betraying the level of anxiety coursing through her.

"Are you okay?" Starr asked, and Catherine was surprised to see genuine concern reflected in her eyes. But she couldn't afford to dwell on it or she'd break down right there.

"Yes," she said.

Pearson cleared his throat and they both looked in his direction. "Sorry, ladies, but I'm just catching up. Would someone mind filling me in?"

Starr started to speak, but Catherine held up a hand to stop her. This was her story to tell and she'd rehearsed exactly what she wanted to say when she'd told Doris to make the call. "When I was young, my name was Jill Winfield. I lived in Albuquerque with my mother. My father left us when I was eight years old. When I was twelve, my mother was killed and I was abducted from our home by a man named Russell Pratt who used to do handyman work in the neighborhood. He kept me captive for a month before I was able to escape. He was never apprehended. I believe," she paused and took a deep breath. "No, I know, that he is the same person who has taken Hannah, and he sent me these flowers to let me know he's back."

"Whoa." Pearson pointed at the other chair. "Mind if I sit down?"

"Go ahead." Catherine folded her hands on her desktop. "I don't want to have to repeat this more than once, so ask me whatever you want to know." While she assessed their incredulous expressions, her mind flashed back to the day after she'd escaped from Pratt.

The road had to be a highway. Cars were driving fast and there were no shops or restaurants along the wooded area bordering either side. She should be relieved to have escaped, but her thoughts were completely occupied by two things: what if his truck appeared on the road, and why hadn't she taken the time to find her shoes? Her bare feet were bruised and bloody from her trek through the woods, and she was torn between hopefulness about the possibility of being rescued and resignation to her fate as a lost soul.

She ducked behind a tree, closed her eyes, and practiced the same ritual she'd employed every day she'd been his captive. She visualized the apartment she shared with her mother as if she could will her way back there. Her mother was probably worried sick and she had enough things in life to be worried about. The apartment would never be the same—it would always be the place where she'd been taken, but they could move, get a new start. They would be more careful and be on guard.

But she couldn't do any of these things unless she returned to her previous life. She dug deep for courage, and although she knew her future life would never be the same after what had happened to her, she vowed to make it the best it could be.

She'd had no idea how difficult that would be.

"I guess the best place to start is, do you have any idea where he might be holding Hannah?" Pearson asked.

Catherine looked up at Pearson and Starr, disconcerted by their intense scrutiny. Sitting here, facing them, she felt hemmed in and she itched for freedom. She pushed back from her desk and stood. "I need some coffee," she said, knowing coffee was actually the last thing she needed in her current state. When she reached the doorway of her office, she looked back at them. "You can come with if you want." She headed to the kitchenette, not caring if they followed.

They did, practically falling over themselves to catch up, and Catherine wished she'd had a moment longer to be alone. To process. To call Dr. M and tell her she'd finally followed her advice and now what? But all she had instead was a cop and a lawyer, neither of whom cared a lick about her except for what she could do for them. And what could she do really? She knew Hannah's abductor was Pratt, but she didn't know much else. All she could relay was her own experience which was distant and dated. Pratt might have developed different techniques, different needs. Hannah might not be in any danger at all.

But she knew none of that was true. He wouldn't have bothered to send the bouquet if he wasn't following the same regimen. Bouquet. She repeated the word in her mind, substituting bow for bou, and stifled a laugh at the cruelty of the joke. She needed to get a grip. If she didn't Starr and Pearson were going to think she was crazy, and that wouldn't help find Hannah. And they needed to find her. Soon.

Suddenly, she knew exactly what she needed to be able to help them. She stopped abruptly and turned. "I want to see Mayor Turner. Right now."

CHAPTER ELEVEN

S tarr cast a surreptitious glance at Catherine in the rearview mirror. To the casual observer, nothing appeared out of place. Catherine sat ramrod straight with her hands in her lap, staring out the window, her face a mask of nonchalance. But Starr detected the slight quiver of her lips, the pinched lines around her eyes. Catherine was seriously stressed, and Starr wanted to take her hand and tell her everything was going to be okay, but she sensed she would be rebuffed. Someone as buttoned up as Catherine Landauer didn't let her guard down easy, and Catherine already had her reasons, however unjustified, not to trust her.

Thankfully, Mayor Turner hadn't answered the phone when they'd called. Starr had spoken with the family attorney, William, and let him know they were coming by because they needed information not because they had any. Not exactly true, but she wanted to avoid getting anyone's hopes up. Pearson had been dead set against this little meeting, but Starr figured they didn't have much else to go on, and any harm would be worth the risk. Catherine's newly revealed identity was a big piece of information, but Starr wasn't exactly sure yet how it played out in this scenario.

She wasn't sure about a lot of things, and many of them were centered around Catherine's past. When had Catherine changed her name? Probably right before college since the last records of Jill Winfield were from her high school. Starr had asked about her aunt, but Catherine's only response had been she'd lived with her aunt until she left for college and hadn't spoken to her since. How had she gotten accepted into the prestigious undergrad and law school programs at UT without anyone knowing who she really was?

Starr filed her questions away, hoping patience would reward her with information. She'd need to know the answers before she placed Catherine on the witness stand in the case against Pratt, but first they had to find him, and bring Hannah home safe and sound. She wasn't sure how Catherine being here at Hannah's house was going to help, but at this point she'd do anything to facilitate a rescue.

When they arrived, Pearson signaled for them to wait in the car while he spoke to the officer posted at the front door. Starr watched him for a moment before turning to Catherine. "Have you met Mayor Turner before?"

"I've seen her speak, shaken hands, but not a real meeting, no."

"I'll be interested in your assessment."

Catherine cocked her head. "Why?"

Starr wished she could take back the words. She was still operating on dual tracks. Her gut told her Catherine's theory that Pratt was back and responsible for Hannah's disappearance was spot-on, but she couldn't afford to completely abandon her working theory that Ricky might be a suspect. The two ideas weren't mutually exclusive, after all. Far-fetched as it might be, Ricky could be copying some of the clues from the first crime.

But how would he have known about Catherine?

Untangling the twin theories would take some work, but for now she didn't need Catherine thinking they were doubting her story or she might clam up, and the one thing she was certain of was that they needed Catherine's help. "No particular reason. Just getting an overall picture of the case."

Pearson waved at them. "Are you ready?"

"Yes."

Catherine pushed open the door and started walking ahead of her. Starr scrambled out of the car to catch up. She needed to carefully control this interaction since she had no idea what Catherine had in mind, and even though the element of surprise was her idea, Starr didn't want the mayor to feel ambushed, a move likely to have bad implications for her professional future as well as this case. When they reached the door, Starr stepped in front of Catherine. "I'll introduce you. She doesn't know why you're here, and we need to give her some space to process all of this."

"Okay."

Starr had expected more of a protest, considering how Catherine had been controlling their interaction so far, so she was pleasantly surprised by the neutral response. She nodded to the officer who answered the door and followed Pearson to the study where they'd met with the family each time they'd been there before. Like the last time, William was there at her side, ever the doting partner, and her husband was noticeably absent. She watched the mayor's eyes light up as she entered into the room, and she realized William hadn't warned her they had nothing to report because it was clear she expected some news.

"Have you found her?" Mayor Turner said, rising from her chair.

"No."

"Then why aren't you out there looking?"

Starr heard the edge in her voice, but she resisted responding in kind. What she wanted to say was that while she was investigating clues in the case, not a single member of the mayor's family was out looking for their daughter, a fact that the news outlets hadn't mentioned yet. It was only a matter of time before some reporter pointed out that in most missing children cases the family was the first to join the search and rescue teams, and the Turners had been noticeably absent. Starr had worked with crime victims enough to know that everyone reacted differently, and Mayor Turner's decision to hole up here at her palatial house didn't mean she wasn't grieving—everyone reacted to pain in their own way—but it didn't look good. Still she modulated her response to keep the peace. "We have lots of people out physically looking for your daughter. Detective Pearson and I are contributing in other ways."

"Who is this?" Turner pointed at Catherine. Starr started to answer, but Catherine stepped in front of her and thrust out her hand.

"My name is Catherine Landauer. Ms. Rio and Detective Pearson have asked for my help. Can I see her room?"

Starr touched her brow to hide her frustration. She shot a look at Pearson who shrugged as if to say, "Hey, it was your idea to bring her here." She cleared her throat. "How about we talk for a minute first?"

But it was too late. The mayor latched on to Catherine like a beacon in a storm. Why wouldn't she? By showing up here with the lead detective and prosecutor on the case, Catherine appeared to have their tacit approval to be involved. "Her room is upstairs," Mayor Turner said to Catherine. She turned to Starr. "We can talk after."

Starr trudged up the stairs after them, annoyed that the mayor was willing to show such deference to Catherine who she didn't know at all, when she barely gave the law enforcement team assigned to the case the time of day. Before they crossed the threshold of Hannah's room, she said, "Please be careful not to touch any of the contents."

Catherine stopped and slowly turned, her eyes piercing and dark. "Why? Surely, you've processed this room and its contents by now."

Starr smiled to cover her anger. Catherine was right of course, but that didn't mean she wanted her riffling around in what might possibly wind up being evidence. She cast about for a tactful response but, thankfully, Pearson stepped in.

"We *have* processed this room, but as I'm sure you can respect, we'd like to leave everything as is in the event something new comes to light that gives new importance to the way the room was arranged when Hannah was last here."

Catherine nodded curtly. "Will you open the closet for me, then?"

Pearson's glowering face said he didn't want to, but he did anyway. He'd barely stepped back before Catherine was in his place, scanning the contents. "Tell me about her," she said.

Mayor Turner stepped up next to her, her eyes trained on the hanging clothes. "She's a friendly girl, secure. No one was a stranger. People used to joke that she would someday follow in my footsteps and run for office."

Catherine nodded slowly. "He would like that. It would frustrate him because he thinks he wants someone who is obedient and shy, but he prefers someone he can talk to and who isn't afraid of him on sight."

The mayor touched Catherine's arm. "Who is it? Who has my daughter?"

"Russell Pratt. Do you remember the Jill Winfield case? He had her once." Catherine paused for a moment, her expression now distant. "He was gone for a long time, but he's back now."

Turner gasped. "I do remember that case." She turned to Starr. "Wasn't she rescued? Wasn't he arrested? Does he have my daughter? Why isn't he in prison?"

Catherine scowled. "Actually, she escaped. On her own. He was never arrested, never did any time. The task force that investigated that case was incompetent and they let him get away."

She turned as she delivered her assessment and locked eyes with Starr, and Starr felt the look like a punch in the face. Catherine was angry. More than angry, she was fiery mad, and she'd been carrying that anger for many, many years. Starr wished she'd read more about the case. She'd been focused on Jill Winfield's miraculous escape, but there was a lot more there. Starr could hardly blame her, but she wondered—was the adult woman that Jill Winfield had become too angry to help them find this little girl's captor?

Catherine turned back to the mayor, who was clutching her arm. Normally, having a stranger touch her like this would be disconcerting, but she knew the connection was necessary to build trust. Both ways.

Everything about this experience was foreign. She'd agreed to ride here with Starr and Pearson, with barely any protest about leaving her car behind. She couldn't remember the last time she'd gotten in a vehicle with people who were practically strangers, let alone one that was headed to an address she didn't know.

But Starr wasn't exactly a stranger. She'd gotten to know Starr well enough to best her at trial, and it wasn't like she expected a future candidate for district attorney to suddenly morph into a nefarious character, but Catherine had spent her life guarding against a repeat of her abduction, and lowering that guard wasn't something she took lightly.

Catherine walked into the room and could instantly tell it belonged to a young person. Unlike the somber earth tones of the rest of the house, this room was decorated in bright colors, the walls a live version of a Pinterest board that could only be created by a preadolescent girl. Catherine hoped Hannah would get to come back here someday, but she knew that when she did, the carefree charm of this place would never be the same for her.

Catherine had never returned home. The police and her aunt waited a couple of days before telling her the grim truth, that Pratt had killed her mother before he'd taken her captive in the dead of night. The house they'd called home had become a crime scene, and her aunt wouldn't let her return, even to collect her things, telling her there was nothing left for her there. She knew her aunt thought she was doing the right thing, but by never letting her return, by forcing her to leave behind the trappings of her former life, she'd been robbed again, left adrift with only vague memories of the life that had been stolen from her.

Her cousins had never understood why she didn't adapt to her new life. Why would they when it had taken years of therapy for her to understand? She had no anchor, no history. Everything was either before the abduction or after. Even now, after years had passed and she'd changed her life completely, she still thought in those terms. Jill Winfield and Catherine Landauer. The two had everything in common and nothing at all.

"She had free rein to decorate however she wanted," Mayor Turner said. "As you can see, she took full advantage."

"Has," Catherine said. "She *has* free rein. Don't give up on her."

The mayor grimaced. "I didn't mean to." She wiped at a corner of her eye. "It's hard not to imagine the worst."

"Hard is being held by a madman. That's what she's going through right now. Your job is to stand strong and make sure no stone is left unturned until she is found. You're the mayor for crying out loud. If anyone has the power to make sure she's found, it's you." She felt a hand on her back and turned to see Starr shaking her head, clearly telling her to back off. She shrugged her off and stepped away.

"I think we should go," Starr said.

"No," Mayor Turner said. "She's right. I haven't been doing enough. We should be out looking for her instead of staying holed up here, hiding from the press, and hoping for good news." Her voice faltered. "I can't even imagine what she must be going through."

Catherine softened at the first display of sincere feeling she'd witnessed since she'd arrived. "Forgive me for being harsh. The truth is, if he has taken her for the reason I believe he has, then she's being well cared for and she hasn't been harmed. Yet."

"How do you know?"

The moment of truth. Catherine had hoped it would be easier to say it the second time, but the words caught in her throat, and she found it harder to spit them out than when she'd told Starr and Pearson less than an hour ago. She spotted a picture of a young girl across the room and pointed toward it. "Is this Hannah?"

"Yes. It was taken at her birthday party a week ago. She turned twelve."

Catherine picked up the photo and tilted it toward her. Hannah was a cute kid. She had an ice cream cone in one hand and one of those new instant print cameras that reminded her of a Polaroid. Hannah was dressed in dark blue jeans, and a Columbia shirt with tons of pockets, and Catherine imagined she was an explorer, picking up things to store in her pockets to be examined later. She glanced around and spotted a scattering of granite stones. "She collects these, doesn't she?"

"Yes. She spends a lot of time outdoors. The original nature lover. I predict she'll be a biologist someday." Turner met her eyes. "When she comes home."

Catherine nodded at the reference to the future. She set the photo back down on the dresser and pointed at the bed. "Let's sit." She joined Mayor Turner on the edge of the bed, purposely excluding Starr and Pearson from the conversation. "He's not going to harm her." She held back a wince as she said the word "harm," hoping the mayor didn't notice.

"How do you know?"

"Because when I was her age, he took me too." Catherine rushed the words to keep her from commenting. "He took me from my house. He'd watched me for a while, spent time selecting me, or so he said. My name used to be Jill Winfield."

Turner gasped and reached for her hand. She squeezed tight, and Catherine was unsure if she meant to be comforting or if she was just hanging on to something concrete for dear life. "I remember."

Of course she did. Everyone did, which was precisely why Catherine had clung to her anonymity as tightly as she had. But her secret was out now, and she braced for the onslaught of questions. She didn't have to wait long.

"Tell me everything you know. I need to know what she's going through."

Catherine turned to invite Starr and Pearson back into the conversation. "He'll have a place. Something permanent. It might only be a trailer, but it has to be private because he likes to be self-sufficient. It'll be on a piece of land, with a garden where he can grow his own food. Likely near a wooded area, and near water. Whatever he drives will be nondescript." She pressed her eyes shut, summoning the exact words. "It doesn't do in the eyes of the Lord to show wealth. True prosperity is the riches of the soul."

She opened her eyes to see them all staring at her, their expressions a mixture of surprise and sympathy. Her skin started to crawl, and an anxious heat burned under the surface. She stood, desperate to break the spell. "I have to go."

The mayor reached out to pull her back, and Catherine stepped away, desperate to get away from the intensity of her need. "I have to go," she repeated. She pointed at Starr and Pearson. "They have to find her. It's up to them." She strode out of the room, careful not to stumble, intent on escape. What had she been thinking? She'd lived this pain once. She wasn't going to live it again.

CHAPTER TWELVE

Starr rushed down the stairs after Catherine, but Catherine was already out of sight before she reached the landing. The officer in the foyer pointed to the front door and Starr pushed through to find her only to be met with the pounding force of a spring rainstorm.

Crap. She held a hand up to block the rain, a futile gesture, and scoured the front yard for signs of Catherine. She spotted her pacing out front, punching at her phone. Starr looked back toward the warm dry house, but she knew she didn't have a choice. She tugged her blazer up over the back of her head and plunged out into the rain.

"What are you doing?" she yelled as she approached Catherine.

"Leave me alone." Catherine kept moving, her head still bent toward the phone in her hand.

Starr ignored her admonition and continued her approach. "You're soaked. Come back inside. If you want to leave, I'll find a ride for you."

"I can find my own ride with a stranger. Leave me alone."

Starr pulled out her keys. "That's ridiculous. I'll take you back to your office. Pearson can get a ride back with one of the guys." She watched Catherine ponder her offer while the rain soaked them both to the skin. What she really wanted to do was grill Catherine about every last detail of her captivity and escape from Pratt in case the retelling held clues that might lead them to Hannah, but she felt like she was dealing with a skittish animal who'd be spooked away at an abrupt approach. A little bit of alone time might be exactly what she needed to get Catherine to open up. "Let's at least get out of the rain."

Catherine jabbed at her phone and then shoved it in her pocket. "Fine."

Unsure what Catherine had agreed to, Starr decided to assume she was on board with a ride back to her office which would give her about thirty minutes to gain her confidence. She sent a quick text to Pearson, and then led the way to her car, relieved she'd driven her own vehicle to the mayor's house.

Catherine slid into the front passenger's seat and buckled her seat belt. She stared straight ahead. It was going to be a long, quiet drive.

Starr tried a couple of softball questions when they were a few blocks away, but Catherine wasn't warming to any subject she broached, and she finally gave in to the silence. They were ten minutes into the drive when Starr's cell phone rang through the speakers of the car. The dash display announced the call was from her mother. She fumbled for the button to answer and send the call to her phone, but the sound of her mother's voice boomed through the car speakers.

"Starr, honey, are you there? That crazy dog got out and I chased it and now I'm locked out of the house in the rain. I know you're busy, but your father's out of town and your brother isn't answering either. Can you come by earlier than you planned? Are you there?"

Starr caught a slight grin on Catherine's face, and she shook her head. "I'm here, Mom. Hold on for just a second." She pushed the button to transfer the call to her phone and muted it. "Sorry about this. I'll only be a moment." She unmuted the call. "Mom, what about the key you have hidden under the rock by the shed?"

"I used it last week and left it in the house. I hope that dog is okay. He's been skittish ever since he showed up. I'm trying to get your brother to adopt him, but so far he's holding out. I saw some lightning off in the distance."

"I'm sure the dog is fine. I can help you out, but it's going to be a little while. I have to run across town, but I should be able to be there in an hour or so. Is there a place you can hunker down until I get there?" Starr looked up at the touch of Catherine's hand on her arm. "Hang on." She put her hand over the phone. "I'll be done in a sec."

"You should help your mother."

"I will, as soon as I get you back to your office."

"Where does she live?"

"Out near Georgetown."

"It'll take you forever in this storm to get back across town." Catherine pointed to a gas station up ahead on the right. "Drop me there and I'll get an Uber back to the office."

Starr looked through the windshield wipers at the shady gas and convenience store up ahead. "Uh, not likely."

"Then I'll ride with you and then you can take me back."

Starr held back her surprise at the suggestion. It was the perfect solution since it would save her from zigzagging across town, plus more time in the car with Catherine might lead her to open up. A slight twinge of guilt at taking advantage gripped her. "That's okay."

"Seriously, I don't mind."

"Are you sure?"

"To be perfectly honest," Catherine said. "I don't want to be alone right now."

"Okay." She got it and she appreciated the vulnerability of the revelation, and wished she'd been more sensitive during this entire process. Catherine had just spent the past few hours having to relive what had to have been a horrific experience that had transformed her entire life from that point. She'd lost her mother, been held by a madman, and basically rescued herself only to be cast in the role of celebrity victim. That she was even walking around, let alone that she'd achieved the success she had over the years, was a huge accomplishment.

"But I don't want to talk about it."

"Understood." Starr steered the car back in the direction they'd come from. "We have two choices. Total silence or radio. Or make that three choices. We could talk about something else."

"I fear our choices in radio may differ vastly."

"Really?" Starr was intrigued. "Tell me what you think I listen to."

"I picture you for a talk radio junkie, mostly news." Catherine cocked her head. "Or eighties."

"I get it. You think I like strong opinions or the tunes of our childhood."

"Am I wrong?"

Starr grinned. "Not exactly. I can definitely rock some Bowie or Hall and Oates, but when it comes to news, I'm more of a NPR kind of gal. What about you? I'm thinking classical."

"Ha. Not even. I too like the eighties, but my go-to artist is Brandi Carlisle. Or the Indigo Girls. Or Shawn Colvin. You know, music with a side of angst."

Catherine smiled as she spoke the words, but her voice held a trace of bitterness that compelled Starr to say, "I know you don't want to talk about it, but I need to tell you how much I appreciate you coming forward and that I understand how difficult it must've been for you."

"Don't."

"That's all I plan to say. I promise."

Silence fell between them and with it came an awkwardness Starr regretted causing. She leaned over and found the local indie station and turned it up just high enough to cover the quiet. Still, it was a long thirty minutes before she turned into the drive that led to her parents' house.

"We're almost there," she announced.

"Okay."

Starr drove carefully on the gravel road, slippery from the rain, grateful to see her mother waiting on the porch. She'd barely turned the car off before she told Catherine she'd be right back, jumped out, and headed to the front door.

"Starr, thank goodness you're here." Her mother waved her arms toward the house. "Hurry out of the rain, you're getting soaked." She leaned forward with a hand on her brow. "Is there someone with you?"

"It's okay, Mom. We're headed back into town."

"Don't be silly. Anything you have to do, you can do on your phone from here. I have a pot of soup in the slow cooker. Get your friend, come in, and have a hot meal. Maybe this storm will die down while you're eating."

Starr placed her key in the lock and released the door. "Seriously, Mom, we're good." She pointed at the open door. "You're all set."

"Wait right there." Her mother charged into the house, leaving the door open behind her. Starr looked back at Catherine, and raised her hands to signal she wasn't sure what was going on. A moment later, her mother appeared with an umbrella and brushed past her on her way to the car.

"Mom," Starr called out, but there was no deterring Mrs. Rio when she was on a mission. She watched, helpless, as her worlds collided.

Catherine jumped at the sharp rap on the window. The woman standing on the other side was motioning for her to lower the window, and she cracked it a bit, leaning back as the rain pelted its way inside the window.

"Come inside," the woman, who looked the spitting image of Starr, said.

"Mrs. Rio?"

"That's me."

"I'll just wait here. Thank you."

"You girls aren't going anywhere in this storm."

Mrs. Rio stepped back and waved her hand up at the biggest umbrella Catherine had ever seen. "There's hot soup and fresh bread inside. Come on."

Catherine paused for a few seconds, but the stern expression on Mrs. Rio's face made it clear she wasn't taking no for an answer. She grabbed her bag and climbed out of the car, ducking under the umbrella while Mrs. Rio led her to the house. When they reached the porch, she shook out the umbrella. "Lose the Mrs. I'm Stella. Do you work with Starr?"

"Uh…" Catherine's brain searched for a suitable reply while she scanned the room, searching for signs of Starr to save her from idle conversation. And instantly she appeared with a ladle in her hand.

"Mom, leave Catherine alone. She's helping me out with a project." Starr placed a finger across her lips. "That's all I can say."

Stella shook her head and wagged a finger at Catherine. "She uses that excuse every time she doesn't want to tell me something. I read the papers. I know you're working on that missing girl case. If Catherine here is helping you then she deserves a good meal as a reward."

"I'm fine," Catherine said.

"You're on the skinny side, if you ask me."

"Mom!" Starr flushed crimson. "See, this is why you can't come to any campaign events. Filter, please."

Stella shook her head. "The voters will appreciate that you come from a family of honest people. I'll meet you in the kitchen." She scurried out of the room, leaving Starr and Catherine standing in uncomfortable silence.

"Sorry about that," Starr said. "My mother has never mastered the art of keeping her opinion to herself."

"It's okay," Catherine said. Despite her protest, she was hungry and the soup smelled divine. As much as she'd rather be back in her familiar surroundings, she knew they'd made the smart decision staying put until the storm passed. Besides, Starr's mother was oddly charming with her straight talk and no-nonsense attitude. "Soup sounds good." She watched Starr's surprised expression and glanced away. All this vulnerability was wearing her down, and after a lifetime of building walls to keep out other people, she was too tired to resist the simple gesture of a hot meal on a day when she'd had to overshare.

But she'd barely shared at all—only enough to pique their interest before she broke down like a silly little girl and ran away. She could hear Dr. M's voice echo in her head, asking what triggered the response, and she barely resisted putting her hands over her ears to keep her out. She'd spent years in therapy, but apparently the counseling had done nothing to actually cure her, but merely served as a way to keep the rest of the world at bay. She shook out of her jacket and handed it to Starr while she cast about for something to say. "This is a nice house. Did you grow up here?"

"I did. Along with my sister and two brothers. It was a great place to grow up. Lots of land to explore and great places for hide-and-seek."

Catherine nodded like she understood, but she had no idea what it would've been like to have this kind of place. "I lived with my aunt after…but her place was fairly small, barely any yard."

"I'm sorry."

"Why?"

"I keep bringing up things that are insensitive."

"You keep bringing up things that are normal for people to discuss. You can't help it that my childhood wasn't normal."

"And neither can you, but I could be more sensitive."

"Not a trait you're known for." Catherine smiled to soften the blow of her remark. "At least not in the courtroom."

Starr laughed. "Truth, but it takes one hard-ass adversary to know one." She pointed down the hall. "Ready for soup?"

"Sure." Catherine followed Starr down the hall, taking note of the stream of family photos hung along the wall, documenting major milestones in the lives of the Rios. Sporting events, graduations, weddings were all represented in a mix of color and black-and-white photos showcasing a happy, healthy family. Catherine couldn't relate, but she wanted to—a longing she thought she'd suppressed forever.

The soup did smell amazing and she said so again to Mrs. Rio when they entered the kitchen.

"Secret family recipe. Chicken tortilla. Tastes like an enchilada in a spoon." Stella pointed to an array of small bowls next to the soup pot. "I'll dish up your bowl and you can pick your toppings here." She leaned close. "I recommend a pinch of cilantro, tortilla strips, cheese, and avocado."

"Who am I to argue with the pro," Catherine said, holding out her bowl. "Soup is my favorite meal." She choked out the words, straining against the emotion that swept through her along with the memory of her mother fixing a pot of soup for the weekend. She called it kitchen sink soup, and it was supposed to last all weekend, so neither one of them would have to cook, but instead of being a throwaway meal, it had become her favorite and something she looked forward to every Friday. Soup wasn't the kind of meal you ate on the fly, it was a sit down experience, meant to be shared over conversation. She would tell her mother all about her day and her mother would do the same.

Catherine felt a hand on her arm, and she looked up to see Stella looking intently at her. "Food is powerful stuff," Stella said. "It carries strong memories."

"It does," Catherine replied, surprised she didn't feel a familiar urge to shake off the physical contact from this woman who was virtually a stranger. She drew her hand back with the now full bowl of soup and added all of the toppings Stella had recommended, and then followed Starr to the rustic table in the center of the kitchen.

Starr handed her a large spoon. "I see you wisely followed Mama's recommendation about toppings," she said.

"And you didn't?"

"I add sour cream. She thinks I'm a heathen, but then she raised me so she's partly responsible."

Stella swatted her on the head with a rolled napkin before joining them at the table. "You see what I put up with?"

"Who saved you from being locked out of the house for the rest of the night?"

Catherine's head switched back and forth at their playful banter. She missed this kind of close affection. She'd had some limited exposure to real friendship in her adult life—a casual outing with acquaintances and the occasional personal interaction she shared with Doris, but those were only glimpses of what she could have had if she'd been willing to open up, a risk she'd never deemed worth taking. Could she have more now that the risk had been taken for her?

"You don't like the soup?" Stella asked.

"Sorry," Catherine said. "I was daydreaming." She plunged the large spoon into the bowl, careful to skim up a helping that included all of the requisite ingredients. When the spicy, warm mixture with its deep flavors and variety of textures hit her tongue, she moaned with pleasure. "This might be the best soup I've ever tasted."

"Might be?"

Catherine grinned and plunged her spoon back into the bowl. "I'll keep eating and let you know."

Stella patted her arm again, and this time it didn't faze her at all. "Enjoy. Now what can you two tell me about this case you're working on?"

Starr's soupspoon clattered against the table. "Mom, you know we can't talk about the case."

"You can surely tell me if you're close to finding that poor girl." Stella shuddered. "I can't imagine what the mayor is going through, wondering if she will ever see Hannah again. What is it they say on those shows? If they don't find her in the first forty-eight hours, the chances go down severely."

"Mom!"

Catherine set her spoon down. "It's okay." She turned to Stella. "That statistic is true in most cases, but we have reason to believe this case is different. She's out there and she's alive. We just have to find her, and everyone is working to get that done." She deliberately didn't look at Starr as she spoke the words but put all her energy into hoping what she said was true. She'd come close to saying why she knew this to be true. This soup, this cozy kitchen, the memories all these things evoked were almost enough to make her forget she should always be on guard and careful. She took another bite of soup, hoping her full mouth would keep her from having to answer any questions, but it was the buzzing of Starr's phone that saved her.

"Crap. I have to go." Starr pushed back the bowl while she read the screen on her phone. "Sorry, Mom."

"But you just started eating."

"I know, but I really have to go."

Catherine's gut clenched at the realization there probably had been a break in the case. She set down her spoon and stood. "Let's go." Starr motioned for her to sit down.

"I'll get someone to come get you and take you back to your office."

"I'll take her," Stella said.

"Thank you, but no," Catherine said. She pointed at Starr. "I'm going with you." She stared at Starr until she elicited submission.

"Fine." Starr grabbed her keys off the counter. "Come on. I'll drop you at your office on my way."

Catherine thanked Stella for her hospitality and reluctantly followed Starr out of the warm, comfortable house into the thunderstorm raging outside. She had no idea where Starr was headed, but she knew one thing for sure—she was going with her.

Chapter Thirteen

Starr steered the car out of her mother's long drive wishing her mother had chosen another day to misplace her keys. By the time she drove Catherine back to her office, she'd be the last one at the scene, and she hated showing up late, but she hadn't wanted to leave Catherine alone with her oversharing mother. When she reached the highway, she contemplated the best direction to take.

"I'm going with you," Catherine said.

"No, I'm taking you back to your office."

"You have a lead, right?" When Starr nodded, Catherine said, "Then I'm going with you. If you don't take me, I'll follow you in my own car."

Starr contemplated how much she should share. The correct answer was nothing. By virtue of her own experience, Catherine was potentially a witness in this case. Involving her in official police business could create sticky complications she'd have to deal with later if and when they brought Hannah's abductor to trial. But Catherine's past also gave her added insight to this case that might prove valuable. Starr weighed the pros and cons and tossed in Catherine's fierce determination as a factor in her decision.

"Okay," she said. "But when we get there, you stay in the car. Don't talk to anyone. I'll fill you in as much as I'm able, and you can help us out if you have anything to add, but if you get in the way or question anyone on the task force, I'll have no choice but to send you packing. Understood?"

Again, with the icy stare. "Understood. You want my help, but on your terms because you know best."

"Close enough." Starr resented the implication that she was a know-it-all, but decided to go with it rather than wasting energy on a fight she wasn't likely to win.

"Did they find her?" Catherine asked, her voice then dropping to a whisper. "Is she alive?"

Starr gripped the steering wheel hard. "They found what looks like a freshly dug grave. That's all I know." She heard Catherine suck in a breath, and she instinctively reached out a hand, surprised when Catherine gripped it for a second before letting go. When Catherine's hands were back in her lap, Starr added, "It could be nothing."

"Was it Pearson who called you?"

"Yes."

"He's a pretty good detective."

"High praise from you."

"What's that supposed to mean?" Catherine asked.

"You have a reputation for thinking none of us know how to do our jobs."

"I come by it honestly."

Catherine delivered the statement and turned to look out the side window, signaling she was done talking. Starr wondered if Catherine was talking about her own case or cases she'd handled since she'd started practicing. She made a mental note to go back and reread the file, but in the meantime, she had another question. "Why did you decide to practice law?"

"Why did you?"

"I'm never going to get to know you better if you always answer a question with questions." Starr smiled, hoping her words would be viewed as a friendly overture. "But I'll play along if you will." Catherine's only response was to raise her eyebrows, but Starr pushed on. "When I was young, around ten, my grandmother's property down in the valley was seized so that the government could put a barrier on the border. She hired a lawyer to fight it, and he took her money and did practically nothing other than make her empty promises. Her farm was divided, and the value of her property plunged."

"And that inspired you?"

"Absolutely."

"To become a prosecutor?" Catherine shook her head. "Seems a bit off to me. Shouldn't you be working against the government, not for it?"

"What better way to affect change than from within?"

"Is that why you're running for DA? So you can have a kumbaya moment with the public?"

"Are you always this cynical?" Starr snapped, instantly regretting her reaction when she saw Catherine's shocked expression. "That was out of line. I'm sorry."

"You don't need to treat me with kid gloves just because you know about my past," Catherine said. "I'm not some kind of delicate flower. I've spent my entire adult life making sure I was on a level playing field. If Hannah wasn't missing, you would have no idea what I've been through."

Starr wasn't sure what to say in response. Catherine had kept her secret well. So well in fact that everyone, including her, had assumed she was an icy bitch rather than a woman who had legitimate reasons to mistrust the system. The facts from Jill's, make that Catherine's, abduction played on a reel in Starr's head. Over a month missing while law enforcement focused all their energy on a teacher at her school. The local sheriff's office had visited the trailer where she'd been held but had failed to notice anything awry. Catherine had managed to escape on her own, and even after she relayed all the information the authorities would need to arrest Pratt, he'd managed to elude capture for over twenty years.

Taking into account all of this, Starr was willing to admit she'd been wrong in her initial assessment of Catherine. "You're right. I don't have personal knowledge of what you've been through, but I have worked enough cases like yours to have some idea of how it might have affected you, and I know that you're a survivor."

"I had no choice."

"Sure you did." Starr slowed for a red light and took the opportunity to turn in her seat to face Catherine. "You could've basked in your fame and assumed the role of permanent victim. Or you could have kept the anonymity you chose and picked a different career—one that didn't put you face-to-face with law enforcement professionals who represent the same kind of people who failed you."

Catherine averted her eyes, but not before Starr read shocked recognition, and she knew she'd identified a sore spot. "It has to be hard for you." A sudden realization occurred. "This is why you don't take child abuse cases."

Catherine twitched and Starr knew she'd gone too far. "I'm sorry. That's none of my business."

Silence hung between them for a few minutes. Starr watched the traffic crossing back and forth across the intersection, biding her time to move forward. What was Catherine thinking? Would she ever speak to her again? She should have taken Catherine back to her office instead of agreeing to take her to the scene. Her desire to know more about this enigmatic woman was causing her to be reckless.

The light changed and she pulled forward, determined to be more guarded when it came to involving Catherine in this case.

"I don't trust myself to defend anyone accused of child abuse," Catherine said, her voice quiet and wistful. "I don't have the level of skill required to be objective in those cases. I think that in the back of my mind, I would always be wondering if they are really guilty, and if they are then they deserve whatever they have coming to them, even if their rights were violated in the process. People like Pratt shouldn't have rights."

And just like that, Starr's resolve to be more guarded fell away. "I think that's pretty natural, don't you?"

Catherine sighed. "I don't know what's natural, or normal. I've lived my whole life inside and outside of the bubble of those few weeks. They were transformative, and not in a good way. Everything I think and do is either because of or in spite of what happened to me. I gave up a long time ago trying to escape my past. The best I can do is figure out how to live my way around it."

"Well, it appears you've done a whole lot more than that. You're a successful lawyer, you have your own practice." Starr wished she could reel off other things, but she didn't know anything else about Catherine aside from her career. She cast about for something to add. "You like puppies."

Catherine cracked a smile. "Who doesn't?"

"Truth. Lots of people like puppies. And kids, although some people think they're a mixed bag."

"You must like them, or you wouldn't have worked in child abuse for as long as you did. Or do, since I guess you're back there."

"For now," Starr said. "For this case. Murphy wanted someone experienced with the unit to handle this case for obvious reasons."

"Of course." A few beats passed. "But you didn't answer the question."

"About whether I like kids? Sure, but it's hard not to have an affinity with the ones I meet. It's hard to believe the range of violence adults inflict on the innocent, and it's hard not to let these kids get into your heart." She shook her head. "But when it comes to kids in general, I guess I'm like most—it depends. I'm as likely as the next person to roll my eyes at people who think their kid is the cutest, the smartest, the you name it." She pointed up in the distance and picked up her phone. "I see a bunch of cars. I think that's the spot."

She eased up close to the line of vehicles, recognizing Pearson's vehicle, and pulled in behind it. "Wait here and I'll be back in a few minutes to give you an update." She bailed from the car before Catherine could answer and contemplated their conversation as she headed toward the line of cars parked ahead of her. For a few minutes, it felt like she and Catherine were actually connecting, and she'd wanted to embrace the feeling, but caution about what they were about to find warned her to hold back. If Hannah was buried in a grave here in the woods, there was no telling how Catherine would react. She shouldn't have brought her here, and the question about why she had nipped around the edges of her mind.

Pearson popped out from behind a tree and waved in her direction. "About time you got here."

"Sorry, my mother is a hard woman to get away from."

He pointed toward her car. "Tell me that's not Catherine Landauer in your car."

"I would, but I'd be lying. There wasn't time to drop her off."

"Uh-huh," he said, clearly conveying his doubt. "I'm going to trust you know what you're doing, but no way should she be here. If you want, I can have a patrol unit take her back to her office."

"You're right," Starr said. His idea was sound, but she didn't want to hand Catherine off to some stranger, not when she'd just started to open up. "But I don't plan to linger. Show me what you've got and I'll get her out of here. Murphy is going to want a report and he's going to want it in person."

"Let's go." He motioned back to the tree behind him and Starr followed him, wishing she had dressed for a trek in the woods. They walked about twenty feet until they were standing in front of a cordoned off area surrounded by crime scene techs wearing yellow slickers. Starr glanced around, taking in every detail. She rarely got to visit crime scenes in person, and when she did, she liked to take full advantage of the entire sensory experience, imprinting it on her mind so she could recall every detail when it came time to make an opening statement to a jury. They were a long way off from that now, but it was never too soon to start formulating her plan of attack.

The first thing that struck her was the mound of fresh earth, like a newly-filled grave in a cemetery, and the exact opposite of a burial site someone was trying to hide. It wasn't covered with leaves and sticks, but fresh red soil, loamy and pungent in the rain. The mound was fairly small, about two feet by four feet. The size gave her chills. The techs were scraping soil samples and taking photos, but otherwise leaving the mound undisturbed.

"Any evidence on the surface?" she asked.

Pearson pointed to a tree about five feet from the mound, and Starr followed the direction of his finger up the length of the trunk until the white bow caught her attention. Her adrenaline had been pumping up until this point, but now it plummeted, filling her body with lead, and she was already starting to think of ways to tell the mayor her daughter was dead.

"It's him."

Starr turned toward the quiet, firm voice, and faced Catherine who was staring behind them, staring directly at the bow. Her face was a hardened mask of neutrality, but Starr wasn't fooled. Catherine was scared and justifiably so, and Starr wished she'd listened to her instincts and never exposed Catherine to this scene.

Catherine stiffened the moment they'd pulled up to the wooded area, any comfort she'd taken in her conversation with Starr faded at the realization they were on the verge of a big break in the case. Starr said something before she left the car, but her words were white noise against the backdrop of Catherine's memories.

The rain had stopped, but water still fell from the trees in big, spattering drops, smacking against the saturated ground. Starr spoke briefly with Pearson before they both disappeared into the brush. Catherine stared after them, her mind consumed with possibilities, each one more horrible than the last.

He'd rousted her in the early morning hours, a finger placed over her lips to keep her quiet, while he whispered in her ear that her mother had asked him to take her to a special place and she would meet them there. She recognized him. He'd been at their house several times, most recently the week before, helping her mother fix the stopped-up sink. Unlike most of the men her mother hung around, he'd spoken to her directly instead of acting like she wasn't in the room. But however friendly he'd seemed in the daylight hours, his sudden appearance at her bedside was dark and strange, and she hadn't wanted to go with him, but his urgency was contagious. If her mother hadn't let him in, then how had he gotten into the house? "I want to talk to her."

She hadn't waited for an answer, instead calling out to her mother, tentatively at first, but then louder when her calls were met with silence. "She's not here," he said, shaking his head.

Looking back, she wished she'd questioned more, fought if she had to, but her mother disappearing in the night and leaving a stranger to care for her wasn't outside the realm of her experience. Setting her instincts aside, she hoped for the best, changed her clothes, and followed him out of the house and into his pickup truck.

It was still dark outside, and she could barely make out the vehicle, but she could tell it wasn't a current model. It took a few turns of the key to get it started, and in that length of time she got a glimpse of what he was like when he was frustrated, his anger seeping around the edges of a smile. Don't ask questions, don't make him mad—the caution became an affirming chant echoed throughout the ride.

The sun was beginning to edge its way past the horizon when he turned off the main road, the truck bucking against the uneven surface of the dirt path lined with trees. They drove for a while longer, and then he pulled into a space between two large trees. Larger than she'd ever seen. "Is Mom meeting us here?" she asked, but her question was ignored. He came around and opened her door, and led her through the woods, roughly pushing his way past low hanging branches, but holding them so they wouldn't snap back and strike her. She appreciated the courtesy at the same time she feared his intentions, and the dichotomy of emotions only confused her more. She was a city girl, unaccustomed to tromping around in nature.

There had been that one time last year in Girl Scouts—her mother had enrolled her so she'd have a place to go after school—when her troop had gone camping to earn as many badges as they could in a single weekend, but camping at a lodge with classes designed to teach basic survival techniques was way different from forging through the forest without a trail or any of the equipment suitable for the trek. Her worn out, off brand tennis shoes slipped on the leaves and rocks still wet from yesterday's rain. Once, she'd fallen hard, almost hitting her head on a large rock, but he'd caught her just in time. Later, she would wish he hadn't.

Catherine pushed the car door open and stumbled out of the vehicle, gasping for breath. The memories were nothing new. The nightmares had abated, but they still lurked in the background, and lately they'd found firm footing in her obsession about this girl's disappearance. She leaned against the car and fought for breath. She had to know if Hannah was in the grave in the woods, Starr's admonition be damned. She took a deep breath and walled off the little girl inside, assuming the armor she wore into court. No tears, no fears, only fierce strength and fortitude. After a few mental chants of this mantra, she followed the path Starr and Pearson had taken.

She counted her steps, a habit established during the time she'd been with Pratt, a skill she hadn't needed or used since then. Each step was a vital piece of information, filed away to calculate the exact parameters of her escape. One thousand steps on the day they went to retrieve water from the stream. Five hundred and one when they went to check the traps. Every step had a purpose, a story, a path out of the nightmare her life had become. One day she would count the steps to her freedom.

"Catherine."

At the sound of her name, Catherine stopped cold, confused and trapped between then and now. She'd been counting. What for? She ran her hands down her side. She was taller, her clothes were new, not the old rags he'd made her wear. That was then and this was now. She wasn't Jill Winfield. She was Catherine Landauer, strong and free.

"Are you okay?"

She looked at Starr who'd stepped in front of her. She knew this woman. Where had she been when she'd needed help? Even now the sound of her voice was muffled, like one or both of them were under water. "What is happening?"

Starr gently steered her a few feet away. "I asked you to wait in the car."

Her voice was gentle, but concern edged through, and Catherine's memory of the past receded into her recollection of the present. "I need to know what's going on."

"We're not sure yet. I'll get someone to take you back to your office, and we'll call you when we know more."

Catherine nodded. Being here was taking its toll and her presence wasn't helping. Hell, she couldn't even keep track of whether things were happening in the past or present. "Okay."

"Wait here," Starr said, her voice comforting and calm. "I'll be right back."

Catherine watched her walk back toward the huddle of people. She couldn't see what they were gathered around, but she assumed it was the grave. Was Hannah buried a mere few feet away? How many steps would it take to find out?

She shook her head. No. She couldn't think about that. She glanced around, seeking something, anything to focus on instead of the possibility they'd been too late. She stared again at the bright white bow fixed halfway up the trunk of a large cedar tree. All she could think was that it was placed too tall for Hannah to have put it there. Unable to stop herself, she started walking toward the tree, ignoring the call of one of the techs for her to stop. She stood beneath the bow, staring upward. Her rational attorney brain told her it was evidence and would wind up in a sealed and labeled plastic bag to be produced in court, but her base level emotion told her to grab a stick from the ground, knock the bow down, and crush it beneath her heel. It had been years since she'd succumbed to these violent thoughts, but now that they were back, they flooded her entire body, filling her with a bristling rage.

"Take it down."

The tech moved toward her, but Starr pushed him aside. "Catherine, it's okay."

"It's not okay." She dropped her voice to a whisper. "He could be watching."

Starr nodded slowly, the kind of placating gesture you offer a toddler whose imagination has conjured the unbelievable. "He's not. They've searched the area." She held out her hand. "Let's go back to the car."

"I'm not leaving until you take it down." Catherine couldn't articulate the why and hoped Starr wouldn't ask, but she couldn't abide the bow displayed in plain sight like a mocking laugh designed directly for her. *You can't catch me. I've come for you.* Her adult self wasn't the least bit scared of Pratt, but the little person inside had never truly healed, and no amount of therapy and medication could possibly have prepared her for his return. "It has to come down." She hated the begging tone, but she had no choice. She locked eyes with Starr until Starr signaled for the tech to take it down. She watched his gloved hand reach high above her head and slowly extract the bow from the surface of the tree. She watched as he slipped the bow and the pin that had held it in place into a plastic bag and tucked it into the box that held all the other bits of evidence they'd gathered so far. Her ears filled with a dull roar partly masking the conversation happening behind her, but she could sort of make out the words.

"You have to get her out of here."

"I know."

"If you want to stay, one of the patrol guys can run her back."

"No, I've got it."

"I'll call you when we...I'll call you after."

"Okay. Thanks."

A hand pressed lightly against her back, and she knew without looking it was Starr. When had she developed such an awareness of her rival, and when had the balance of power shifted between them? She wanted to fight it, but she couldn't muster the energy it would take to resist. Not right now. She turned to face her. "What now?"

"We have to go."

"I know." Catherine didn't wait for Starr to respond before taking off back in the direction she'd come. She felt like a fool for her indecision—a moment ago she refused to leave and now she couldn't wait to get out of here. Her emotions were scattered like fallen leaves in a swirl of wind, and she had no more control of her reactions than she did over the forces of nature. She could hear Starr's footsteps behind hers and she rushed to stay ahead. The ride would be painful enough, and she prayed Starr would be insightful enough to realize she didn't want to talk or otherwise deconstruct what had just happened. She came out here to be of help, but she was nothing more than a shivering mess of emotion, full of fear and dread. Pratt might have tread this very ground. Would the path he'd chosen to take forever define her?

CHAPTER FOURTEEN

S tarr pulled onto the road and turned back in the direction they'd come, uncertain about what to do or say. Catherine hadn't spoken a word since she'd led her out of the woods, and she was currently staring out the side window. They rode along in silence for a few moments before Starr ventured into innocuous conversation. "I can drop you at your house if you want," Starr said.

"Just take me to my office," Catherine said.

"Do you think that's a good idea?" Starr had told the crime scene techs to take the bouquet, but the memory of it was likely to linger. After the way Catherine had behaved in the woods, she didn't need any more triggers.

"Are you seriously patronizing me?"

"I'm not patronizing you at all." Starr stopped for a light and turned in her seat. "You've had a couple of really traumatic events today, both of them digging up a past you've apparently worked really hard to keep buried. If I'd had the day you've had, I'd want to be as far away from work as possible and huddled up in the comfort of my home."

"Maybe my home isn't all that comfortable."

"That's an easy fix. Some bubble bath and a bottle of wine can be transformative. Why don't I take you home and you take the rest of the day for some pampering?"

Catherine's eye's widened and Starr played back her words through an objective lens. "Sorry, I didn't mean that the way it sounded. I mean you do deserve a day off, and wine and a bubble bath come highly recommended, but I wasn't implying—" She shut up abruptly for fear she was digging a bigger hole. She really hadn't meant to imply that she wanted to share in the comfort making. Or did she?

She could concede that Catherine was an extremely attractive woman. She was smart and highly accomplished, but totally not her type. She could almost hear her mother telling her that in order to have a type, she would have to actually be dating. Mom was right, but that didn't change the fact that even if Catherine were her type, by virtue of her connection to this case, she was off limits. If the police managed to catch Pratt, Catherine would be a witness at his trial—a good reason to stay on her good side but keep things professional, which meant no sharing wine or a bubble bath or anything else for that matter.

"The office is fine," Catherine said. "I need to check in, although Doris has probably already gone for the day."

"Office it is." Starr could tell by Catherine's tone there was no point in pushing. She didn't make eye contact for fear Catherine might read the disappointment she felt. The rest of the ride went by in silence, and it seemed like forever before they pulled up in front of Catherine's office building. There was only one car in the lot.

"Is that you?" Starr asked, pointing at the vehicle.

"Yes. Doris must have left." Catherine sighed. "Probably not a bad idea. I may do the same." She pulled the door handle but paused before getting out of the car. "Thanks for letting me come with you today. Tell your mother thanks for the soup."

"I will." Starr searched for something to say that would keep her there longer, but nothing came to mind that didn't sound silly in her head. "I'll call you if there's anything to report."

"Thanks."

Catherine held her gaze for a moment longer and the air was full of portent, but a moment later, she pushed open the door. Starr watched her go with the nagging sensation that something was off. She glanced around the empty parking lot for a moment before it hit her. Pratt knew where Catherine worked. Did he also know where she lived? Starr pressed the button on her car phone and tapped her hand against the steering wheel until the call connected and Pearson's gruff voice said hello. "Why don't we have someone assigned to Catherine Landauer? I mean Pratt knows where she works. Who's to say he won't have her house staked out. She needs protection, and if we have someone watching her, they might be able to get a lead on Hannah."

"Good point," Pearson said. "I'll see if we can get someone assigned." He cleared his throat. "They're about to start digging. Are you going to come back out here?"

Starr started to answer, but a high-pitched whine from across the parking lot startled her. "Hang on a sec." She moved the phone away from her ear and watched Catherine slam her steering wheel with both fists. Car trouble? She pulled the phone back toward her. "Don't wait for me, but call me later when you know something. And let me know about the protective detail. Thanks." She hung up quickly, climbed out of the car, and strode toward Catherine's car. She rapped on the window, instantly sorry when Catherine jumped at the sound. When Catherine lowered the window, she leaned in. "That doesn't sound good."

"It won't start."

"Not sounding like that, it won't." Starr motioned for her to try again and winced when it made the same screeching sound. "Sounds like a loose belt. You're going to need a ride."

Catherine sighed. "I'll call the auto club."

It was going to be dark soon, and Starr tensed at the thought of Catherine waiting here in the parking lot by herself for some stranger to come to her aid. "They won't be able to jump the car. They're going to have to tow it in. Let me give you a ride home, and you can call them from there."

Catherine's brow furrowed and Starr was certain she was going to say no, but when she finally spoke, she said, "Okay."

Starr held the door open, secretly pleased Catherine had acquiesced. It solved the problem of leaving her without a guard, and she looked forward to seeing where Catherine lived, hoping it would give her some insight into what made her tick. But she held in her enthusiasm for fear she would spook Catherine back into her shell.

❖

Catherine stared out the window, hoping Starr wouldn't notice she was practicing her breathing exercises as an effort to avoid the panic threatening to overwhelm her. No one came to her house. Ever. She knew that fact was strange, but it was what it was, and up until now she'd been perfectly content to wall off her personal life so completely. She should've called a car service, walked, anything to avoid this situation, but she'd been caught off guard by Starr's kind gesture. Lots about Starr had taken her by surprise.

Seeing Starr interact with the mayor, with Pearson, with her mother had given Catherine several different perspectives. Starr treated colleagues with respect, victims with compassion, and her mother with the good-natured ribbing of an affectionate relationship. The only version of Starr she'd ever known was the one who would do anything to win, even if it meant breaking the rules that ensured everyone got a fair shot. Now Catherine was beginning to question her assumptions.

"Are you hungry?" Starr asked. "Mom's soup is good, but I usually eat seconds and there wasn't time."

"I am actually," Catherine said. "But after this day, I don't feel like going out."

Starr nodded knowingly. "I'm starving. How about I swing through a drive-thru and get us both something since until your car gets fixed, you're going to be in for the night?"

"That would be nice. Thanks."

Starr named a couple of places, but although she was hungry, making a decision seemed overwhelming and Catherine told Starr to choose. Starr drove to Flyrite Chicken, placed both their orders, and insisted on paying. A short while later, they pulled up in front of Catherine's house. Starr put the car in park. "I'll walk you to the door"

Catherine paused for a moment, the prospect of coming home to an empty house disturbing her for the first time in as long as she could remember. Impulse seized her. "Why don't you bring your food and have dinner with me?"

"I don't want to impose."

"Nonsense. By the time you get to the police station, your food will be cold. They'll call you if they find anything, won't they?" Catherine looked down at her lap. "Besides, I could use the company while we wait." She looked back up and found Starr staring intently at her. The long silence that followed should've been uncomfortable, but instead it was electric with anticipation. Catherine put her hand on the door handle. She'd ask one more time, and then she was done. "Are you coming?"

"Sure."

Catherine led the way up the walk, immediately having second thoughts. She did a mental rundown of the interior of the house, but she knew for a fact it was perfectly clean and everything was in its place. That wasn't the issue at all, and she knew it. This house was her sanctuary, the place she was able to retreat from the rest of the world, away from the fears of her past that still crept up despite the time and distance since they'd held her in their grip.

She turned the key in the deadbolt, opened the door, and punched her code in the keypad inside. Starr followed her in and Catherine noted her approving glance at the high tech security system, complete with a video screen displaying a wide-angle view of the entire front porch. "Can I take your coat?" she asked.

Starr shrugged out of the black wool coat. "That would be great. Thanks."

Catherine motioned down the hall. "The kitchen's over there. I'll be right back." She hurried down the hall ahead of Starr and hung both of their coats in the hall closet before ducking into her bedroom. Now that Starr was in her house, her anxiety rose. She considered calling Dr. M, but she already knew what she would say.

"We've talked about you taking the step of inviting people to your house. It's a big step, but an important one."

"Yes, but we've talked about 'people.' This is different."

"How so?"

Catherine didn't have an answer for that question. Well, she did, but not one she wanted to admit. Starr wasn't anything like what she'd thought she would be. She was kind and compassionate and protective in a way that wasn't smothering. It was almost enough to make her lower her guard. Almost.

Dinner, a bit of conversation, and then she'd send Starr on her way. She squared her shoulders and took a deep breath. She could do this. The alternative was being alone, and after the day she'd had, the solitary blanket she'd wrapped around her life felt more suffocating than comforting.

Starr was sitting on one of the barstools by the kitchen counter when Catherine entered the room. She'd half expected her to be snooping through her stuff because who wouldn't be curious to meet celebrity survival girl Jill Winfield?

"I probably should've grabbed some plates and silverware," Starr said, "but I didn't want to go through your cabinets without permission."

Mind reader. "No worries." Catherine was surprised to find that the idea of Starr rummaging around in her kitchen wasn't an unwelcome thought. She reached for some plates and pointed to a drawer. "Grab whatever you want and I'll get us something to drink." She opened the fridge. "I have iced-tea, water." She pushed aside a few items. "A nice Pinot Grigio."

"The wine sounds great, but I probably shouldn't since I need to go back to the station after we eat."

Catherine heard the wistful tone in Starr's voice. "A tiny glass won't hurt. Besides, I need a drink, and it's not nice to make a girl drink alone." She winced the moment the words left her lips—a cross between desperate and flirty. "But no pressure."

"You're right. A drink is in order." Starr pointed to the cabinet. "Glasses up here?"

Catherine remembered the Balcones single malt ordered at Guero's after the Knoll trial. "I have something stronger if you'd like."

Starr cocked her head like she was considering the idea. "Rain check on a whiskey? I think if I have one now, I might curl up in a ball and fall asleep on your couch."

The image of Starr lying on the couch sent a flood of warmth through Catherine, and she ducked her head to hide the blush warming her face. She picked up the plates and carried them over to the kitchen table, having decided the living room was now off limits. Starr joined her with the wine and the bags of food, and they dug in. Catherine was surprised at how hungry she was, but she took the time to savor the taste of the food, curious about the insight it would give her into what Starr liked. The sandwich was delicious, not at all what she would have expected from a drive-thru. Left to her own devices, she would have been sitting in front of the television, scraping a spoon against the bottom of a yogurt container. Another reason she was glad she'd invited Starr in. When they were done eating, she gathered their plates and motioned for Starr to stay seated while she took the dishes to the kitchen.

"I'm curious about something," Starr called out after her. "And if it's impolite to ask, just tell me to mind my own business."

Catherine braced for an onslaught of voyeuristic questions, glad Starr couldn't see her expression from the other room. "Shoot."

"Why criminal defense? I mean, considering everything you've been through, it seems like you'd be a shoo-in for a prosecutor."

It was a fair question, considering Catherine had asked a version of it to Starr earlier. Dr. M had asked the same question years ago, so she should be prepared with an answer. She was, kind of, but she'd rarely had a chance to test it out loud. She set the plates in the sink and returned to the dining room, mulling over potential responses. She sat back down at the table and proceeded carefully. "I actually interned with the Williamson County DA's office after my second year in law school as part of the clinic program at UT. You know how it was back then, way before the Michael Morton case was catching headlines, and the motto of the day was do whatever it takes to win, defendants have no rights." She paused and Starr nodded. Everyone in this part of the country knew the story of the murder case. Michael Morton's wife had disappeared only to show up dead and the former DA and police department that focused all their attention on the husband, certain he had committed the crime. In their quest to shore up the foregone conclusions, they not only ignored evidence that might lead them to other suspects, but they actively hid exculpatory evidence from Morton's defense attorney.

Michael served years in prison for a crime he didn't commit. When he was finally exonerated, instead of crawling away and licking his wounds, he lobbied tirelessly for reform, and just a few years ago the Texas legislature had passed laws to ensure that prosecutors would share evidence with defense attorneys.

"I helped out herding witnesses during trial for a similar case," Catherine said. "Another husband accused of killing his wife, Deke Tyson. He was convicted, but the case was overturned on appeal and sent back for a retrial."

"I remember that case. It's never been closed, has it?" Starr asked.

"No, and I doubt it ever will be. The prosecutor was anxious to retry Tyson right away, but then a slew of evidence came out that pretty much proved he couldn't have committed the crime, so they dismissed the charges. By then, too much time had passed. Even if they ever do find the real killer, the momentum is gone, and it's unlikely a jury would view the crime through the same lens as they might have when it was fresh. That experience and a few others left me feeling jaded about the process."

"You're saying you decided to work the other side to keep us law-and-order folks in line?"

Catherine searched Starr's face for any sign she might be making fun with her broad summary of her intent, but all she saw were gentle eyes reflecting real concern. "Something like that. I started working for Neil Daniels right out of law school. Neil was an old family friend of my aunt and uncle. After I graduated from high school in Albuquerque, I told them I wanted to change my identity and apply to UT, so they contacted him because he was a big deal alumnus and he helped me get accepted under my new name. I moved away from New Mexico and never looked back."

"Were your aunt and uncle upset that you left?"

"I think they were actually relieved. They never really knew what to do with me. Every time we'd meet someone new there would be this contorted explanation of how I'd come to live with them, and I never felt like part of the family. But I connected instantly with Neil. He was smart and kind and patient, and he taught me that our job as defense attorneys was to ensure the system worked. I was too young when my father left to remember what he was like, but I liked to imagine that if I'd had a dad who'd stuck around, he would be like him—the exact opposite of Russell Pratt."

"I met Neil once. He was good people."

"Thanks. He died without family and left me the law firm. I was surprised, but it was a godsend not to have to start from scratch in my own practice, and going to work for someone else would've been a nonstarter."

"Because you didn't want to have to explain your life story?"

"Explain, and then continue to explain. You don't realize how much your past plays into your everyday life until you're trying to hide it. Where did you grow up? Do your parents live nearby? Do you have any siblings? Seemingly innocuous questions that everyone else answers as a matter of routine are sharp tools chipping away at all you have left of your privacy. You can't let anyone close because once your life has been on display twenty-four seven, everyone thinks they own a piece of you."

"I can't even imagine. How do you have a life at all?"

Catherine wondered if she was imagining a personal angle to Starr's question, but pushed the thought away instead of overthinking it. "I keep to myself mostly. I've dated occasionally, but inevitably the background and family questions pop up around the second or third date. My evasive answers usually send the women running in the other direction." She watched for a reaction to her coming out, and thought she detected a trace of recognition, and slight nod of approval at the admission. Why had she thrown in the detail about her sexuality? This wasn't a date and it wasn't important that Starr had that information for any reason having to do with the case.

Because some line had been crossed. With Starr in her house, discussing her past, they'd moved from professional to personal with no stops in between. Why wasn't she more uncomfortable at the shift?

"Thank you for telling me all this," Starr said. "It's helpful to have some context. And I can't even begin to tell you how much I appreciate you coming forward."

Catherine took a moment to assess Starr's words. On the surface, nothing about them could be construed as anything other than a prosecutor talking to a witness, but she felt a simmering heat emanating from Starr, and for the first time in a long time, Catherine savored the intense thrill of a human connection. Tentatively, she reached out a hand and touched Starr's arm. It was a light touch that could be construed as a simple pat, but she lingered a few seconds longer than necessary if she was merely trying to acknowledge Starr's words, and as the seconds passed, the intensity of the moment became palpable. She tore her attention away from Starr's arm and looked up into her dark and intense eyes. Something was happening between them and instinct told her to shut it down, but every cell in Catherine's body was begging her not to break the connection. The room suddenly shrank and the space between them compressed. They were close, extremely close. On any other occasion, faced with the same set of circumstances, Catherine's first response would've been to flee, but even though it was contrary to every impulse she'd had before, she didn't want to be anywhere else but in this space with this woman.

And then Starr pulled away. "I should go," she said, standing up and edging away from the table.

Catherine looked up at Starr, wondering how much of the spark between them had been her imagination. This feeling was so new it was hard to know what was actually real and what was conjured out of wishes. But whatever it had been, it was apparently over. At least as far as Starr was concerned. "Okay."

"I'll call you tomorrow," Starr said. "To give you an update." She started toward the door.

Catherine searched for something to say, something that would restore the moment, take them back to allow her to slow down time and see if she could capture more detail in the replay. "Wait."

Starr turned slightly.

"Your coat." She stood and hurried down the hall to her bedroom. A small delay, but it would give her a moment to think. A moment to compose her emotions. Starr's abrupt exit was for the best. Starr had a job to do, and she could do more good out there than sitting in here, no matter how much Catherine wished she would stay. She took Starr's coat from the hanger and pulled it to her face, drinking in the soft scent of lavender. The sense memory would have to be enough. It was better this way, leaving her less vulnerable, less exposed. Once Starr left, Catherine could find a way back to the safety her private, solitary self had worked a lifetime to build.

❖

Starr resisted the urge to look back on the way to her vehicle. She spotted a patrol car at the end of the block and hoped it was the one she'd asked Pearson to send to keep watch over Catherine until Russell Pratt was in custody.

If you really cared about her safety, why did you leave? The internal voice baited her, but she wasn't about to play that game. Perhaps she'd imagined the heat in the room when Catherine had looked deeply into her eyes, touched her arm, and shared details about her personal life that she'd likely not divulged to anyone else, but even if the spark between them was something she'd conjured out of thin air, it was no less dangerous. Catherine was a witness in this case, and more than that, she was a victim of a horrible crime at the hands of the suspect. Starr had no business engaging with her on any level that wasn't purely professional.

She probably thinks I'm crazy for running out on her. Before she drove away, Starr reached for her phone, thinking a quick text could smooth things over, but she changed her mind before she could send the message. Best not to blur the lines any further. She'd communicate with Catherine only if she had something specific to report about the case and nothing more. She did see a text from Pearson asking her to call him. Relieved for the distraction, she dialed his number and waited through the rings, about to give up before he finally answered.

"Where are you?" he asked.

"Why?" she hedged. "Did you find anything?"

"No body, but forensics is still combing through stuff just in case there's anything there we can use."

"I don't get it," she said. "What was the point of the grave? Is he letting us know he plans to kill Hannah?" Or Catherine? She shook the thought away, unwilling and unable to go there. "I'm headed back to the station now."

"No point really. Why don't you get some sleep? I'll call you if anything turns up. Chief called a meeting for first thing tomorrow morning. Did you get the message?"

Starr scrolled through her messages and spotted two crucial texts she'd missed while she was having a leisurely dinner with Catherine. One from Murphy letting her know about the meeting and the other from Nelson asking if she wanted him to attend the meeting in her place if she had other things to do. "Sorry, my phone must be acting up." She offered a silent apology for the lie. "Murphy's asking for an update, so I better give him a call. I'll see you in the morning."

She clicked off before he could ask her anything else and texted Nelson that she wasn't sure what he was talking about, but she would absolutely be at the task force meeting. Next she called Murphy and brought him up to speed on the flower delivery to Catherine Landauer's office, and their new working theory that Russell Pratt had emerged from wherever he'd been hiding out the last twenty years. "The lab has the bouquet, but I doubt this guy was dumb enough to leave any useful evidence that will tie it to him."

"But you think he's involved in Hannah Turner's disappearance?"

"I do. I'm not sure how everything is connected yet, but after that call to the tip line that led us to a bow exactly like the ones Catherine received in her office, it's clear the kidnapper is dropping hints, and they point toward Pratt."

"All right. I trust your judgment on this, but watch your step. The mayor called and said that you brought Landauer to her house. That was a pretty risky move."

"I know," Starr said. He didn't immediately respond, and she knew he was waiting for her to explain her actions, but she had a feeling he wasn't going to be too impressed with "I've become really attracted to Catherine Landauer, and she must've cast a spell over me." She let a few seconds pass while she came up with something else to say. "Respectfully, sir, I think we're at the point where we're going to have to take some risks. For what it's worth, Mayor Turner didn't object. In fact, I think having Catherine meet her actually allayed her fears that we don't have anything to go on yet."

He grunted. "And that could backfire if this connection doesn't pan out. I trust you, but be careful. Whenever this thing busts wide open, it will be all over the news, and neither one of us needs bad press right now. I'll talk to you later."

He hung up before she could get in another word, leaving her to stew over the implication that her actions should be directed by her political ambition. She cared about only one thing, and that was finding Hannah Turner, alive and well, and putting away the man who had robbed Catherine of a huge chunk of her life, not to mention killing her mother. Sure, the decision to take Catherine to the mayor's house had been reckless, but she'd do it again in a heartbeat if it led to clues they could use to find Hannah. And free Catherine from living under the shadow of Russell Pratt's looming presence.

Out of the corner of her eye, she spotted the patrol car again, and she wondered if Catherine had seen her sitting outside on the phone after she'd left so abruptly. Apparently, she was willing to take risks, but not when it came to crossing lines with witnesses. Starr started the car and pulled away from the curb. In order to help Catherine, she needed to put some distance between them.

Chapter Fifteen

Early the next morning, Catherine left a message for Doris that she was closing the office for the day and that she shouldn't come in. She still hadn't heard anything from Starr or Detective Pearson about the bouquet Pratt had sent her, but she wasn't about to put Doris's life in danger by putting her in proximity to the problems from her past. Maybe she could convince Doris to finally take a vacation. For her part, a late-night call to Dr. M had secured her an appointment for this morning, after which she'd do her best to resume life as usual, whatever that meant.

She wondered what Starr was doing this morning. She wanted to text her, but after no communication from her since she'd rushed out the door last night, Catherine wasn't sure how to navigate the space between them which had seemed to be getting closer, but now seemed more distant. What she did know was that the simple takeout dinner with Starr last night had been the first normal interaction she'd had with another woman in a very long time, which either meant her regular life was very sad or there was something very special about Starr she'd overlooked up until now.

Catherine stopped at Jo's on the way to Dr. M's, telling herself the break with her routine had nothing to do with the anticipation that she might run into Starr now that she knew she frequented the popular spot too. She took a moment to sip her coffee while watching the crowd of people mill around, all of them going about their day as if everything was normal, but her life was completely upended.

Her worst nightmare might be anywhere right now, watching her, waiting for an opportunity to swoop in and…She had no idea why Pratt would revisit her. Yes, she'd run from him, but she had a feeling that the trusting little girl she'd once been was more to his liking than the strong and powerful adult woman that she'd become. What possible reason would he have for coming out of hiding after all these years?

And the nightmare was balanced by the strange feelings she was having for Starr, though she acknowledged they were really only strange because she was stunted when it came to romantic relationships. After a hit and miss, mostly miss, few years of dating when she'd graduated from law school, it had gotten to the point that she'd stopped trying, resigned to the fact her plagued past meant she would never be decent relationship material.

She repeated the thought in Dr. M's office an hour later and braced for the response.

"Maybe you're right." Dr. M said.

Catherine felt her jaw drop. It was so unlike Dr. M to respond definitely to anything she said. Besides, she'd expected a dreaded pep talk in response to the depressing admission she was doomed to never have a normal romantic relationship. She supposed she should be grateful for the honesty, but all she felt was stunned. "Tell me how you really feel."

"It's not about how I feel. It's about how you feel."

"What does that even mean?"

"You've had a really hard week, so I'm going to shortcut this for you. Maybe you aren't relationship material in the way that you think relationships should be."

"That's clear as mud. I feel like I should get a discount for this session."

"Work with me here. Why don't you describe a perfect relationship to me."

"No such thing."

"Okay, how about as close as you believe one can be."

Catherine sighed. "Two people in love. Commitment. Happily ever after, and all that sweet, sappy, perfect stuff that comes with it."

Dr. M nodded. "Let's work with that. Love, commitment, sweet, sappy, perfect stuff. Are all of those things necessary?"

"I don't know."

"Why not?"

Catherine fiddled with her coffee cup. She'd been coming here long enough that Dr. M should know the answer to pretty much any questions she posed, so she was certain the good doctor was only asking for some didactic reason. She should be used to this method by now, but it never failed to make her want to stick out her bottom lip and stubbornly refuse to answer. But for once she really, really wanted to get past this. Catherine shifted in her chair. "Because I've never had any of those things."

"Fair enough. Do any of them sound appealing to you?"

"Maybe."

"Can I get something more definitive?"

Catherine rolled her neck, willing away the tension. "I could go for the love part. And I guess the commitment too, but the rest seems unrealistic."

Dr. M feigned a shocked look. "No sappy for you?"

"As if. But seriously, what's your point?"

"My point is that you get to define what a relationship is to you. If you can't see ever fitting into the definition you've heard all your life, then you get to change it to fit you. Does that make sense?"

"What if her definition is different than mine?" Catherine quickly caught the slip and added, "I'm talking global 'her' in case you start thinking I have someone specific in mind."

"It's just like negotiating a plea deal for one of your clients. If *her* definition is different, you get to either work it out or walk away."

"Except I have no personal stake when I'm advocating for a client."

"True, but without risk there's no reward. The thing to remember is that your reward gets to be whatever you want it to be. Doesn't have to have a sappy moment involved."

Catherine laughed. She hadn't meant for this session to turn into an hour long dating advice, but now that it had, she was calmer and more at ease than she had been when she arrived. Could it be that the feelings Starr was stirring had her more off kilter than the threat of Pratt? She shook her head. No, it had to be the combination of everything at once. Too many sensations, too many feelings to process. What she thought she was feeling for Starr was likely just a symptom of the loneliness in her life that was being magnified by the visit from her past. Dr. M's advice was useful and she hoped that one day she would get to apply it, but nothing was going to happen between her and Starr Rio. Not now, not ever.

The entire bleary-eyed task force was gathered in the war room, and Pearson was leading the discussion. He reviewed what they had so far, most of which Starr already knew, but she listened with rapt attention just like everyone else. White pickup truck. White satin bows. The delivery to Catherine's office. As they'd suspected, there was no forensic evidence on the bouquet, but they were working with the florist to determine who might have placed the order.

"We have reason to believe that the suspect may be this guy." Pearson motioned to an officer sitting nearby who pressed a few buttons on a computer, and an old driver's license photo of Russell Pratt appeared on the screen. Starr stared at the picture of the innocuous looking man, and thought about how easy it had been for him to entice Catherine from her bed in the middle of the night. No surprise really. Catherine's mother had often worked late nights and her father had left when she was very young. When the nice neighborhood handyman showed up and said he'd been sent by her mom, Catherine did what a lot of kids would—trusted the familiar face and obeyed what she thought was her mother's directive. She had no way of knowing that Russell Pratt was a sick and twisted man.

Starr wished people like Pratt were a rarity, but the truth was there were tons of Russell Pratts, lurking where children gathered. Nowadays they found most of their prey online, but the electronic interface didn't diminish their evil. She'd put lots of these guys away, but she knew for every one she sent to prison, there were dozens who would never be apprehended. Russell Pratt would not be one of those. Not on her watch.

Pearson put up a slide showing all the credible clues they'd gathered so far, many of which had come from Catherine. The task force had added more officers and widened the focus of their investigation, which meant they were looking at everyone who'd had contact with the Turners over the last few months including delivery people, contractors, neighbors, and friends. They were also searching for private plots of land relatively close to town where someone like Pratt could hide Hannah in plain sight. It was only a matter of time before Pratt made a mistake. Starr hoped Hannah had enough time for that to happen.

When the meeting was over, she pulled Pearson aside. "Murphy called me. He wants answers now, of course, and I can tell he thinks we're taking a risk by redirecting our energy to Pratt. I need you to tell me if you think we're on a wild goose chase."

"What does your gut tell you?"

Starr took a moment to assess. Her gut was telling her all sorts of things, but many of them were wound up in how she felt about Catherine which caused her not to trust her usual instincts. She swiped the doubt away. Catherine may be a hard-ass, but she had a reputation for being honest and forthright. "I think we're headed in the right direction. I mean how else do you explain the flowers that were sent to her office?"

Pearson averted his eyes for a second, but it was enough to tell her something was off. "What? You don't believe Pratt sent her the bouquet? What about the call to the tip line?"

He raised his hands. "Don't be mad at me because I'm simply playing devil's advocate here. It's possible that Pratt didn't do either of those things. What happened to Catherine when she was a kid— that was the kind of thing that can cause a person to break, even years later. We have to consider the possibility that she might've seen this story about Hannah Turner, and it brought up old wounds, caused her to regress or whatever fancy term you want to call it when people act out."

Starr heard his words, but they skittered along the surface of her brain without sinking in. Catherine Landauer was formidable, not the kind of woman who broke down and tried to draw attention to herself. Hell, she'd spent her entire adult life trying to hide who she was.

Then how did Pratt find her? She pushed away the question. "I hear what you're saying. We can keep all our options open, but this is a strong lead and we need to follow it wherever it leads."

"Roger that." Pearson looked over his shoulder at the war room. "I need to get in there and start divvying up assignments. You need me for anything right now?"

"No, I'm good. I'm going to the office to check in, but I'll be close by in case you need anything from me." Starr strode off briskly, her confident stride a direct contrast to the swirl of emotions inside her. What if her trust in Catherine was misplaced? Once outside, she paused to let the cool air hit her in the face, and it was exactly what she needed to snap out of any conflict. The idea that Catherine had lied just didn't ring true. She'd seen the genuine emotion on Catherine's face in her reaction to the flowers, the bow on the tree in the woods, and the faux grave site. Catherine hadn't faked those feelings, and while it was possible they were the side-effect of psychosis, Starr believed she'd seen enough in her career as a prosecutor to know when she was being played. She'd keep her mind open, but her focus was on Russell Pratt and keeping both Hannah Turner and Catherine Landauer safe from his clutches.

"Ms. Rio, can we have a moment?"

Starr turned at the sound of her name and was ambushed by Gloria Flynn from the local news station accompanied by a cameraman. Before she could reply, Gloria shoved a mic in her face.

"We received a tip that the police are looking into the mayor's brother-in-law as a possible suspect. Can you confirm this?"

Starr stopped in her tracks, hoping her face didn't reflect the oh shit feeling storming through her head. Treading carefully, she looked at Gloria instead of into the camera. "Gloria, you know me well enough to know I'm not going to comment about an ongoing investigation."

"Should we take that as a yes? Doesn't the public have a right to know if there is a predator who has access to the top elected official in the city?"

Starr barely resisted the urge to choke her. She'd had plenty of experience dealing with the press, and most were measured in their questions, but Gloria's schtick was surprising her prey on camera and going for the gotcha moment. She'd rarely been caught in her net, and never at a more critical moment in time. All she could hope to do would be to extricate herself as quickly as possible. "We're doing our best to keep everyone informed about the status of the case, but we have a duty to make sure that we guard against releasing information that could affect our ability to conduct a thorough investigation. Now, if you'll excuse me, I need to go."

Gloria wasn't so easily deterred. "Are you following up on a lead?"

"I have nothing further to say at this time." Starr rushed off before Gloria could ask another stupid question, mindful of the fact she had her back to the camera—never a good thing—but she didn't know how else to shut her down. She only hoped that she'd been boring enough not to make the cut for the evening news because that definitely hadn't been her best moment.

Chapter Sixteen

Tuesday evening, Catherine stared at the television screen, wishing she'd taped the news so she could replay what she'd just seen. Gloria Flynn was annoying as hell with her gotcha techniques, but even she wouldn't make an allegation that the mayor's brother-in-law was involved in Hannah Turner's kidnapping without some evidence to back it up.

What was going on? She hadn't heard from Starr since last night and there'd been no news from the police or DA's office as to the status of the investigation. Had Starr abandoned the search for Russell Pratt in favor of this new theory? And on what basis?

Catherine picked up her phone to call Starr and confront her about the abrupt turn of events, but she couldn't quite figure out what to say. At the root of her anger was fear she hadn't been believed and that Russell Pratt would never be caught. It was like she was reliving her childhood all over again, except it was almost worse this time because she had a voice and still no one heard her.

When the doorbell rang, she considered ignoring it, but a quick check of the video doorbell revealed Starr standing on her doorstep. She should leave her standing there. Starr had betrayed her. She'd shared deep, dark secrets with Starr, and Starr had cast aside the relevance for the more salacious angle. She watched as Starr paced on the doormat and raised her hand to ring the bell again. Finally, she decided to confront her and get it over with.

She cracked the door open, barely wide enough to see Starr. "What do you want?"

"I want to talk to you."

"There's nothing for us to talk about."

Starr leaned in and her face filled the small space between the door and the doorjamb. "I'm guessing you watched the news."

Catherine heard a contrite undertone, but she wasn't interested in Starr's excuses. "Good thing I did or I would've missed the latest update on the case."

"Don't believe everything you hear. Gloria caught me off guard. I was only trying to deflect her, and I didn't want to say anything that might cause her to show up on your doorstep with a herd of other reporters looking for Jill Winfield. I'm here now and I want to talk to you. Please."

Catherine considered the plea. Starr certainly sounded earnest, and she supposed it was possible Starr was telling the truth, but she suspected there was more to it. The only way to find out was to hear what Starr had to say, and having this conversation on her front door step wasn't ideal. She eased the door wider. "Come in, but you can't stay long. I have work to do."

"Thanks." Starr stepped into the room. "It's nice and warm in here."

"You're not wearing a coat." That explained why Starr had been shivering on the porch. "That's crazy."

"I was in a hurry to get over here and I forgot it."

Catherine wanted to believe Starr's story, but she couldn't afford to feel sympathy or anything else where Starr was concerned. She'd already exposed too much too fast, and for what? Apparently, Starr and her task force hadn't believed what she'd told them about Pratt and were searching elsewhere for suspects. Well, they could search all they wanted but she knew without a doubt Russell Pratt had Hannah Turner, and the more time the task force wasted, the more danger Hannah faced. She'd been a fool to let Starr get close to her, but she wasn't going to make that mistake again.

"Can we sit down?" Starr asked.

"I suppose." Catherine led the way to the living room and motioned for Starr to sit in one of the chairs across from the couch, while she perched on the edge of one of the couch cushions. "Say what you have to say."

Starr fiddled with her hands in her lap, apparently struggling for words. Finally, she met Catherine's eyes. "I shouldn't be telling you any of this, but I feel like you need to know." Again with the restless hands.

"What is it?"

"Ricky Turner, the mayor's brother-in-law, was our first suspect. He drives a white pickup like the one Hannah was last spotted near, and he has a record. Nothing violent, but he's been in prison. We didn't make any of that information public for several reasons, one of which was it was the very early stages in the investigation."

"And the other being politics. Wouldn't want to taint the mayor."

"Sure, that factored in," Starr admitted, to Catherine's surprise. "But it wasn't the sole factor. You're savvy enough to know how these things work."

"With a suspect that juicy, I'm surprised you were willing to listen to my theory."

"It's not that simple."

"And what I told you wasn't just a theory," Catherine said, her voice rising. "Tell me you're still looking for Pratt."

Starr wore a pained expression. "We are, but we have to keep all our options open. Didn't you tell me before that one of the reasons you were so frustrated with the way your case was handled was that the cops focused on one suspect and didn't look at anyone else. You don't want that to happen here, do you?"

Catherine hated having her own words tossed back at her, but Starr was right. The task force should explore all potential suspects, but she also knew that Russell Pratt was the one who had taken Hannah, and she worried that spreading their resources would allow him to get away.

"I promise you, if he's out there, we won't let him get away."

Starr's words, delivered with quiet conviction, were exactly what she needed to hear, and Catherine nodded. "I'm going to hold you to that."

"Thanks for hearing me out." Starr half rose from the chair. "I should go and let you get back to your evening."

The idea of Starr leaving again so suddenly tore a hole in the comfort Catherine had drawn from her promise. "You keep doing that."

"Doing what?"

"Dashing out." They locked glances for a few seconds and the air between them became thick and heavy. "I know you're probably busy, but if you can stay for a little bit, I could use the company."

A slow smile slid across Starr's lips. "I guess I do owe you."

"Are you hungry?"

"Starving."

"Probably because you've been working around the clock," Catherine said. She led the way to the kitchen and Starr followed.

"I could let you believe that, but it wouldn't be true. Ask my mother, I'm always hungry. She used to complain that it was me, not my brothers, who ate her out of house and home."

Catherine reached into the fridge and pulled out a carton of eggs, some cheese, and a bell pepper. "Was she right?"

"Mostly. I do have an appetite."

"Is an omelet going to fill you up or should we add in some pancakes?"

"Omelets are perfect."

Catherine whipped the eggs in a bowl and set it aside and started cutting the vegetables. She could feel Starr's intense observation of her every move, and it was both disconcerting and oddly inviting. "You act like you've never seen someone cook before."

"It's possible I didn't take you for a chef."

"Well, I'm no Iron Chef, but I do know my way around a kitchen. I've been on my own for a while, and eating out alone gets old. It was either learn to cook or starve. I might be a spinster, but at least I won't be hungry."

"Any woman would be lucky to have you."

Catherine looked up and met Starr's eyes again. "For my mad omelet skills? Yes, but once they find out the whiz in the kitchen is damaged goods, they run as fast as possible in the other direction."

"Not everyone is that shallow."

"I suppose, but I have yet to meet anyone I thought would stick around after the big reveal. Oh, they'd probably stay for a while at first, enjoying the novelty of sleeping with the girl who escaped her captor, but after a few times of waking up to the sound of my nightmares, the newness would wear off and they'd go in search of someone who didn't have that kind of baggage."

"Everyone has baggage. It's how you carry it that counts."

"A nice platitude, but everybody doesn't see things that way."

"Not everyone is worthy of being with someone as strong as you are, who has gone through as much as you have."

Catherine paused, her knife midway through one of the peppers. "You don't know me that well."

"I'd like to, if you'd let me."

For all her lack of relationship skills, Catherine knew flirting when she heard it, and there was definitely a hint of flirtatiousness in Starr's voice. But there was a serious edge to it, like Starr was truly attracted to her, like she respected her, and Catherine basked in the warmth of the feeling. She'd been wrong about Starr. Starr was a passionate, caring person who'd thought enough about her feelings to come here tonight to mend the harm done by the newscast. That Starr even realized the broadcast would bother her was huge. Perhaps letting Starr get close wasn't that risky after all. She decided to venture a small step toward bridging the gap between them.

"Here," Catherine said, handing Starr the knife. "You chop while I grate the cheese. And you get three questions about anything you want as long as they don't have anything to do with this case."

"Sound's fair." Starr took the knife and dutifully started chopping. "Although three isn't a lot."

"Quit trying to get more than you're offered. This isn't a negotiation. Take off your lawyer hat."

"That's like asking me to cut off one of my arms."

"Are you going to ask or not?"

"Yes. Question number one: name two of your heroes."

Catherine was impressed. "That's a good one. Hard to narrow down to two, but I accept the challenge." She sifted through the many examples that sprang to mind and settled on a couple of Texans Starr was sure to know, Barbara Jordan and Ann Richards.

"Good choices. Not predictable, but definitely solid."

"What about you? Who would you pick?" Catherine asked.

"This isn't about me."

"Come on, I want to know," Catherine said, surprised at how much she really did want to know about Starr. "Tell me."

"The first one's definitely obvious, RBG, but don't dis my choice because it's a worthy one and you know it."

"Fair enough," Catherine said, enjoying their playful banter. "Who's the second?"

A loud ring pierced the air, and Starr reached into her pocket and pulled out her phone. She stared at the screen for a moment. "Sorry, I have to take this."

Catherine watched, transfixed, as Starr had a cryptic exchange with whoever was on the other end of the line. By the time Starr hung up, Catherine was certain she was going to come unglued. "Who was it? Have they found her? What's going on?"

Starr stood. "I've got to go, but I'll contact you as soon as I know more."

Catherine was on her feet. "Please don't leave without telling me what's going on, even if it's just a hint. I won't be able to stand waiting here, not knowing." She watched the conflict play out in Starr's expression, surprised at her own admission of weakness, but it was too late to take it back. As if she could sense her need for reassurance, Starr stepped toward her, clutched her hand, and pulled her close.

"Pearson said they have a strong lead on Pratt." Starr squeezed her hand. "I promise, I'll let you know more as soon as I can."

"Okay." It was and it wasn't, just like it was both comforting and disconcerting to have Starr standing so close to her. Catherine wanted Starr to find out what was going on, find Pratt, and bring him to justice, but she also didn't want to break the connection between them. "As long as you promise."

"I do." A few beats passed before Starr eased her hand away. The moment they were no longer touching, it was as if a cold wind had swept between them, and Catherine longed to be warm again. She watched Starr leave, already counting the moments until she heard from her again, knowing her longing had nothing to do with the case.

❖

Starr punched in Pearson's number as she sped away from Catherine's house. When the line connected, she didn't wait for him to speak. "What's the situation?"

"We've got eyes on a duplex on the east side, over near Montopolis," he said, referencing one of the sketchier neighborhoods in Austin. A patrol cop in the area spotted a guy matching Pratt's description at the convenience store down the block and followed him back here. He's been holed up in the house ever since."

"Please tell me he was driving a white pickup."

"No, he was on foot, but that doesn't mean anything. The store's just down the street. He'd have to be stupid to drive the truck around after all the news coverage."

Starr knew he was right, but she was still disappointed not to have that clue locked up. "What's the plan? Are you going to wait for him to make a move?"

"Not much longer. If she's in there, we need to get inside sooner, rather than later."

"If Hannah Turner is in that house and you go in guns blazing, she could die."

"You're preaching to the choir," Pearson said. "Hey, I don't suppose Landauer would be willing to show up on his doorstep?"

"And do what exactly?" Starr struggled to keep her voice neutral, but she wanted to scream at the idea of putting Catherine in harm's way. "Remember he wants her more than he wants Hannah. Catherine showing up on his doorstep is only an invitation for him to take two victims, instead of one."

"You're right, I know. I doubt the chief would go for it anyway."

Starr heard the edge in his voice, and she could empathize. They were all on edge, and hers was fueled further by her growing connection to Catherine that came with a strong desire to bring her good news that would allow her to put her past back where it belonged. The only way she was going to make it through the anxiety of waiting, was by doing something. "What do you need me to do?"

"I guess check in with the rest of the task force and see if there are any other leads," Pearson said. "If this is Pratt, we've got him cornered. When he comes out, we can arrest him based on the New Mexico warrant, but we might need a warrant of our own to search his place for anything to do with Hannah. You want me to text you the address?"

"Yes." She knew he meant so that she would have the information for the warrant, but she couldn't imagine sitting at the police station waiting around while he and the others on the task force closed in on the man whose actions had altered the entire course of Catherine's life. The very least she could do was to see the place where he lived. "I'm going to meet you there. I've got my iPad, and I can type out a warrant just as easily from my car as at the office." Her phone chimed with the sound of his incoming text. "I'll see you in a few."

She hung up the phone before he could protest. She really had no business showing up at a stakeout, but she needed to lay eyes on Pratt's place, if only because she knew that Catherine would want to hear every detail and she wanted to be able to comply. She steered into an illegal U-turn, daring anyone to stop her and raced through the ten-minute drive to the address Pearson had sent. As she drove up to the duplex, she spotted his car right away, along with a couple of patrol units parked along the side street, out of view of the front of the house. Taking her lead from the cops on sight, she parked nearby, and made her way to Pearson's vehicle.

He looked up as she approached, shook his head, and lowered his window. "Taking a stroll, counselor?"

"Better than sitting around in the office, waiting for shit to go down," she replied, knowing he would understand.

He pointed to his passenger seat. "Get in."

Once she was settled into the seat next to him, she asked, "What's the plan?"

"It depends. Do you think we have enough to get a warrant to search his house?"

"Probably not, unless you know for sure it's his. You said the patrol cop recognized him from the photo we circulated at the briefing?"

"Yes. Officer Burns spotted a guy matching Pratt's description buying some snacks at the convenience store down the street. He called it in right after Pratt left the store," Pearson pointed to his right, "and he followed him here."

Starr shook her head. "As much as I'd like to believe it's him, that picture was old. It's not enough. Who owns the duplex?"

"Some corporation. We're running it down now, but if Pratt lives there he probably leases, and likely under a different name."

"We need him to come out so we can confirm his ID," Starr said. "I think that's the only way we're going to convince a judge to let us search the house."

"Or we could find exigent circumstances," Pearson said.

Starr wanted to agree. All they'd need was to allege that they'd heard a young girl calling for help or that they'd spotted one of the creepy white satin bows in the window to justify pushing their way into the house. The courts made an exception for warrantless searches when someone's life was in danger or evidence was likely to be destroyed if the police were forced to wait, but if they forced their way in and didn't find Hannah or any of the bows, they wouldn't be holding Pratt for long and the misstep could do serious damage to their credibility if they eventually wound up at trial. She was about to tell Pearson no, when he pointed toward the front door of the house.

"He's on the move."

Starr looked up to see a tall, lanky man dressed in jeans, boots, and a heavy jacket locking the door of the duplex. She held her breath that he would stay outside long enough for Pearson to approach and ask to see his ID. Pearson radioed to the patrol units to stand by, and he motioned for her to stay put. He quietly opened the door of his car and eased out. Starr watched in the rearview mirror as Pearson crept around the back of the car, while glancing surreptitiously at the sidewalk in front of the duplex as Pratt exited the house. The next few moments played out in slow motion.

Pearson walked up the street toward the duplex, feigning nonchalance. Pratt looked up as they were about to pass. Pearson said something to him that Starr was too far away to make out, but whatever it was, it sent Pratt running back toward the house with Pearson in hot pursuit. Pearson tackled Pratt and suddenly uniformed officers swarmed them both. Seconds later, Pratt was in handcuffs in the back of one of the patrol cars. Starr climbed out of the car and rushed over to Pearson.

"It looks like him," Pearson said before she could get a word in. "Plus, he took off running the minute I said his name. No ID though. At least not on him."

"Maybe it's in the house?" Starr said. She was convinced they had the right guy, and she wanted desperately to prove it.

"Do we have enough to go in?"

Starr knew he was referring to searching the house, and that he was asking if they could go on in without a warrant. She could make a case either way, but her mind flashed to Catherine, and she knew she had to do this the right way to make sure that the case against Pratt was airtight. "Send one of the detectives on the task force to Judge Tatum's house. She lives near the station." She paused long enough to grab her phone and send the judge a text, grateful she knew Lisa Tatum well enough to have her address in her phone. "Tell him to wait there until he hears from us. In the meantime, surround Pratt's house. If you hear anything to indicate someone is in there and in trouble—for real—then bust in."

Starr opened her iPad and pulled up one of the search warrant templates she'd used in the past. Pearson peppered her with facts and she crafted the arguments, and within twenty minutes, she had a search warrant she hoped would hold up in court. She had him sign it and emailed a copy to the judge. "Tell your guy the warrant's on the way. He can call us when it's signed, and you can go on in.

It seemed like forever before they got word, but it was actually only fifteen minutes. Starr waited outside in deference to Pearson while half a dozen police officers performed an initial sweep of the house. The wait was excruciating. She wanted to call Catherine, tell her they had Pratt and were close to rescuing Hannah, but she wanted to be absolutely certain Catherine's nightmare was over before she shared the good news.

When Pearson emerged from the house thirty minutes later, she could tell by his grim expression she'd been right to wait. "She's not here?" she asked, although she was certain she knew the answer.

"Not a trace. If she's been here at all, he's hidden it well. We'll get the crime scene techs out here, but my gut says they're not going to find anything."

"Okay." Starr cast about for something to give them hope. "This place doesn't fit his MO anyway. Maybe he's keeping her somewhere else."

Pearson nodded. "We'll take him in and question him, but unless we arrest him, we won't be able to hold him long."

"Arrest him for the kidnapping of Jill Winfield." She took note of his pained expression. "What?"

"There's something else." He sighed and shoved a driver's license toward her. "We found this."

She stared at the card in her hand and her gut roiled with dread. The picture was of the man they had in handcuffs a few feet away, but the name next to the photo was Albert Stevens. She cast about for an explanation. "She changed her name. He could've changed his."

"Maybe. What do you want to do?"

She wanted to leave this chaotic scene and all the answered questions and go back to Catherine, but she knew she couldn't face her if her only news was that they'd let Pratt go free. "I know what I don't want to do. I don't want to let him get away. Arrest him. I'll contact the original jurisdiction and work out the details later. Do whatever it takes to hold him long enough for us to find Hannah Turner. Take him in and set him up in a video room. Let him sit there while we formulate a strategy for questioning him. I want to proceed very carefully."

"Roger that. Meet you back at the station?"

Starr felt her phone buzz and it reminded her she'd promised to update Catherine. She made a mental note to call her back from the privacy of her car while she checked her phone to see who was calling. She gasped when she read the text from Fred Nelson. *Where are you? Hannah Turner just showed up at the south substation. Murphy wants to see you now.*

Her elation at the news Hannah had been found was dampened by the obvious tone in Nelson's text. She told Pearson the news. "Why didn't anyone call you?" she asked.

"Good question. Does this change our plans?"

A small voice inside told Starr she should hold off on having Pratt/Stevens arrested, but the voice urging her to protect Catherine was louder. "No." Starr fished for her keys. "I better get going. First one of us that finds out what the hell's going on, fill the other in." At Pearson's nod, she hurried to her car, wishing she knew what she was rushing toward.

CHAPTER SEVENTEEN

Catherine leaned back in bed and read the texts from Starr for what had to be the hundredth time. Two texts about an hour apart. *Pratt's in custody. Hannah's safe.*

She'd texted back: *Can't wait to hear more. Come by if you can.* She paused before adding. *Even if it's late.*

It was two a.m. She'd gotten in bed an hour ago, but she didn't hold out much hope of getting any sleep until she heard the whole story. She didn't want to admit it, but she'd kind of expected Starr to call instead of text to deliver the news. Her warm voice would've eased the discomfort she felt every time she thought about Hannah Turner in Pratt's clutches. She read the text again and tried to suppress a growing sense of unease. Was her discomfort because she thought Starr wouldn't be back now that she'd gotten resolution to her case?

No, that wasn't it. Surely she was reading too much into the terse phrasing, but she couldn't help but wonder what was going on. How had they located them? Had they found Hannah with Pratt? If not, had Pratt confessed to kidnapping Hannah? Had he confessed to kidnapping her? Had they even asked him that? As the questions mounted, she felt foolish for asking Starr to come by.

The doorbell rang, startling her out of her endless loop of questions. She picked up her phone from her nightstand and opened the video app to see Starr standing on her doorstep for the second time that evening. She spoke into the phone to tell her she'd be right there, and she jumped out of bed and headed to the door before she realized she was only wearing a slinky tank and too short shorts. She rushed back into her room, snatched a robe from the closet, and tugged it on as she made her way to the door.

Starr was by herself and she looked haggard and worn. "You must be exhausted." Catherine pulled her in and shut the door behind them. She wanted to touch her, hug her, provide some comfort, but she decided it would be best to keep a safe distance for now. "Come, sit down." She reached for Starr's jacket, and set it on a chair. "Can I get you something to eat or drink?" She smiled. "It's been a while since the omelets and knowing you, you're probably hungry again."

Starr smiled. "That's for sure. Believe it or not, I'm not hungry, but I could use a drink if you don't mind."

Catherine reached into the cabinet and pulled down a bottle of Balcones single malt. Without asking, she poured them each a few fingers in short, heavy glasses and handed one to Starr.

"I love this stuff," Starr said, and took a healthy swallow.

"I'd never heard of it before that first night we kind of shared drinks." At Starr's questioning look, Catherine said, "After Knoll pled out. At Guero's."

Starr nodded. "I remember."

"I bought a bottle right after that. I have to confess, I didn't think I'd ever be sharing it with you in my kitchen, but I'm glad you're here." The admission was big, but it felt natural. Now that she'd made it though, she was anxious to find out more. "I hate to kill your buzz, but can you tell me anything? I'm kind of dying without the details." She sensed hesitation from Starr and started to backpedal. "Look, I get it if you can't talk. I don't want you to compromise the case against Pratt by sharing things out of school. But anything you can tell me would be welcome."

Starr took another sip of whiskey and set the glass down. "I want to tell you everything, and I will when I can. For now, just know that he's in custody and Hannah's back home with her parents. He won't ever be a threat to you, or Hannah, or anyone else again."

Catherine let out a pent-up breath. "Thank God." She sagged against the counter and a second later felt Starr's arms around her, supporting her from behind.

"Are you okay?" Starr whispered in her ear.

She was and she wasn't. She felt relief at Pratt's arrest and Hannah's safe return, but there was a buzzing in her ears and the room was suddenly intensely hot. Was she having a panic attack? If so, it was nothing like the ones she'd had before because instead of feeling like she was coming out of her skin, she felt at home in her own body for the first time in a very long while. She pressed into Starr's embrace, longing to be closer to her, touched by her, held.

Starr shifted slightly. Catherine turned to find out why and suddenly their faces were inches apart. She stared into Starr's dark, hazy eyes for several seconds before turning her attention to Starr's full lips. It had been a long time since she'd been with another woman, and never one she'd felt such a strong emotional connection to, but she recognized the signs of passion. Did Starr see the same thing reflected in her expression? Catherine leaned in and took Starr's lips between her own. Soft yet firm, they were as hungry as hers, and slow touches quickly built to flaming heat, searing and then ebbing back to a gentle caress. When she pulled away to breathe, Catherine was heady with desire and unwilling to let that be the end.

Starr pulled back. "Wow."

"I need a little more information," Catherine said. "Is that a good wow, or a wow, I wish we hadn't done that?"

Starr stepped back into her arms. "Seriously, can you not tell you are making me melt?"

"I may be a little too busy melting myself."

"I want you."

"I hear a 'but.'" Catherine wanted to gloss it over, but it was important they get this right.

"Some people might say I'm taking advantage. This is a big night for you for obvious reasons. I imagine you're feeling all kind of things, and sometimes those kinds of feelings can lead a person to do things they might not otherwise do."

"Are you done?" Catherine waited until Starr nodded. "I'm an adult. I've been in therapy for years. I know what I want, and right now I want you. Russell Pratt has absolutely nothing to do with that.

Understood?" She waited and watched Starr's face shift through a few different emotions until she arrived at the right one.

"Understood. Now kiss me again, please."

Catherine pulled Starr closer, the feel of her body against her skin welcome and inviting. This time the kiss spiked with intensity, and Catherine needed more. The chains from her past and the stress of this day fell away, and she no longer cared about anything other than the way Starr felt and her compelling need to make love to her. Right now. She grasped Starr's hand. "Bed. Now."

She led the way to her bedroom, uncharacteristically unconcerned her bed was unmade and she'd left her clothes in a pile on a chair. She felt both confident and reckless, not knowing where this night would lead, but excited to find out. When they crossed the threshold to her room, she reached for Starr's sweater and pulled it over her head, sucking in a breath at the sight of her ivory skin against the burgundy demi cup bra. She traced her fingers along the edges of the satin trim before dipping her head and following the path of her fingers with her tongue, stroking gently at first and then more rapidly as her hunger grew. When Starr sagged against her, she lifted her head and gazed into Starr's dazed eyes. "Are you okay?"

Starr cleared her throat. "Okay? No. Unbelievably aroused? Absolutely." Starr reached for the ties on her robe and twisted them loose. She ran her hands up underneath Catherine's tank top, and traced her thumbs across her nipples. Catherine gasped for breath and pressed closer. Starr leaned in and whispered in her ear, "That right there. That is what you do to me."

Catherine caught Starr's lips between her own. "I can't remember the last time I've felt so aroused." She hesitated a moment before venturing a more vulnerable truth. "Maybe never."

"I want to do whatever makes you feel good." Starr's hands remained on her breasts, but still now. "I want you to be comfortable."

Comfortable. Catherine rolled the word around in her head, trying to figure out what exactly about it bothered her. Starr cared about her feelings, her comfort, her well-being. Her tender gestures should be soothing and welcome, but instead Catherine felt slightly agitated, and fairly certain comfort was the opposite of what she craved. Dr. M's words from their last session echoed. *Without risk there's no reward. The thing to remember is that your reward gets to be whatever you want it to be.*

Suddenly, she knew exactly what she wanted. She wanted Starr in every way possible, from tender touches to wild abandon, but right now she wanted to put aside the role of victim and take complete charge of everything that was about to happen between them. She reached up and placed her hands over Starr's, motioning for her to resume her touch. "I don't want to be comfortable. I want to feel every inch of your hot, naked skin sliding over mine, and I want us both to be so aroused we're on the verge of exploding. I want to come with you, again and again, for the rest of the night, to hell with the rest of the world." She paused and met Starr's darkened gaze. "That is what would make me feel good."

Starr answered by stepping back and removing the rest of her clothes. Catherine watched intently, savoring every moment. When Starr was finally naked, she stepped back into Catherine's arms and pushed the robe from her shoulders. Before it hit the floor, Starr had pulled the tank over Catherine's head and was running her hand along the inside of Catherine's boxers. "I want to make you feel all kinds of things," she said.

Catherine grabbed Starr's hand and led her to the bed. She gently pushed Starr back against the covers. "Me first." She bent down and slowly ran her tongue from Starr's navel to her chest, shuddering with pleasure when Starr arched up into her touch. She marveled at Starr's trust, her vulnerability, since she'd always guarded her own trust like treasure. Feeling Starr respond so readily to her touch brought with it a rush of confidence, and all the powerlessness she'd felt since Pratt had surfaced fell away like outdated armor. In this moment, with this amazing woman, she had complete and total control outside of the persona she projected, and it felt good. No, better than good. It felt amazing.

She took her time, lavishing Starr's breast with attention, slowly, but with increasing pressure. Encouraged by Starr's writhing body, Catherine reached down and brushed the back of her hand against Starr's thigh before running her fingers through her slick sex. She mirrored the attention with Starr's breasts, thrilled at the way Starr began to buck beneath her.

"You're incredible," Starr whispered, punctuated by a groan of arousal. "I'm so close."

Catherine slowed her pace. "Should we slow down?"

Starr clutched her wrist. "Please don't. I don't think I can hang on much longer."

Catherine spent a split second wavering between giving Starr what she wanted and taking her time to enjoy a slower build, but ultimately she decided power could be used to bestow or to control, and she didn't have to choose. She stretched her body upward and faced Starr. The trust, the vulnerability was still there, but now there was something else. Something powerful and wild.

Desire.

Starr wanted her fiercely—it was clear in the dark, urgent hunger reflected in her eyes. Catherine had no idea what her own expression told Starr, but she was desperate to show her that she desired her too, and with the same level of intensity. She leaned down and brushed her lips against Starr's, and murmured, "Are you ready to let go?"

Seconds later, as Starr's body rose to meet hers and then shuddered with orgasm, Catherine experienced the most incredible sense of release, and she too was ready to let go of a past that had held her captive to explore wherever this passionate journey with Starr might lead.

Starr woke to the sound of a phone buzzing and found Catherine's head tucked into her shoulder. She liked the sensation of waking up with Catherine nestled next to her, and willed whoever was calling to go away.

"What is it?" Catherine murmured, her eyes still closed.

She kissed Catherine's cheek. "Nothing." She reached for the phone, wishing it was true, but the text was from Fred Nelson. *Meeting in Murphy's office at nine.* Crap.

"Tell me you don't have to go."

Starr looked down at Catherine, her eyes now open and filled with a hopeful expression, and for the first time she could remember, she wished she could set aside duty for pleasure. Last night had been amazing. From the moment Catherine had taken control, she'd surrendered to the pleasure of powerlessness—not at all her normal role—but one she'd relished more than she thought possible. A flash of Catherine bent over her, lavishing her with ardent strokes of her hands and tongue, sent heat surging through her entire body, and it was as if the ripple of their last orgasm was lingering still.

She let the feeling last for a moment while she contemplated what her life might be like if she hadn't spent it being entirely focused on her career. Perhaps she could've met someone like Catherine, smart, accomplished, beautiful, years ago, and settled down into a normal life where she wasn't always on call and didn't have to deal with the gruesome side of life on a regular basis. Where she would have a sexy, passionate lover to come home to each and every night.

But she'd chosen differently, and as much as she wanted to stay here, tangled in the sheets with Catherine Landauer, she had a job to do, and it was bigger than her and her desire for her own pleasure. "I wish I could stay."

Catherine slipped out of her embrace and drew slightly away. "I get it. Can you tell me anything?"

Starr hesitated for a second before deciding Catherine deserved to know something about the case that had plagued her her entire life. "A patrol cop spotted Pratt at a convenience store in Montopolis last night and followed him to a house down the block. While we were scoping out the house, Hannah Turner showed up at the south substation. She couldn't tell us much. She'd been picked up by a man in a white pickup and taken somewhere. She was blindfolded the whole time and can't ID her abductor. At some point, he drove her to a spot in the woods and dumped her and she managed to find her way to a nearby farmhouse and the owners brought her in."

"That doesn't sound like enough to arrest Pratt. How did you manage to get a warrant?"

Starr ducked her head, contemplating the best approach. "We arrested him on the outstanding warrant for your kidnapping and your mother's murder." She saw Catherine tense up, and she rushed to explain. "It's enough to hold him until we can sort out what happened with Hannah. I know in my gut he kidnapped her, it's just a matter of getting him to confess or trip up. Besides, you and your mother deserve justice for what happened to you." She didn't bother telling Catherine about the ID with Stevens' name or that he'd refused to say a word after his arrest or that they hadn't found any evidence at the house to tie him to any crime. Instead she reached for her phone and pulled up Pratt's photo, wishing she could avoid this, especially now, but knowing it was necessary if they ever wanted closure on Catherine's past. "I can show you his picture if you want."

Catherine nodded slowly and reached for the phone. Starr waited patiently while Catherine examined it from all angles, hoping she wasn't causing Catherine additional trauma by exposing her to this step of the process.

"It's been a long time," Catherine said and her voice carried the slight lilt of a question. "But it's him."

Starr breathed a sigh of relief at the definitive response. "We're meeting this morning to review strategy." She reached out for Catherine's hand and pulled it to her lips, kissing her softly and injecting all the confidence she could muster into her words. "Trust me, we got this."

"I trust you."

Three little words, but Starr felt the portent behind them. The list of people Catherine Landauer trusted was likely very short, and Starr was proud to be among them. She vowed that she would do everything in her power to prove she was worthy of Catherine's trust. First step, leave this warm bed and meet with her boss to figure out the next steps. "I have to go."

"I know." Catherine leaned in and kissed her gently on the lips. "Call me when you can?"

"Absolutely." Starr squeezed her hand. "What are you going to do today?"

"I suppose I should go back to work now that Pratt's in custody. How long do you think I have before word gets out that I'm Jill Winfield?"

Right. Starr hadn't contemplated the publicity storm that would descend as soon as the press got wind that Jill Winfield's kidnapper had been caught. They would only be able to shield Catherine from exposure for so long before her testimony would be necessary to put Pratt away for the rest of his life. Starr only hoped that before that happened, they would be able to find enough evidence to charge him with Hannah Turner's case and then Catherine might not have to be exposed to all the scrutiny that went with a public trial. "As long as I can manage."

Catherine nodded. "Fair enough." She stared deep into Starr's eyes. "And when will I see you again?"

Starr stared back, ignoring the voice in the back of her brain whispering that Catherine was now a witness in a major case, and they had no business seeing each other on a personal level, at least not until Pratt was behind bars for good. She'd worked her whole life to see justice done, no matter what steps she'd had to take to accomplish the ends. Why should now be any different? Was putting Pratt away more important than hanging on to the incredible way Catherine caused her to come alive? She didn't know the answer, but she did know that she wasn't ready to give up on whatever this was growing between them. "As soon as I can manage."

CHAPTER EIGHTEEN

"I don't know why I'm here," Catherine said, leaning back into her favorite chair in Dr. M's office. She was midway through her session and she was well aware she'd mostly rambled away her time. "Things are going well. Pratt's in custody. Hannah Turner's safe and sound."

Dr. M nodded. "You seem a little agitated."

"Well, that's normal, right? I mean, I've spent my whole life looking over my shoulder. Suddenly, there's no longer any need to hide, but it's like I'm two different people. The little girl who was powerless and the adult who spent her life protecting her. I don't know who I am anymore."

"Maybe you're both. And that's okay. Jill is safe now, and Catherine can finally have a life."

Catherine picked at a piece of lint on her pants while she contemplated Dr. M's assessment. "I want to. Have a life that is. I don't ever remember feeling that way before. I've spent all these years merely existing."

"It's natural that you're hesitant. There's no rush."

The word rush caused Catherine to slip into a memory of last night in bed with Starr. She'd been in a hurry to embrace their attraction, and also in the mood to slowly savor every minute of their love-making. She'd never experienced anything like the passion they'd shared, and all she could think about was doing it again and how devastated she'd feel if she couldn't. She blamed her

CARSEN TAITE

euphoria for the words that spilled out. "I slept with Starr Rio last night. It was amazing, but I don't have a clue what comes next." She delivered the statement without making eye contact, certain that if she witnessed Dr. M's reaction firsthand, she'd lose her nerve, but once the words were out, she slowly raised her head and met Dr. M's surprisingly neutral expression. "Aren't you going to say something?"

Dr. M cleared her throat. "Wow."

Catherine felt a smile slide across her lips, pleased to have elicited the reaction. "Yeah, that's pretty much what I felt."

"I'd ask you how you feel about it, but it's pretty clear you're happy."

Catherine paused before answering. She *was* happy—a level of happy she didn't think she'd ever felt before, and while the emotion excited her, it scared her too. "No judgment?"

"Do you really think I sit here judging you, ever?" Dr. M didn't wait for an answer. "Look, I can tell you're happy, but I can also tell you have other feelings as well. Do you want to talk about them?"

Like always, Dr. M had honed right in on the crux of the issue. Yes, she was happy. Ecstatic even, but like any bits of happiness in her life, they were mixed up with other feelings: uncertainty, caution, fear. The difference now was that she wasn't focused on what might go wrong, only on the possibility that she might have a future where she could be with someone who knew and accepted her for everything she was. "I do have other feelings, but I don't want to talk about them. Not right now, anyway. Right now, I'd like to stick with happy."

Dr. M smiled. "Fair enough. I'm here whenever you're ready."

A few minutes later, Catherine pulled out of the parking lot of Dr. M's office building, feeling for the first time in her life like there might be an end to her therapy. Not now of course, but someday. In the meantime, she was ready to embrace whatever came next, and she hoped Starr was a part of it.

She reached for her phone to check and see if Starr had texted any updates, or really just texted anything at all. The blank screen left her feeling somewhat disappointed, but she refused to let it quell her mood. She would go to the office and occupy her mind with work until she heard from Starr. For the first time she could remember, the idea of work took a back burner to what she really wanted to do.

Starr paused at Murphy's door and stared at the second text in a row from Pearson. Like the first one, it simply said, *Call me.* She briefly considered complying, but she was already a few minutes late for this meeting, so she made a mental note to contact Pearson as soon as she was done. She entered Murphy's office without knocking, a first for her, but she figured she deserved some deference for having helped apprehend Hannah Turner's kidnapper. What she didn't expect was the stern look on Murphy's face and the smirk on Nelson's when she entered the room.

"Sit down," Murphy said, pointing to the chair directly in front of his desk.

"What's going on?" Starr asked, ignoring his command.

"How about you tell us?" Nelson said. "Not only did you authorize an arrest for a suspect over whom we don't have any jurisdiction or evidence, but then you spent the night with the only witness in the case against Pratt. Would you like to explain?"

Starr's stomach fell, and she suddenly knew why Pearson had been trying to reach her. She should've known the patrol unit assigned to watch Catherine would've reported any unusual activity, and a prosecutor staying the night definitely constituted unusual. How could she have been so stupid? A couple of hours ago, she'd celebrated her ability to finally let her personal life take precedence over her professional life. Would she have celebrated if she'd known how quickly her career dreams would come tumbling down around her?

Damn it. She'd handle this the same way she handled everything else in her life—head-on. "I don't have anything to explain. I went to Catherine Landauer's house to talk to her about the case."

"And that took all night?" Nelson said, his tone incredulous.

"It took as long as it took." She met his stare with as much defiance as she could muster. "I don't see how that's any of your business."

"Because if you're personally involved with the only witness who claims that Pratt is our guy, then we've got a huge conflict." Nelson turned to Murphy. "If it were up to me, I'd replace her right now."

Starr started to protest, but Murphy spoke first. "Let's dial things back a bit," he said in his well-practiced politician's way of trying to balance all sides. "Starr, is there anything I should worry about here?"

She had a choice and it was a big one. If she were in Murphy's position and one of her prosecutors had just slept with a witness, she'd remove them from the case without a second thought. But she wasn't just any prosecutor. She was a star player, and she'd spent her entire life dedicated to putting criminals behind bars. Murphy had to know she would never intentionally jeopardize an investigation. But no matter what her intention, she had placed this prosecution in jeopardy, and apparently her indiscretion was about to not only cost her this case, but it could potentially tank her chance to take over Murphy's job. Nelson was staring at her waiting for her to answer, and she knew he was salivating, but she couldn't lie. She had to come clean and trust that Murphy would believe that she hadn't compromised her ability to handle this case. She took a deep breath. "May we have a moment alone?"

Nelson started shaking his head, but Murphy motioned for him to leave the room. When Nelson was finally gone, Starr rushed to explain. "Whatever my personal feelings for Catherine Landauer, I would never let them get in the way of how I handled this case."

Murphy sighed. "That may be true, but you know as well as I do that it's the appearance of impropriety that matters, not whether you actually did anything wrong."

"I know."

"What the hell were you thinking?"

She wanted to face him, to give him some rational explanation, but the plain truth was she hadn't been thinking at all. She'd given in to feelings of attraction and lust without any regard for how her actions might impact this case. Not just her own role in it, but the case overall. A good defense attorney would have a heyday if they knew she'd been sleeping with the key witness within hours of Pratt's arrest. They would play it like Starr had brought home a trophy to gain a lover. "It just happened. I wish it hadn't."

Even as she spoke the last words, she wasn't sure if they were true. Did she really regret her night with Catherine or only the fallout? She didn't know the answer, but this wasn't the time to ruminate on her mistakes. It was time to face the consequences. "What happens now?"

"I'm pulling you from the case. Pearson can work with Nelson. The task force will dig in and do their best to find out who kidnapped Hannah Turner before the mayor fires the chief of police and makes this office look incompetent."

Starr cycled through his words, trying to make sense of what he was saying. "But what about Pratt?"

"You mean the guy you think is Russell Pratt? Pearson will keep an eye on Albert Stevens. If he really is Russell Pratt, we'll notify Albuquerque so they can come get him, but your decision to have him arrested last night was premature. We don't have anything to tie him to Hannah Turner or the Winfield case, and Albert Stevens has no criminal record."

"But Catherine ID'd him as her kidnapper." Starr tried hard to keep the desperation out of her voice, but she couldn't quell her rising fear.

"When? During pillow talk with the lead prosecutor on the case?"

"You could put him in a lineup and let her ID him there."

He waved his hand to indicate he was done discussing the matter. "That's Albuquerque's decision, not ours, but I'll be damned if we're going to taint their case any further. We need to get out of it and fast. Besides, for all you know, Hannah Turner's abduction is a copycat crime. We'll keep a close eye on Stevens or whoever he is, and if Albuquerque wants to send someone out to question him about the Winfield case, we'll assist in any way we can. If we turn up credible evidence he was involved in Hannah's case, we can rearrest him. Right now, we're focused on damage control. He was released this morning."

Starr's knees buckled and she braced a hand on the chair. "What?"

"It's not your problem anymore. I'm not going to take any disciplinary action against you, and I'll make sure Nelson keeps his mouth shut, but you're off this case. Understood?"

Starr nodded slowly, but the only thing she completely understood was that she'd let Catherine down and she may very well have tanked her career at the same time.

❖

Catherine was just pulling into the parking lot of her office when Starr called. She answered on the first ring, not caring if she appeared too eager. "I was just thinking about you."

"And I haven't stopped thinking about you since I left this morning. I wish I could've stayed in bed."

Catherine's heart skipped at the idea Starr had been thinking about her and the time they'd shared, but she thought she also heard some reservation in Starr's voice. "Is everything okay?"

"We should talk. Where are you?"

And just like that, Catherine's heart went from skipping beats in a good way to thudding into the quick pattern she associated with the desire for flight. "What's wrong?"

"Nothing. Are you at home?"

Starr was lying. Catherine was certain, and she wasn't about to wait for answers. "I need to know what's wrong. Tell me now." She heard Starr sigh and counted the seconds until Starr replied, wishing she could reach through the phone and claw the words from her throat.

"Pratt's been released."

"On bond?" Catherine asked, sure she must've misunderstood the meaning.

"No. He's been released free and clear. Murphy isn't going to charge him. Not now anyway."

Starr's words echoed in her head like booming thunder, and like thunder, they warned of a storm to come. Catherine braced against the torrent of thoughts Starr's revelation had unleashed. She started to ask Starr to repeat what she'd said, because surely she'd misheard, but she couldn't bear hearing the words again if they were true. "You have to fix it. You're the prosecutor assigned to the case. He'll listen to you."

"He won't. I'm no longer on the case. Apparently, someone told Murphy I spent the night at your house and now they think I have a conflict. He tossed me off the case, and since Nelson knows all about it, any chance I had at election is probably doomed."

The dull roar subsided and now all Catherine felt was anger. "Russell Pratt is free and on the loose and all you care about is your electability?"

"No, of course not. You're the first person I called because I care about you. I wanted you to hear about Pratt from me. I promise I'll do whatever I can."

Catherine wanted to shout that whatever Starr could do it wouldn't be enough. They'd arrested Russell Pratt and let him go. It was like her childhood all over again, except this time she should've known better than to trust the authorities, but she'd done it anyway. And now the press would get wind that Jill Winfield was alive and well in Austin, Texas, and they'd start knocking on her door, ready to mine for reader gold, deep in the pages of her life.

"Catherine, are you still there?"

She stared at the phone in her hand. She was here and she wasn't. She was Catherine and she was Jill. She'd tried so hard to separate the two, but despite all her efforts, here she was, forced to confront her past no better armed now than she had been then.

"Catherine, please say something. Tell me where you are. I need to see you, make sure you are okay."

She wasn't okay, and that was something no one else could fix, not Dr. M, not Starr. She'd been foolish to believe she could have a life outside of the past that framed her. All she wanted was to be alone, which was what she'd done effortlessly for years. Why was it so difficult now? She braced for the strength to do the only thing that would protect her from any more harm. "I'm hanging up. Please leave me alone."

She heard Starr protest, but didn't keep the call connected long enough to make out the words. It was for the best. She turned her phone off, slipped it in her pocket, got out of the car, and made her way into the office, thankful she'd given Doris time off. Solitude was exactly what she needed to sort out where she'd go from here, both literally and figuratively. Maybe it was time for a move. Time to find a place where no one knew her past and where Russell Pratt could no longer taunt her.

She'd barely reached for the light switch in her office when she heard the unmistakable sound of someone racking the slide of a gun. She froze in place, certain she knew what was about to happen and powerless to stop it. The next sound she heard confirmed her deepest fears.

"Little Jill Winfield is all grown up now."

CHAPTER NINETEEN

Pearson picked up on the first ring. "I've been trying to reach you for hours."

"I know," Starr said as she left Murphy's office and headed to her own. "Believe me, I know. I had to meet with Murphy, and I'm pretty sure you know why."

He sighed into the phone. "Don't say I didn't try to warn you."

"I appreciate the attempt." Starr paused, unsure exactly how to broach the real reason for her call. She'd been going nuts since Catherine had hung up on her. She contemplated driving to Catherine's house or office, but she didn't need the patrol unit watching either to report back to Murphy that she was ignoring his orders. Still, she needed to know where Catherine was, if only so she could rest assured she was being watched over now that Pratt was a free man. She had to trust Pearson if she wanted the information, and she plunged in. "I need to know where Catherine is."

"Don't you think it's best if you stayed away for a while?"

She appreciated the gentle way he admonished her. "Yes, but this isn't about that."

"I think I know what it's about, and I get it, but you need to lay low for a bit."

"I just want to know that she's safe," she spoke the half-truth with as much strength as she could muster. "If I knew where she was, I could stop worrying."

"I'm guessing she's probably at home."

"Can you check with the patrol unit?"

"What?" A pause, then, "Oh, they were pulled this morning. Chief's orders."

"What?" It was Starr's turn to be surprised. "But what about Pratt? He knows where she works, probably knows where she lives. What's to stop him from going after her, especially now that he thinks he's in the clear?"

"We're going to keep tabs on Stevens for a while."

Starr heard the equivocation in his phrasing, and she barely resisted screaming into the phone that Stevens's real name was Pratt. "Do you know where he is right this second?"

"Last thing he said when he left was that he was going to his attorney's office. Chief had us stand down for now. Don't need a lawsuit claiming we harassed him by following him to his lawyer's office after the charges were dropped. But I promise you we'll keep an eye out."

Starr barely heard most of what he'd said after he said the words "attorney's office," and dread swept through her. Could it be so simple? She had to know. She started to ask Pearson to join her, but hesitated. No sense getting both of them in trouble, and she'd rather see Catherine for the first time alone. She'd check out her hunch and maybe, just maybe, she'd be able to get Catherine to listen to her, forgive her for the way she'd botched the case and whatever had happened between them.

A few minutes later, she started her car and while it was warming up, she sent one more text to Catherine. *I know I'm the last person you want to talk to right now, but I need to know you're okay.* She hit send and managed not to look at the screen again until she pulled up outside Catherine's office. She parked beside Catherine's car, pleased her instincts had been correct and hoping that because the rest of the parking lot was empty, she would be able to talk to Catherine alone. The first thing she did when she shut off the ignition was check her phone, but Catherine hadn't responded to any of her texts. She could hear Murphy's and Pearson's voices in her head, telling her to drive away, but she was already committed. She'd go in and say her piece. What happened next would be entirely up to Catherine.

❖

Catherine stared at Pratt, marveling at how much he had changed, but how familiar he seemed. His hair was gray now and his skin was weathered, but the familiar smile was present—the one she'd found engaging when she'd first met him, but later learned was a mask designed to trick her into submission.

"Come in. Have a seat."

The gun in his hand made it clear his words weren't a request, but a command. Her gun. The one she kept in her desk for emergencies. The irony almost made her laugh. "What do you want?" she asked, pushing as much strength into her voice as she could muster.

"I want you to sit down and talk to me. It's been a long time, and I'd like to get reacquainted with you."

Standing felt like the only advantage she had, and she was loath to give it up, but her few seconds of hesitation had him waving the barrel of her gun, and she reluctantly complied, selecting the chair farthest from him and closest to the door. Her mind started spinning with possibilities. No one knew where she was, and the circle of people who might care was so small it was unlikely anyone would notice her missing for days. She'd canceled meetings and postponed court appearances for the rest of the week, and just this morning she'd told Doris not to come in until next Monday. Her next appointment with Dr. M wasn't until late next week. Starr had been persistently texting her, but she'd made it crystal clear she wanted to be left alone.

Whatever Pratt chose to do to her, no one would know about it until it was too late to help, and for once the isolation she used to embrace felt more like a restraint than a comfort. She was on her own, and if she wanted to survive this encounter, she would have to do the rescuing all on her own.

But the past weighted her down, and she sunk farther into the chair as if she were the girl she'd once been, trying desperately to keep from drawing Pratt's prurient attention.

"Tell me how you've been," he asked. "I want to hear all about your life since you decided to walk out on me and the plans that I had for us."

Catherine struggled to hide her shudder, but he was watching her so intently, she feared he would pick up on her revulsion for him. Her younger self had survived by being compliant. Never raising her voice, never crossing him. Biding her time until the opportunity to escape presented itself and she could slip away. But as she stared down the barrel of her own gun, she realized there would be no such opportunity now. She didn't know exactly what Pratt wanted, but she suspected he wasn't here to take her as his bride. No, now that the cops had released him, he was here to get rid of any evidence of the crime he'd committed so many years ago. The tactics she'd once employed would be of no use to her now, and she reached deep to summon every bit of strength she'd gained back over the years.

"I've been great. Never better than since I escaped your filthy den. What do you care anyway? You moved on, or was Hannah Turner not what you were looking for?"

His grin was feral, no longer reminiscent of the friendly handyman who'd lured her from her bed in the middle of the night. "Little Hannah was exactly what I was looking for. High profile, guaranteed to arouse your curiosity. It was a bit of a challenge finding the exact same bows, but I managed."

"You expect me to believe you've been lying in wait all these years for the perfect opportunity to bust back into my life? How did you even find me?" She asked the question to goad him, but she really did want to know how he'd managed to track her down. At some point, years ago, she'd stopped furtively looking over her shoulder, but she'd kept her circle small not only to keep her privacy, but as a protective measure. Had her efforts been completely in vain?

"At first, I had to hide because of the lies you told the police, but that was simply a test of my patience and faith. Your defiance robbed me of my promised life. I never married. God said I wasn't worthy after I'd let the pure gift he'd sent to me escape. I wandered the country, lost and desolate, but then I came across that interview where you got so angry with that reporter, and I knew then that God had led me back to you."

Catherine racked her brain, and then it came to her. She'd always been careful about avoiding the press, using Doris to fend them off, but the week before Peter Knoll's trial started, she'd been accosted by Gloria Flynn as she left the courthouse. In Gloria's usual style, she fired off incendiary questions designed to provoke, and that day, after a particularly grueling day hashing out pretrial motions, Catherine had lost her cool. Her responses had been terse and temperamental—the exact kind of sensationalist sound bites pseudo journalists like Gloria loved to air on the evening news. She recalled her dismay that the clip of her interview was picked up by one of the cable news channels featuring stories of domestic abuse, but she'd simply been annoyed at the fact she'd lost her cool, when apparently, she should've been worried about the fact she'd be recognized. "I can't believe you could tell that was me."

He stood and walked toward her. Catherine braced against his approach, wanting to run, but knowing she couldn't outdistance a bullet. She counted his steps while her eyes swept the room, searching for something, anything she could use to defend herself, finally landing on a heavy crystal paperweight, a gift from Doris, on the far edge of her desk. She glanced away to keep Pratt from noticing, but she mentally calculated how many of her own steps it would take to reach the paperweight. As he drew closer, she feigned a stumble and clutched the edge of the desk to right her balance, her hand almost within reach of her potential weapon.

He was right next to her now and she could feel his warm, jagged breath on her neck as he reached up and touched the skin just to the left of her eye, caressing it with his thumb. "You still do that thing when you get angry, where you can't stop blinking. You were so angry when we first started to live together until you realized it was meant to be. I thought you would've outgrown that little tic, but I'm glad you didn't since that was what led me back to you."

Catherine flinched at his touch and her first instinct was to shut down, to let whatever was about to happen unfold outside her body, while she curled inward, the same way she'd done time after time when she was Jill Winfield, small and powerless. She felt her eyes drift shut and a dull roar drowned out her thoughts.

He ran his thumb down the side of her face. "Your voice, your eyes. I memorized everything about you. It wasn't chance that I saw that interview. It was divine intervention that lead me back to you."

His words were like sharp tacks, piercing through her defenses, stabbing her awake. Jill would've burrowed deeper, resisting the urge to inflame the monster, but she wasn't a small, helpless little girl anymore. She was a strong, fierce, independent woman who'd fought to keep her past from defining her. Jill had managed to escape her captor, but she'd never been free. Catherine had to finish the job, and this was her chance, her moment. With a quick glance at the gun hanging at Pratt's side, she lunged for the paperweight and in a perfect arc of motion, swung it against his head.

Starr pushed open the door to Catherine's building, a little surprised to find it unlocked. Of course, Catherine probably didn't realize she no longer had a patrol unit watching out for her, but Starr planned to remedy that as soon as possible. First order of business, make amends for her careless way of breaking the news about Pratt's release, and then assure Catherine she planned to do everything in her power to make sure he was brought to justice for the harm he'd inflicted on her, her mother, and Hannah Turner. There was no doubt in her mind that Pratt was responsible for Catherine's mother's murder, and both kidnappings—she didn't give a damn what anyone had to say about memory loss or lack of evidence. Her gut was all she needed, and she trusted her instincts implicitly.

She was only a couple of steps from Catherine's office when she heard the sound of voices. Thinking perhaps Catherine was on the phone, she debated her options. It wasn't cool to eavesdrop, but she didn't want to leave and miss this opportunity to catch Catherine alone. She was just starting to back away when she heard a man's voice say, "It was divine intervention that lead me back to you."

Pratt. He sounded as slick and smooth as he had last night when he'd politely refused to answer their questions. But he wasn't in a holding cell now. He was here in Catherine's office. Holy shit. Starr's first instinct was to call Pearson, but he was miles away at police headquarters. She could go out to her car and get her gun, but what if he heard her or did something to Catherine while she was out of the building? She did a quick scan of the room, and settled on a large vase with a dried flower arrangement. She carefully extracted the flowers, hefted the vase on her shoulder, and tiptoed toward Catherine's office, but before she reached the door she heard a loud cry followed by sounds of a scuffle. Being careful was no longer a priority, and Starr rushed toward the sounds, vase over her head, ready to be launched in Catherine's defense.

But when she entered the room, it took her a moment to process the scene. Pratt was lying on the floor next to an overturned chair, bleeding from a large gash on his face, apparently unconscious. Catherine was a few feet away, bent down and reaching for a gun on the floor. She looked up and met Starr's eyes.

Starr looked away for a second to make sure Pratt was still down before asking Catherine, "Are you okay?"

"Yes, but you should leave."

Starr looked at the gun, at Pratt, and back at Catherine, and the pieces clicked into place. She saw Catherine reach for the gun again. "Wait."

"Starr, this doesn't concern you."

"It does." She injected calm she didn't feel into her voice. She set the vase down and reached for her phone. "I'm going to call for help. Pearson will be right here, and he'll arrest Pratt."

Catherine looked at the gun and back at Starr. "They already did that. It didn't take."

"That's my fault. I acted prematurely. If I'd been more thorough, followed the rules, we could've made the charges stick."

"I need you to leave because you can't be here for what I'm about to do."

"You want to kill him. You think I don't understand that urge, but you're wrong." Starr read surprise in Catherine's eyes, and she seized on it to try to distract her. "I want to kill him too. It would be easier if people like Pratt didn't exist at all. I have a great conviction rate, but the defendants who walked are the ones I remember the most. The ones that keep me up at night." She risked taking a step closer to Catherine. "After what you've been through, I can only imagine how you would want to absolutely destroy him."

"Then you must know that I have to do this, and you can't stop me."

Starr heard the hard edge in Catherine's voice and hated the man who had put it there just like she hated everything Catherine had had to endure, and with that realization came the confidence she would do anything in her power to protect Catherine, to keep her safe. The intimacy they'd shared was only a taste of what they could have together, and she was hungry for more. She would not stand in Catherine's way, but she had to fight for a chance at a future with her. She raised her hands in the air.

"I won't stop you. If you want to kill him, I'll stand here and watch you do it. I'll tell Pearson you did it in self-defense. I'll keep your secret until my dying day." She took a breath to steady her voice. "But, Catherine, I know in my soul that killing him will wreck you. You've spent your entire career fighting to make sure justice is done, and while right now, in this moment, you may think that killing him is just, you know in your heart it isn't. He deserves to be punished, and I will do everything in my power to see that he is, but if you take on the role of executioner, you will die inside because you are not a killer. You're not like him. I couldn't have fallen in love with you if you were."

She stopped abruptly at the surprised expression on Catherine's face. She'd surprised herself by the admission, but now that the words were out, she had no regrets. She had fallen in love with Catherine, with her fierce independence and strength, and she prayed she would get a chance to see her feelings through.

"Do you mean it?" Catherine asked.

"I absolutely do," Starr said.

At that moment, Russell Pratt grunted and started to sit up. Starr saw Catherine flick a glance at the gun, and then back at her. She shook her head and delivered a swift kick to what she hoped was Pratt's kidney. He groaned and curled up in a ball, while Starr ran over, grabbed the gun in one hand, and put her arm around Catherine. "Let's call Pearson and get this piece of shit back behind bars."

CHAPTER TWENTY

S tarr pulled the car alongside the curb and cut the engine. "Are you sure you're up for this?"

Catherine looked up into her eyes, and Starr was touched by the strength she saw reflected there. It had been a month since Pratt's rearrest, but Catherine had dealt with every aspect of the case like a heroine instead of a victim.

"I promise, I'm good," Catherine said. "I want to do this."

"Okay, but if you change your mind, we're out of here."

As they climbed the steps to Mayor Turner's front door, Starr reflected on how much had changed since she was last here. The lack of urgency was the first thing that she noted. Russell Pratt had plead guilty and was awaiting sentencing, and Hannah Turner was safe at home, although Starr knew from experience in the child abuse unit that Hannah's life would never be quite the same. This time the idea to visit had come from the mayor, and curiosity caused them both to comply with the request. Linda Turner opened the door before they could knock.

"Thank you for coming." She reached out a hand to Catherine and welcomed them both in. "I know you've been through a lot."

Catherine nodded, and Starr gently pressed her hand in the small of Catherine's back as a show of support.

"I'm glad to see you under different circumstances," Catherine said.

"Most definitely." The mayor ushered them back to the den and invited them to sit. "Would either of you like some tea or coffee, or anything at all really?"

Starr cleared her throat. "I don't want to appear rude, but I think we're both very curious about why we're here."

"I've always admired your ability to cut to the chase." Linda folded her hands in her lap. "I have two matters to discuss. The first one involves you directly, so I'll start there. Starr, I would like to pledge my support to your campaign for district attorney."

Starr flicked a glance at Catherine who raised her eyebrows. They'd had several discussions about their future, but in all of them Starr had insisted she was done with the political side of criminal justice. She'd settled on continuing her work as a career prosecutor, in the trenches, where she felt she could do the most good. Catherine told her she supported whatever she chose to do but had encouraged her not to abandon her dreams too quickly.

"I appreciate your offer, Madam Mayor, but I've decided not to run."

Linda brushed the air with her hand as if she could erase Starr's words from existence. "Call me, Linda. Both of you. And as for you not running, well, that would be a travesty. If it wasn't for you, Russell Pratt would be a free man. Murphy's gotten too gun-shy, pardon the term, and that first assistant of his, Nelson, is cut from the same cloth. We need new blood. Someone creative who is willing to take risks, when it matters, to see that justice is done."

Starr reflected that this was the first time in her career she was actually being praised for skirting the rules, but she wanted to make sure credit went where it was due. "The truth is, Catherine here is the reason Russell Pratt is in custody. She risked her life to take him down."

"I'm aware, but since I doubt Ms. Landauer has any interest in running for public office, you'll have to do." Linda grinned. "Seriously, Starr, the party has already conducted polling, and you're easily the front runner. I'm merely taking the side of a winner. It's an easy decision." She glanced purposefully at the two of them seated so close together. "And not to be a total political hack, but if

Catherine is by your side during the election, it's only going to boost your numbers."

Starr shook her head. "There's absolutely no way I would use the press about Catherine's case to try to win an election."

"You don't have to. The press is already there. And for the record, I was referring to the fact that you make a stunning couple."

Starr looked at Catherine who merely smiled and shook her head. Linda was right—they did make a stunning couple, but Starr didn't believe that was the sole motivation for endorsement. "I've already made up my mind." Starr turned to Catherine. "It's the best thing for both of us. Right?"

Catherine inclined her head. "Are you asking for my honest answer?"

"Of course."

"There was a time when I thought your methods were a bit, shall we say, questionable. That you'd do just about anything to win a case, even if you wound up trampling on a defendant's rights."

"And now?"

"And now, I think it's possible that I was viewing you through a jaded lens, based on my own experience. What I know now is that you are incredibly passionate about getting justice for the victims you represent. You're not perfect, but you care, and you care deeply. About people. Someone like Nelson only cares about clearing cases and winning stats. The citizens of Travis County deserve better than that." Catherine reached over and grabbed her hand. "They deserve someone like you."

Starr met Catherine's eyes and, in that moment, she knew she'd do anything and everything Catherine wanted her to do. She opened her mouth to answer the mayor, when she heard a voice behind them.

"Mom, Sally said you wanted to see me."

She turned to see Hannah Turner standing in the doorway. Unlike the photo they'd shown around when she was missing, this version of Hannah was somber, more somber than a young girl should be, a natural consequence of what she'd been through. Starr had had very little interaction with her since she'd turned up. Pam had worked with Hannah before her grand jury testimony, and although all Hannah had to offer was circumstance and an ID of Pratt's voice, her testimony, along with Catherine's had been sufficient enough to indict Pratt on some serious charges, including the murder of Catherine's mother, that would keep him behind bars the rest of his life.

"Hi, Hannah," Linda said, beckoning her to enter. "There's a couple of people here I want you to meet." She pointed to Starr. "This is Ms. Rio. She works for the DA's office, and she helped look for you when you were missing." She turned to Catherine. "And this is Ms. Landauer. She…" Her voice faltered, and she turned to Catherine. "I'm sorry, but I just realized how rude it is of me not to have checked with you about this first, but I was hoping maybe you and Hannah could talk about, well…"

Starr raised a hand to protest. If she'd known she was bringing Catherine here for an ambush, she never would've agreed, but Catherine answered before she could get her words out.

"I'd love to talk to you, Hannah. Any chance I could get you to show me your room?"

Starr watched as Hannah's eyes brightened for a second and then dimmed again. "I guess."

Catherine stood. "Excellent. Your mom and Ms. Rio have a lot to talk about. Show me the way."

Starr watched her walk away, more in awe of Catherine than she'd thought possible.

"She's amazing," Linda said.

"She is."

"She'll make a great asset on the campaign trail."

"I haven't decided yet," Starr said, but Catherine's little speech from before echoed loud, and she knew she was leaning toward a run.

"You have some time still. I'm confident you'll make the right decision."

Starr stared at the doorway Catherine and Hannah had just passed through. She'd already made one very excellent decision and that was admitting she'd fallen in love with Catherine. Should she try her luck again?

❖

Catherine followed Hannah into her room and pretended she was seeing it for the first time. Hannah pointed at the bed. "You can sit there if you want."

"Thanks," Catherine said, setting aside one of the pillows to make room.

"Mom says that the same man who took me took you when you were little."

"That's true. I was around the same age as you. Obviously, since I'm old now, it was a long time ago." She offered a small grin, hoping a tinge of levity would score her some points.

Hannah returned the grin, but after a few seconds, it faded. "Why did he do it?"

Because he's crazy? Because he could? Catherine could opine all day about the motivations of Russell Pratt, but at the end of the day, she was only left with more questions than answers. "I wish I knew. There are some people who think the rules don't apply to them and they do things that don't make sense to the rest of us. That guy? He's one of those people." She smoothed the quilt on the bed. "I'm sorry about what happened to you."

"I'm sorry about what happened to you too."

"Thanks. Like I said, it was a long time ago."

"How long?"

"Over twenty years."

Hannah kicked at the carpet with the toe of her sneaker. "Does it still bother you?"

"I wish I could say no, but it does sometimes. I go see someone to talk about it when it gets bad."

"Like a shrink?"

Catherine hid her surprise at the frank question and answered in kind. "Yep. It helps."

"Mom wants me to see one. Maybe I will."

"I'm no shrink, but if you ever want to talk, I'm here for you."

"Thanks. Mom wants me to tell her everything, but when I start to talk, she gets upset, and I know it sounds selfish, but then we wind up talking about her feelings…Was your mom like that?"

Catherine reached out a hand and Hannah clasped her fingers. Her aunt had been the same. And as for Hannah's question about her mother, she decided telling Hannah that Pratt had killed her mother would defeat the purpose of telling her she got where Hannah was coming from. "Everyone was like that for a while. It's hard to understand unless you've been through something like this yourself." She looked Hannah straight in the eyes. "I mean it. You can call me anytime."

Hannah nodded soberly. They talked for a few more minutes about how surreal it was to reenter normal life after what they'd both gone through. The conversation felt natural, and Catherine found it easy to share feelings with Hannah she'd rarely shared with anyone else. When they finally went back downstairs to where Starr and Linda Turner were waiting, Catherine's heart ached for the painful memories this little girl would carry with her for the rest of her life. Her only comfort came from knowing that Hannah wasn't alone because she had family and a community that cared about her and who had surrounded her with love and protection.

Catherine's mind strayed to Doris who'd fussed over her since Pratt's arrest, Jack Pearson who stopped by the office on a weekly basis ostensibly just to check in, and her friends from law school, Lisa and Pam, who'd worked at the courthouse with her all these years without knowing her past, but now that they did, they'd banded together to make sure she knew she had friends she could confide in. For the first time in her life, Catherine knew she too had a family and community that cared about her, and the most important member of her circle was Starr, who'd saved her life by convincing her it wasn't worth throwing away to seek revenge, who loved her unconditionally, and with whom Catherine couldn't imagine living without. As she descended the last step, she took Starr's hand, not caring about appearances or elections or conflicts of interest. She leaned close to Starr and whispered, "Are you ready to go, Ms. DA?"

Starr's eyes darkened. "Yes, please."

Once they were back in the car, Catherine asked Starr to take her to Jo's.

"Are you craving coffee?" Starr asked as she placed the key in the ignition.

"I'm craving you, but I want to talk first, and I'm scared if we go right back to my place, there will be no talking."

"Sounds ominous." Starr didn't start the car, instead turning in her seat to face Catherine. "Don't you think we've had enough ominous lately?"

Catherine smiled at the wistful tone in Starr's voice and found it hard to remember why she'd wasted any time thinking they had nothing in common. "You're not at all what I expected you to be."

"Tell me that's a good thing. Come on, don't leave a girl hanging."

"It's a very good thing. I've spent my life seeing people through the lens of what happened to me. But since I've met you, I see the world in a different way." She reached out and drew Starr's hand to her lips and gently kissed her fingers. "A good way. A way with a bright future."

"This is no longer sounding ominous. I like it." Starr wiggled her fingers. "I like this too."

"Promise me you'll run."

Starr pretended to pout. "And here I was thinking you were talking about us."

Catherine closed her fingers over Starr's. "I was. I am. But promise me. We all need more Starr Rios running point on making the world a better place, present company included."

"Who could turn down such an impassioned plea?" Starr grinned. "I'll do it under one condition."

"Name it."

"You'll be by my side every step of the way. Not just through this election, but through everything. Falling deeper in love, making a family, growing old together. Nothing we can do to make the world a better place will matter if we don't get to share the journey."

Overcome with emotion, Catherine closed her eyes and breathed deep, telling herself this was really happening. That little Jill would one day grow up to break the chains of her past and find true love was a possibility she'd never considered, never thought possible.

When she opened her eyes, Starr was still there, patiently waiting for her response, and Catherine knew she was finally free to have the life she'd never let herself dream, and there was no one else she wanted to share it with more. "Let's go make a life together."

THE END

About the Author

Carsen Taite's goal as an author is to spin tales with plot lines as interesting as the cases she encountered in her career as a criminal defense lawyer. She is the award-winning author of over twenty novels of romance and romantic intrigue, including the Luca Bennett Bounty Hunter series, the Lone Star Law series, and the Legal Affairs romances.

Books Available from Bold Strokes Books

30 Dates in 30 Days by Elle Spencer. A busy lawyer tries to find love the fast way—thirty dates in thirty days. (978-1-63555-498-4)

Finding Sky by Cass Sellars. Skylar Addison's search for a career intersects with her new boss's search for butterflies, but Skylar can't forgive Jess's intrusion into her life. (978-1-63555-521-9)

Hammers, Strings, and Beautiful Things by Morgan Lee Miller. While on tour with the biggest pop star in the world, rising musician Blair Bennett falls in love for the first time while coping with loss and depression. (978-1-63555-538-7)

Heart of a Killer by Yolanda Wallace. Contract killer Santana Masters's only interest is her next assignment—until a chance meeting with a beautiful stranger tempts her to change her ways. (978-1-63555-547-9)

Leading the Witness by Carsen Taite. When defense attorney Catherine Landauer reluctantly becomes the key witness in prosecutor Starr Rio's latest criminal trial, their hearts, careers, and lives may be at risk. (978-1-63555-512-7)

No Experience Required by Kimberly Cooper Griffin. Izzy Treadway has resigned herself to a life without romance because of her bipolar illness but wonders what she's gotten herself into when she agrees to write a book about love. (978-1-63555-561-5)

One Walk in Winter by Georgia Beers. Olivia Santini and Hayley Boyd Markham might be rivals at work, but they discover that lonely hearts often find company in the most unexpected of places. (978-1-63555-541-7)

The Inn at Netherfield Green by Aurora Rey. Advertising executive Lauren Montgomery and gin distiller Camden Crawley don't agree on anything except saving the Rose & Crown, the old English pub that's brought them together. (978-1-63555-445-8)

Top of Her Game by M. Ullrich. When it comes to life on the field and matters of the heart, losing isn't an option for pro athletes Kenzie Shaw and Sutton Flores. (978-1-63555-500-4)

Vanished by Eden Darry. A storm is coming, and Ellery and Loveday must find the chosen one or humanity won't survive it. (978-1-63555-437-3)

All She Wants by Larkin Rose. Marci Jones and Tessa Dalton get more than they bargained for when their plans for a one-night stand turn into an opportunity for love. (978-1-63555-476-2)

Beautiful Accidents by Erin Zak. Stevie Adams and Bernadette Thompson discover that sometimes the best things in life happen purely by accident. (978-1-63555-497-7)

Before Now by Joy Argento. Can Delany and Jade overcome the betrayal that spans the centuries to reignite a love that can't be broken? (978-1-63555-525-7)

Breathe by Cari Hunter. Paramedic Jemima Pardon's chronic bad luck seems to be improving when she meets police officer Rosie Jones. But they face a battle to survive before they can find love. (978-1-63555-523-3)

Double-Crossed by Ali Vali. Hired thief and killer Reed Gable finds something in her scope that will change her life forever when she gets a contract to end casino accountant Brinley Myers's life. (978-1-63555-302-4)

False Horizons by CJ Birch. Jordan and Ash struggle with different views on the alien agenda and must find their way back to each other before they're swallowed up by a centuries-old war. (978-1-63555-519-6)

Legacy by Charlotte Greene. When five women hike to a remote cabin deep inside a national park, unsettling events suggest that they should have stayed home. (978-1-63555-490-8)

Royal Street Reveillon by Greg Herren. Someone is killing the stars of a reality show, and it's up to Scotty Bradley and the boys to find out who. (978-1-63555-545-5)

Somewhere Along the Way by Kathleen Knowles. When Maxine Cooper moves to San Francisco during the summer of 1981, she learns that wherever you run, you cannot escape yourself. (978-1-63555-383-3)

Blood of the Pack by Jenny Frame. When Alpha of the Scottish pack Kenrick Wulver visits the Wolfgangs, she falls for Zaria Lupa, a wolf on the run. (978-1-63555-431-1)

Cause of Death by Sheri Lewis Wohl. Medical student Vi Akiak and K9 Search and Rescue officer Kate Renard must work together to find a killer before they end up the next targets. In the race for survival, they discover that love may be the biggest risk of all. (978-1-63555-441-0)

Chasing Sunset by Missouri Vaun. Hijinks and mishaps ensue as Iris and Finn set off on a road trip adventure, chasing the sunset, and falling in love along the way. (978-1-63555-454-0)

Double Down by MB Austin. When an unlikely friendship with Spanish pop star Erlea turns deeper, Celeste, in-house physician for the hotel hosting Erlea's show, has a choice to make—run or double down on love. (978-1-63555-423-6)

Party of Three by Sandy Lowe. Three friends are in for a wild night at billionaire heiress Eleanor McGregor's twenty-fifth birthday party. Love, lust, and doing the right thing, even when it hurts, turn the evening into one that will change their lives forever. (978-1-63555-246-1)

Sit. Stay. Love. by Karis Walsh. City girl Alana Brendt and country vet Tegan Evans both know they don't belong together. Only problem is, they're falling in love. (978-1-63555-439-7)

Where the Lies Hide by Renee Roman. As P.I. Camdyn Stark gets closer to solving the case, will her dark secrets and the lies she's buried jeopardize her future with the quietly beautiful Sarah Peters? (978-1-63555-371-0)

Beautiful Dreamer by Melissa Brayden. With love on the line, can Devyn Winters find it in her heart to stay in the small town of Dreamer's Bay, the one place she swore she'd never remain? (978-1-63555-305-5)

Create a Life to Love by Erin Zak. When sixteen-year-old Beth shows up at her birth mother's door, three lives will change forever. (978-1-63555-425-0)

Deadeye by Meredith Doench. Stranded while hunting the serial predator Deadeye, Special Agent Luce Hansen fights for survival while her lover, forensic pathologist Harper Bennett, hunts for clues to Hansen's disappearance along the killer's trail. (978-1-63555-253-9)

Death Takes a Bow by David S. Pederson. Alan Keys takes part in a local stage production, but when the leading man is murdered, his partner Detective Heath Barrington is thrust into the limelight to find the killer. (978-1-63555-472-4)

Endangered by Michelle Larkin. Shapeshifters Officer Aspen Wolfe and Dr. Tora Madigan fight their growing attraction as they work together to destroy a secret government agency that exterminates their kind. (978-1-63555-377-2)

Incognito by VK Powell. The only thing Evan Spears is focused on is capturing a fleeing murder suspect until wild card Frankie Strong is added to her team and causes chaos on and off the job. (978-1-63555-389-5)

Insult to Injury by Gun Brooke. After losing everything, Gail Owen withdraws to her old farmhouse and finds a destitute young woman, Romi Shepherd, living in a secret room. (978-1-63555-323-9)

Just One Moment by Dena Blake. If you were given the chance to have the love of your life back, could you ignore everything that went wrong and start over again? (978-1-63555-387-1)

Scene of the Crime by MJ Williamz. Cullen Mathew finds herself caught between the woman she thinks she loves but can no longer trust and a beautiful detective she can't stop thinking about who will stop at nothing to find the truth. (978-1-63555-405-2)

Accidental Prophet by Bud Gundy. Days after his grandmother dies, Drew Morten learns his true identity and finds himself racing against time to save civilization from the apocalypse. (978-1-63555-452-6)

Daughter of No One by Sam Ledel. When their worlds are threatened, a princess and a village outcast must overcome their differences and embrace a budding attraction if they want to survive. (978-1-63555-427-4)

Fear of Falling by Georgia Beers. Singer Sophie James is ready to shake up her career, but her new manager, the gorgeous Dana Landon, has other ideas. (978-1-63555-443-4)

In Case You Forgot by Fredrick Smith and Chaz Lamar. Zaire and Kenny, two newly single, Black, queer, and socially aware men, start again—in love, career, and life—in the West Hollywood neighborhood of LA. (978-1-63555-493-9)

Playing with Fire by Lesley Davis. When Takira Lathan and Dante Groves meet at Takira's restaurant, love may find its way onto the menu. (978-1-63555-433-5)

Practice Makes Perfect by Carsen Taite. Meet law school friends Campbell, Abby, and Grace, law partners at Austin's premier boutique legal firm for young, hip entrepreneurs. Legal Affairs: one law firm, three best friends, three chances to fall in love. (978-1-63555-357-4)

The Last Seduction by Ronica Black. When you allow true love to elude you once and you desperately regret it, are you brave enough to grab it when it comes around again? (978-1-63555-211-9)

Wavering Convictions by Erin Dutton. After a traumatic event, Maggie has vowed to regain her strength and independence. So how can Ally be both the woman who makes her feel safe and a constant reminder of the person who took her security away? (978-1-63555-403-8)